Praise for
JOE HALDEMAN
Winner of the Hugo, Nebula

"If there was a Fort Knox for the science fiction writers who really matter, we'd have to lock Haldeman up there."
—Stephen King

"Haldeman has long been one of our most aware, comprehensive, and necessary writers. He speaks from a place deep within the collective psyche and, more importantly, his own. His mastery is informed with a survivor's hard-won wisdom."
—Peter Straub

"Haldeman remains a nimble, necessary figure in sci-fi's pantheon."
—*Entertainment Weekly*

THE ACCIDENTAL TIME MACHINE

"Curiosity and some unfortunate accidents send Matt through a series of vividly described, wryly imagined futures, where he gradually becomes more adaptable and resourceful as experiences hone his character . . . Rather than being a riff on H. G. Wells's *The Time Machine*, this novel is closer in tone to Neil Gaiman's *Anansi Boys*, another charming yarn about a young man who's forced out of a boring rut. Producing prose that feels this effortless must be hard work, but Haldeman never breaks a sweat."
—*Publishers Weekly* (starred review)

"The ever-inventive Haldeman offers a new twist . . . [His] ingenuity delivers cutting-edge technological speculation and irresistibly compelling reading."
—*Booklist*

"This is a book that manages to conflate flavors of Stephen Baxter, Walter Miller, Keith Laumer, and Cyril Kornbluth into one unique and potent cocktail that is unmistakably Haldeman."
—Paul Di Filippo, *Sci Fi Weekly*

continued . . .

"I've always admired Haldeman's ability to write short yet compelling novels . . . Haldeman's sparse yet action-packed novels rarely have a slow moment . . . *The Accidental Time Machine* packs a large story into that small space; it's a fast and amusing book."
— *The Davis Enterprise*

"Haldeman delivers a succinct cautionary fable while ultimately spinning a humorously thought-provoking tall tale. A good choice."
— *Library Journal*

"A fascinating extrapolation of the future in the way only Joe Haldeman can do. It's a relatively swift read, and I found it hard to put down once I'd started, eager to find out what mess our hero would get into next. Haldeman's look at these societies of the centuries to come is intriguing and even plausible . . . I really enjoyed *The Accidental Time Machine*. Haldeman has some great ideas."
— *SF Site*

"A time-travel yarn in the classic style . . . A great deal of fun and compulsively readable while it lasts, it leaves the reader wanting more."
— *Kirkus Reviews*

"Joe Haldeman is a solid and experienced writer, and *The Accidental Time Machine* is, overall, a well-crafted story. And that's no accident."
— *SFRevu*

"Haldeman has crafted a rollicking, fun joyride through the intricacies of time travel while gently developing a good-natured but decidedly unmotivated grad student into a smart, world-wise adult. The relationship that grows between the two protagonists is sweet without being overdone, with smooth prose, imagination, and a neat ironic twist."
— *Monsters and Critics*

"This terrific science fiction time-travel tale feels like a throwback thriller starring a disingenuous antihero."
— *Alternative Worlds*

"An offbeat time-travel story . . . one of the classic SF themes given new life. I'm not sure if it's possible to feel nostalgic about something new, but if so, this is the book that will do it."
— Don D'Ammassa, *Critical Mass*

"Haldeman takes you on an amusing and thought-provoking trip through science and culture. His sharp wit and engaging characters make this book an energizing read." — The Maine Edge.com

"Written with a tongue-in-cheek style that is chock-full of humor, mystery, ironies, hard science, speculative musings, ruminations on religion, and all sorts of provocative ideas, *The Accidental Time Machine* features one of SF's most engaging protagonists: Matt Fuller is something like a shaggy, obsessively inquisitive though somewhat naive Tom Sawyer on Ritalin (as if he were also hardwired into Kurt Gödel's and Albert Einstein's DNA) . . . [This is] one of those must-read books of the year that will entertain, amuse, and occasionally frighten readers who join Matt Fuller on his fascinating odyssey." —*BookLoons*

"In Shakespearean terms, [*The Accidental Time Machine* is] really a comedy—a romp, even. The time machine gets Fuller into and out of various jams and pickles, and the far-distant futures that he encounters are grim, hilarious, and brilliant speculation. Time travel is an oft-plowed field in the genre, but Haldeman surpasses most of the other efforts with rock-solid characterization, great speculation, and a deft writing style. He has so perfected his conversational style of prose that the novel reads more like a dialogue between writer and reader . . . He has his own opinion of what modern science fiction should be and, in executing his ideas, is doing his part to define the genre." —*Bookgasm*

"Haldeman deftly weaves the elements of physics, religion, and technology together in this tautly imagined and plot-driven story . . . compelling, completely unpredictable, and un-put-down-able." —*Romantic Times Book Reviews*

A SEPARATE WAR AND OTHER STORIES

"Unlike some other writers of hard science fiction who are too busy trying to wow readers with their knowledge of applied physics or molecular biology to be bothered with such trivialities as plot and character, Haldeman never forgets that even in science fiction it's all about us humans . . . Readers will be hard-pressed to find a subpar effort by science fiction master Joe Haldeman in *A Separate War and Other Stories*." —*The Baltimore Sun*

"A must-have collection." —*The Philadelphia Inquirer*

" 'For White Hill' is one of the most memorable tragic love stories ever written as SF . . . Haldeman's work is never less than clever and sometimes much more." —*Publishers Weekly*

THE
ACCIDENTAL
TIME MACHINE

JOE HALDEMAN

ACE BOOKS, NEW YORK

THE BERKLEY PUBLISHING GROUP
Published by the Penguin Group
Penguin Group (USA) Inc.
375 Hudson Street, New York, New York 10014, USA
Penguin Group (Canada), 90 Eglinton Avenue East, Suite 700, Toronto, Ontario M4P 2Y3, Canada
(a division of Pearson Penguin Canada Inc.)
Penguin Books Ltd., 80 Strand, London WC2R 0RL, England
Penguin Group Ireland, 25 St. Stephen's Green, Dublin 2, Ireland (a division of Penguin Books Ltd.)
Penguin Group (Australia), 250 Camberwell Road, Camberwell, Victoria 3124, Australia
(a division of Pearson Australia Group Pty. Ltd.)
Penguin Books India Pvt. Ltd., 11 Community Centre, Panchsheel Park, New Delhi—110 017, India
Penguin Group (NZ), 67 Apollo Drive, Rosedale, North Shore 0632, New Zealand
(a division of Pearson New Zealand Ltd.)
Penguin Books (South Africa) (Pty.) Ltd., 24 Sturdee Avenue, Rosebank, Johannesburg 2196,
South Africa

Penguin Books Ltd., Registered Offices: 80 Strand, London WC2R 0RL, England

This is a work of fiction. Names, characters, places, and incidents either are the product of the author's imagination or are used fictitiously, and any resemblance to actual persons, living or dead, business establishments, events, or locales is entirely coincidental. The publisher does not have any control over and does not assume any responsibility for author or third-party websites or their content.

THE ACCIDENTAL TIME MACHINE

An Ace Book / published by arrangement with the author

PRINTING HISTORY
Ace hardcover edition / August 2007
Ace mass-market edition / August 2008

Copyright © 2007 by Joe Haldeman.
Excerpt from *Marsbound* copyright © 2008 by Joe Haldeman.
Cover art by Craig White.
Cover design by Annette Fiore DeFex.

All rights reserved.
No part of this book may be reproduced, scanned, or distributed in any printed or electronic form without permission. Please do not participate in or encourage piracy of copyrighted materials in violation of the author's rights. Purchase only authorized editions.
For information, address: The Berkley Publishing Group,
a division of Penguin Group (USA) Inc.,
375 Hudson Street, New York, New York 10014.

ISBN: 978-0-441-01616-7

ACE
Ace Books are published by The Berkley Publishing Group,
a division of Penguin Group (USA) Inc.,
375 Hudson Street, New York, New York 10014.
ACE and the "A" design are trademarks belonging to Penguin Group (USA) Inc.

PRINTED IN THE UNITED STATES OF AMERICA

10 9 8 7 6 5 4 3 2 1

If you purchased this book without a cover, you should be aware that this book is stolen property. It was reported as "unsold and destroyed" to the publisher, and neither the author nor the publisher has received any payment for this "stripped book."

For Susan Allison:
about time.

1

The story would have been a lot different if Matt's supervisor had been watching him when the machine first went away.

The older man was hunched over his oscilloscope screen, staring into the green pool of light like a tweedy and corpulent bird of prey, fiddling with two knobs, intent on a throbbing bright oval that wiggled around, eluding his control. Matt Fuller could have been in another room, another state.

Sleet rattled on dark windows. Matt put down his screwdriver and pushed the RESET button on the new calibrator, a shoe-box-sized machine.

The machine disappeared.

He stared for about one second. When he was able to close his mouth and open it again, he said, "Dr. Marsh! Look!"

Dr. Marsh pulled all of himself reluctantly from the round screen. "What is it, Matthew?"

The machine had reappeared. "Uh . . . the calibrator. For a moment there, it . . . well, it looked like it went away."

Dr. Marsh nodded slowly. "It went away."

"I mean like it disappeared! Gone! Zap!"

"It appears to be here now."

"Well, yeah, obviously. I mean, it came back!"

The big man leaned back against the worktable, tired springs on his chair groaning in protest. "We've both been up a long time. How long for you?"

"Well, a lot, but—"

"How long?"

"Maybe thirty hours." He looked at his watch. "Maybe a little more."

"You're seeing things, Matthew. Go home."

He made helpless motions with his hands. "But it—"

"Go home." His supervisor turned off the 'scope and heaved himself up. "Like me." He took his thermal jacket, a bright red tent, off the hook and shrugged it on. He paused at the door. "I mean it. Get some sleep. Something to eat besides Twinkies."

"Yeah, sure." Look who's giving dietary advice. Maybe it was the sugar, though, and the coffee, and the little bit of speed after dinner. Cold french fries and a chocolate-chip cookie and amphetamines—that might make you see things. Or not see them, for a moment.

He waved good night to the professor and sat back down at the calibrator. It was prettier than it had to be, but Matt was funny that way. He'd found a nice rectangle of oak in the "Miscellaneous" storage bin, and cut out the metal parts so they fit flush on top of it. The combination of wood with matte black metal and glowing digital readouts pleased him.

He always looked kind of scruffy himself, but his machines were another matter. His bicycle was silent as grease and you could play the spokes like a harp. His own oscilloscope, which he had taken apart and rebuilt, had a sharper display than the professor's, and no hiss. Back when he'd had a car, a Mazda Ibuki, it was always spotless and humming. No need for a car at MIT, though, and plenty of need for money, so somebody back in Akron was despoiling his handiwork on the Mazda. He missed the relaxation of fiddling with it.

He ran his hand along the cool metal top of the machine, slightly warm above the battery case. Ought to turn it off. He pushed the RESET button.

The machine disappeared again.

"Holy shit!" He bolted for the door. "Professor Marsh!"

He was at the end of the hall, tying on his hat. "What is it this time?"

Matt looked over his shoulder and saw the calibrator materialize again. It shimmered for a split second and then was solid. "Uh . . . well . . . I don't guess it's really important."

"Come on, Matt. What is it?"

He looked over his shoulder again. "Well, I wondered if I could take the calibrator home with me."

"What on Earth would you calibrate?" He smiled. "You have a little graviton generator at home?"

"Just some circuit-board tests. I can do them at home as well as here." Thinking fast. "Maybe sleep in tomorrow, not come in through the snow."

"Good idea. I may not come in either." He finished putting on his mittens. "You can e-mail me if anything comes up." He pushed open the door against a strong wind and looked back, sardonic. "Especially if the thing disappears again. We do need it next week."

Matt went back and sat down by the calibrator and sipped cold coffee. He checked his watch and pushed the button. The machine shimmered and disappeared, but only the metal box; the oak base remained, a conical woodscrew hole in each corner. It had done that the last time, too.

What would happen if he put his hand in the space where the box had been? When it came back it might chop him off at the wrist. Or there might be a huge nuclear explosion, the old science fiction version of what happens when two objects try to occupy the same space at the same time.

No, there were plenty of air molecules there when it came back before, and no obvious nuclear explosions.

It shimmered back, and he checked his watch. A little less than three minutes. The first disappearance had been about one second, then maybe ten, twelve seconds.

His watch was a twenty-dollar dime-store Seiko, but he was pretty sure it had a stopwatch function. He took it off and pushed buttons at random until it behaved like a stopwatch. He pushed the button on the watch and the RESET button simultaneously.

It seemed to take forever. The rattle of sleet quieted to a soft whisper of snow. The machine reappeared and he clicked the stopwatch button: 34 minutes, 33.22 seconds. Call it 1, 10, 170, 2073 seconds. He crossed over to the professor's desk and rummaged around for some semilog graph paper. If you took an average, it looked like the thing went missing about twelve times longer each time he pushed the button.

Do the next one, about six hours, at home. He found a couple of plastic trash-can liners to protect the machine, but before he wrapped it up he put a cardboard sleeve around the RESET button and fixed it in place with duct tape. He didn't want the machine disappearing on the subway.

It was one unholy bitch of a night. The sleet indeed had turned to snow, but there were still deep puddles of icy slush that you couldn't avoid, and Matt hadn't worn boots. By the time he got on the Red Line, his running shoes were soaked and his feet were numb. When he got off at East Lexington, they had thawed enough to start hurting, and the normal ten-minute uphill walk took twenty, the sidewalks slippery with ice forming. Wouldn't do to drop the calibrator. He could build a new one in a couple of days, if he could find the parts. Or his successor could, after he was fired.

(All the calibrator was supposed to do was supply one reference photon per unit of time, the unit of time being the tiny supposed "chronon": the length of time it takes light to travel the radius of an electron. Nothing to do with disappearing.)

He managed to take off a glove without dropping the machine, and his thumbprint let him into the apartment building. He trudged up to the second floor and thumbed his way into his flat.

Kara had only been gone for a couple of days, and most of that time he'd been in the lab, but the place was already taking on bachelor-pad aspects. The stack of journals and printouts on the coffee table had spilled onto the floor, and though he had sorted through it twice, looking for things, it hadn't occurred to him to stack it back up. Kara would have done that the first time she walked through the living room. So maybe they weren't exactly made for each other. Still. He put the calibrator on the couch and stacked the magazines. Half of them slid back onto the floor.

He went into the kitchen and didn't look in the sink. He got a beer from the refrigerator and took it into the bathroom along with the new *Physical Review Letters*. He ripped off his shoes and ran a few inches of hot water into the tub and blissfully put his feet in to thaw.

There was nothing in *Letters* that particularly interested him, but reading it let him pretend to be doing something useful while he was mainly concerned with thawing out and drinking beer. Of course that made the phone ring. There was an old-fashioned voice-only in the bathroom; he leaned over and punched it. "Here."

"Matty?" Only one person called him that. "Why can't I see you?"

"No picture, Mother. I'm on the bathroom phone."

"I'm sending you money so you can have a phone in the *bathroom*? I wouldn't mind a phone in the bathroom."

"It was already here. It would cost extra to take it out."

"Well, use your cell. I want to see you."

"No, you don't. I look like I've been up for thirty-six hours. Because I have."

"What? You're killing yourself, you know that. Why on Earth would you stay up that long?"

"Lab work." Actually, he was disinclined to come home to the empty apartment, the empty bed. But he'd never told his mother about Kara. "I'm going to sleep in tomorrow, maybe not even go to the lab." He kept talking and pushed the HOLD button down for a moment. "Call coming in, Mother. Buzz you tomorrow on the cell." He hung up and raised the beer to his lips, and there was a perfunctory knock on the apartment door. It creaked open.

He wiped his feet inadequately on the bathroom throw rug and stumbled into the living room. Kara, of course; no one else's thumb would open the door.

She was pretty bedraggled, pretty *and* bedraggled, and had a look that Matt had never seen before. Not a friendly look.

"Kara, it's so good—"

"I finally stopped trying to call you and came over. Where have you *been* since yesterday morning?"

"At the lab."

"Oh, sure. You spent the night at the lab. Forgot to route to your cell. With the secret number even I can't call."

"I *did*! I mean I didn't." He spread his arms wide. "I mean I spent the night at the lab and they don't allow you to route calls there."

"Look, I don't care where you spent the night. Really, I don't care at all. I just need something from the bathroom. Do you *mind*?"

He stepped aside and she stomped by him, dripping. He followed, also dripping.

She looked in the medicine cabinet and slammed it shut. Then she looked at the tub. "You're taking a bath in two inches of water?"

"Just, uh, just my feet."

"Oh, of course, of course, your feet." She jerked open a drawer. "You're weird, Matt. Clean feet, though. Here." She pulled out a baby blue box of Safeluv contraceptive discs. "Don't ask." She pointed a finger into his face. "Don't you dare ask." Her face was flushed and her eyes were bright with held-back tears.

"I wouldn't—" She pushed her way past him. "Won't you just stay for a cup of coffee? It's so bad out."

"Someone's waiting." She stopped at the door. "You can take my thumb off the door now." She paused, as if wanting to say something more, and then spun into the hall. The door closed with a quiet click.

2

Matt did know something about time travel, though it wasn't his specialty. He didn't really have a specialty, not anymore, though he was only a couple of hard courses and a dissertation away from his doctorate in physics.

Everybody does travel through time toward the future, trivially, one second at a time. There was no paradox involved in going forward even faster—in fact, modern physics had allowed that possibility since Einstein's day.

Demonstrating that, though—time dilation through relativistic contraction—requires either really high speeds or the ability to measure very small amounts of time. You have the "twin paradox," where one twin stays at home and the other flies off to Alpha Centauri and back at close to the speed of light. That's eight light-years, so the traveling twin is about eight years younger when he returns—to him, his stay-at-home brother has traveled forward in time eight years.

They don't build spaceships that fast, but you can do it on a smaller scale with a pair of accurate clocks. Send one around the world on a jet plane, and when it comes back, the traveling clock will be about a millionth of a second slower than the stay-at-home.

Matt had been familiar with that stuff since before puberty, and then after puberty, the pursuit of physics had exposed him to more sophisticated time-travel models, Gödel and Tipler and Weyland. But they all required huge deformations of the universe, harnessing black holes and the like.

Not just pushing a button.

Matt woke up on the couch, groggy and aching. Past the row of empty beer cans on the coffee table, an old movie capered on the TV screen. It had been Fellini when he fell asleep. Now it was Lucille Ball with a grating laugh track. He found the remote on the floor and sent her back to the twentieth century.

His feet were cold. He shuffled into the bathroom and stood for a long time under a hot shower.

He still had several days' worth of clean clothes hanging in the closet, relics of when there used to be a woman living here. Was Kara fanatically folding and hanging for another man now?

The coffee was ready by the time he got dressed. He sweetened a cup with a lot of honey and made a space at the kitchen table by pushing aside some three-day-old newspapers. He brought his bag to the table and took out the machine, still wrapped in the trash-can liner, his notebook, and the piece of graph paper from the professor's desk.

He plugged in the notebook and scanned the graph paper into it, with the four data points. The first two were guesses, the third approximate, and the fourth timed with a stopwatch. He drew in appropriate error bars with a stylus and asked the notebook to do a Fourier transform on them. As he expected, it gave him a set of low-probability solutions that curved all over the map, but the cleanest one was a straight line with a slope of 11.8—so the next time he pushed the button, the thing should be gone for 24,461 seconds. Six hours and forty-eight minutes, give or take whatever.

Okay, this one would be scientific. He got the digital alarm from his bedroom and set it to show seconds. He put a fresh eight-hour tab into his cell and set it for continuous video, then propped it up on a stack of books so that it stared at the clock and the machine. As an afterthought, he cleared the junk away from the table behind it, and restarted the cell. This would be part of the history of physics. It ought to look neat.

He rummaged through the everything drawer in the kitchen and found his undergraduate multimeter. The calibrator machine's power source was a Madhya deep-discharge twenty-volt fuel cell, and the multimeter said it was 99.9999 percent charged. He showed the result to the camera. See how much power the thing drew while it was gone.

It was 9:58, so he decided to wait until exactly 10:00 to push the button. Out of curiosity, he pulled a two-dollar coin out of his pocket and set it on top of the machine. That would be his dramatic sound track: the clink of the coin falling when he pushed the button.

His eye on the clock, he could feel his heart racing. What if nothing happened? Well, nobody else would see the tab.

A split second before ten, he jammed his thumb down on the button. The machine dutifully disappeared.

It took the two-dollar coin with it. No clink.

That was interesting. Both he and the coin had been in contact with the machine, but the coin had been on the metal box, not the nonconducting plastic button. What would have happened if it had been him touching the metal instead?

He should have put the cell *on* the machine, rather than outside. Get a record of what happens to it when it's not here. Not here and now.

Well, next time.

Of course the phone rang. He peered at the caller ID.

His mother. When it stopped ringing, he called her from the bathroom.

"You're calling from the bathroom again," she said.

"Something wrong with the cell." Let's not tell Mother about the disappearing machine. "Why did you call me?"

"What, you were sleeping?"

"No, I'm up and around. Why'd you call?"

"The storm, silly. Are you doing all right with the storm?"

"Sure."

"What do you mean, 'sure'? You got power and water?"

"Yeah, sure." He went to the little window at the end of the room and pulled the blinds. It was solid gray, snow packed so thick that no light came through.

"Well, we don't. The power went out right after I got up. Now they're telling people to boil the water before you drink it."

He just stared at the window. Snow ten feet deep?

"Matthew? Hello?"

"Just a minute, Mom." He set the phone down on the rim of the tub and stepped to the front room. He peered through the blinds.

There was snow, all right, but only a couple of feet. The wind was fierce, though, rattling the windowpanes. That was it. The bathroom window looked out over a temporarily vacant lot. Wind blowing from the north had an unobstructed path more than a hundred yards long. So the snow had packed up against the north wall, including the bathroom window.

He picked up the phone. "So what's the matter there?" his mother said.

"Just checking. It's not so bad here. Anything I can do?"

"If you had a *car*."

"Well." It had been a graduation gift, and he'd sold it when he moved back to Boston.

"You couldn't rent one."

"No. I wouldn't in this weather, anyhow, Boston drivers. You need something?"

"Candles, milk. A little wine wouldn't hurt." She lived in a dry suburb, Arlington. "Some bottled water—how'm I going to boil it? Without the electric?"

"Let me check on the T. If it's running, I could bring you out some stuff."

"I don't want you should—"

"Make a list and I'll call you back in a couple minutes." He hung up and calculated. If his extrapolation was right, the machine would reappear just before five. Plenty of time, even with the weather.

He should eat something first. Nothing in the fridge but beer and a desiccated piece of cheddar cheese. He popped his last can of Boston Baked Beans—made in Ohio—and nuked them while he chased down a piece of paper and a pen for a list.

Candles, wine, milk, water. He called and she added bread, peanut butter, and jelly. Red currant if they had it. Some sardines and Dijon mustard—don't worry, she'd pay. Fish? She'd better.

He poured the beans over a slice of bread that was dry but not moldy and squelched some ketchup over them. He opened another beer and watched the Weather Channel while he ate. The snow should stop by noon. But more tomorrow. A good time to take a long weekend.

He tried not to think about being bundled up with Kara while the snow drifted down. Hot chocolate, giggles. Some giddy exploration of the outer limits of love. Perhaps.

The beans had turned cold. He finished them and dressed in layers and went out to slay the wily groceries.

The combat boots he'd bought in Akron were clumsy but dry, good traction, trudging downhill. The wind had gentled somewhat, and he almost enjoyed the walk. Or maybe he enjoyed not being in the apartment alone

No candles at the grocery store except little votive ones.

He bought her a box of two dozen and a five-liter box of cheap California wine. Get one for himself on the way back. Two jugs of water. Everything but the water went into his backpack. He lumbered off toward the Red Line.

His mother was just two stops down, but more than a mile walk after that. By the time he got there, he was regretting the second gallon of water. Mom could brush her teeth with wine.

She was glad to see him in spite of the fact that he didn't get any matches to go with the candles. He searched and found some in his father's old workshop, where Matthew knew he'd sometimes escaped to smoke dope. They sat in the kitchen and had a glass of wine and some chocolate, and he said he had to get back to work, which was true, even though the work was not of an arduous nature.

On the way back he picked up the wine and a couple of days' groceries, and a cheap camera phone in a blister pack. He could have gone on into Harvard Square to Radio Shack for a little button camera, since he didn't need a new cell, but it probably would have cost at least as much. And he didn't want to miss the reappearance.

The wind and snow had started up again when he got off the subway to make his way home. He was shivering by the time he got inside. A glance verified that the machine was still off to wherever it was, so he went straight into the kitchen and started water for coffee and to warm his hands.

A little more than an hour to go, as he sat down on the couch with his coffee. He picked up his notebook and clicked on the calculator, and made a short list:

1. (1.26 sec) (extrapolating back)
2. (15)
3. (176)
4. 2073 s.
5. 24,461 = 6h 48m
6. 3.34 days

7. *39.54 d.*
8. *465 d.*
9. *5493 d. = 15 y.*

So he had to plan. The next time he pushed the button—if the simple linear relationship held true—the thing would be gone for over three days. Next time, over a month; then over a year. Then fifteen years, and way into the future after that.

So it was a time machine, if kind of a useless one. Unless you could find a way to reverse it—go up fifteen years and come back with the day's stock quotations. Or a list of who had won the World Series every year in between. But simply putting yourself in the future, well, you could do that by just standing around. No profit in it unless you could come back.

He calculated two more numbers, 177.5 years and 2094. If you went that far up, if would be like visiting another planet. But you couldn't come back, like the guy in the Wells novel, and warn everybody about the Morlocks. And it might get lonely up there, with nobody but Morlocks to grunt with.

Maybe it would be a high-tech future, though, and they'd know how to reverse the process.

No. If they could do that, we would have seen them around. Playing the stock market, betting on horses.

But they wouldn't necessarily look any different from us. Maybe they came back all the time—made a few bucks and then went back to the future. Of course you had the Ray Bradbury Effect. Even a tiny change here could profoundly affect the future. Don't step on a butterfly.

Through all this rumination, he kept staring at the spot. Four forty-eight came, and nothing happened. He started to panic, but then it shimmered into existence, just before 4:49. Have to adjust the equation slightly.

The two-dollar coin was where he had set it. He should have put a watch next to it. A cage with a guinea pig. And the camera.

He checked the Madhya fuel cell, and it was at 99.9998 percent, a drop of a hundredth of one percent. It might have lost that by capacitance, though; the circuit open. See what the next data point shows.

Three days and eight hours, next time. He counted on his fingers. Just after midnight Monday. He could call in sick that day. Marsh wouldn't miss him.

He would miss the machine, though. Could he build a duplicate by Tuesday? Nothing to it, if he had all the components in front of him and a properly equipped worktable. But it would be hard to gather all that stuff over a weekend when the Institute and the city were mostly shut down. You couldn't go to a pharmacy and pick up a gram of gallium arsenide, anyhow.

Even with the 'tute open, there would be a lot of paperwork. Of course if you were just *borrowing* things . . .

Matt had been a student at MIT for five years, and an employee for three more. He went back to the everything drawer and pulled out a large ring with a couple of dozen keys identified with little paper labels.

One of them would open nine out of ten MIT doors, but those were mostly uninteresting classrooms and labs. The others were special offices and storerooms.

Most students who had been around a long time had access to a similar collection, or at least knew someone like Matt. MIT had a venerable tradition of harmless breaking and entering. When he was a second-semester freshman, Matt had been taken on a midnight tour of the soft underbelly of MIT, crawling through semisecret passageways that crackled with ozone and dripped oily condensate, emerging to tiptoe through experiments in progress—look but don't touch—room after room of million-dollar gadgetry protected only by the hackers' code of honor. You don't mess with somebody else's work.

And you don't steal. But then it wouldn't be stealing if it was for an Institute project, would it?

He brought up a schematic on the computer and made a list of components he wouldn't be able to just pick up in his own lab, or rather Professor Marsh's. He knew where all of them would be, since he'd already built the thing once.

Saturday night in a blinding snowstorm. If he met anybody else, they'd be hackers on similar errands. Or janitors or security guards, neither of whom would be much of a problem. He'd guided freshmen on the tour dozens of times, and they only had to run like hell twice.

He half filled a thermos with the rest of the coffee and made two peanut butter and jelly sandwiches, and put them in his knapsack along with the computer and key ring. He emptied out a multivitamin jar and sorted through the various pills. He broke a large Ritalin in two and swallowed one half. The other he folded up into a scrap of paper and put in his shirt pocket. This would be an all-nighter.

What he really wanted to do was set up the machine with the camera and a watch, and send it off into the future. But not until he had a duplicate.

He had to smile when he imagined the look on Professor Marsh's face when he pushed the RESET button on the duplicate. He tried to hold on to that thought as he barged out into the blowing cold.

3

It turned out to be more than an all-nighter. He
had to sneak into fourteen different labs and storerooms
before he had all the parts in his bag. In some places, he
left IOU notes; in some, he assumed people wouldn't miss
the odd resistor or thermocouple.

A thin gray winter dawn was threading through the window when he gathered all the parts together at his bench.
He hadn't been able to quite match everything precisely—
all the electronic and optical components had the right
characteristics, but they weren't all from the same manu-
facturers as before, which shouldn't make any difference.
But then the machine shouldn't disappear, either.

He had a pine plank instead of the furniture-quality oak
he'd scrounged. Surely that wouldn't make any difference,
the neutral platform. He trimmed it with a table saw to just
the right dimensions, then he found the cardboard template
he'd used as a guide and drilled holes in the board to position the various components. Then he took it to the chemical hood and spray painted it with two coats of glossy

black enamel. It was fast-drying, supposedly, but he set a timer for a half hour and stretched out on the bench for a nap, his more or less dry boots folded for a pillow.

Waking up not too refreshed, he took the rest of the Ritalin and heated up half a 1000-ml. beaker of water for coffee. While it was coming to a boil, he set out all of the components in order next to the drilled and painted plank and then got together the tools and materials he'd need to put it all together.

This last step was the most satisfying, but also one prone to spectacularly stupid error, because of familiarity and fatigue. He got a big mug of coffee and stared at the neat array as the drug came on slowly, waking him up. He assembled the calibrator mentally, writing down the steps in sequence on a yellow pad. He studied the list for a few minutes, then rolled his sleeves up neatly and got to work.

It was a mind-set he remembered from childhood, spending hours in the meticulous construction of airplane and spaceship models, excitement holding fatigue at bay. Now, as then, after he'd soldered the last join and firmly tightened the last tiny screw, he felt a little letdown, the fatigue hovering.

He slid the fuel cell into place and tightened the contacts. Push the RESET button or not?

Had to try it. He set his watch to the stopwatch function and pressed both buttons simultaneously.

Nothing happened. Or, rather, the calibrator emitted one photon per chronon, as designed. Dr. Marsh could have this one.

A heavy lassitude flowed into him. He stretched out on the lab bench again. The thought of his soft bed at home was seductive, but the subway wouldn't start till seven, Sunday. He checked his watch, but it was still set on stopwatch, earnestly adding up the seconds. He left it that way.

* * *

Three hours and seven seconds later, he un-folded, groaning, and sat up. It was after nine, good.

He left the calibrator on the shelf and went out to face the Cambridge winter. It was overcast and bitter, in the teens or single digits. No new snow, but plenty of old. He could hear a snowblower somewhere on campus, but it obviously hadn't made it to the Green Building. He crashed through the snow, more than knee-deep, toward the Red Line. The smell of Sunday morning coffee at Starbucks lured him in.

He put enough sugar and cream in the coffee to call it breakfast, and thought about the next stage of the experiment. The machine would be away for three days and eight hours. There would be the cell camera recording the machine's surroundings, and he'd leave his watch in there to record the passage of time—or buy an even cheaper one that he wouldn't mind losing.

A guinea pig. See whether something alive would be affected by the suspension of time, or whatever was going on.

An actual lab animal would be pretty complicated: cage and water and all. He thought about catching a cockroach, but actually he hadn't seen any of them since Kara made him bring the bug man in.

Something that would survive for three days without maintenance. Something he could buy cheap or borrow . . .

A turtle. When he'd gone to the Burlington Mall with Kara to get new pillows, she'd dragged him into the pet store. They had a terrarium full of the little rascals.

They wouldn't be open on Sunday, though. He toyed with the idea of breaking in, risking months in jail for a two-dollar turtle. No. It wasn't MIT. The security guards would take one look at him, a shaggy drug-addled young male dressed like a street person, and shoot to kill.

The Starbucks had a phone book, though, a much-abused sheaf of dirty yellow paper, and he found the number and punched it up on his cell.

"Go to hell," a woman's voice said. He checked the number and no, he hadn't called Kara by mistake. "Pardon me?"

"Oh! I'm sorry!" She laughed. "I thought you were my boyfriend. Who else would call on a Sunday morning?"

"I just . . . well, I wondered if you were open on a Sunday morning."

"Huh-uh. I got to come in and feed and water and clean up after my babies. They don't know it's six feet deep out there."

"It's your store? You run it?"

"Yeah. Try to hire someone who'll do this. Who has a higher IQ than the animals."

"What if I wanted to buy something?"

There was a pause. "You suddenly need a pet on Sunday morning?"

"Not a pet, exactly." Go with the semitruth. "I'm an MIT researcher. We need a small turtle for . . . for a metabolic experiment."

"Well . . . you're down at MIT now?"

"At the Starbucks, actually, right on the Red Line at Kendall Square. I could get up there in less than an hour."

"Lots of luck." She laughed again, a pleasant sound. "Tell you what. I'll give you exactly an hour. Then I cover up my babies and leave."

"I'm on my way." He paused just long enough to put a lid on his coffee, and ran down the stairs to the platform.

And waited. The only thing to read was the sex and Personals section of the *Phoenix*. He studied the WOMEN DESIRING MEN section, and none of them had the hots for a broke ex–graduate student. Well, he could always run one himself: "Broke, shaggy ex–graduate student desires replacement for inexplicably beautiful girl. Will supply own turtle." If the train would only come.

When it did come, of course, it was jammed full of people who would otherwise be driving or walking. A lot of church perfume, which was pleasant when he stepped into the car but overpowering thirty seconds later. The crowd was unusually tense and silent. Perhaps devout. Perhaps wondering why a loving God would do this to them on Sunday morning.

The T stop was on the wrong side of the mall, and he was five minutes late, so he ran. She was waiting in the door with her coat on. "Hey, slow down," she called. "I'm not going anywhere."

She was a small black woman with a broad smile, wearing tight purple jeans and a shirt that said KILL PLANTS AND EAT THEM. She handed him a white cardboard box with a bail, like a Chinese takeout, and a small jar of Baby Reptile Chow. "Fifteen bucks; three for the food. Can't take plastic; register's closed."

He came up with two fives and two deuces and, checking three pockets, enough change. "Hey, you could owe it to me."

"No, I'll hit the ATM." Impulsively: "Take you to lunch?"

She laughed. "Sweetheart, you don't need lunch; you need some sleep. Give Herman some water and a piece of lettuce and go crash."

"That's his name?"

"I call them all Herman. Or Hermione. How long you been up?"

"I got a nap this morning. Sure? About lunch?"

"My boyfriend's making pancakes. He found out I had breakfast with some turtle wrangler from MIT, he'd up and leave me. Love them pancakes."

"Oh. Okay. Thanks."

She went off in the opposite direction, toward the parking lot. He opened the box, and the turtle looked at him. Where was he supposed to get lettuce on a Sunday morning?

He hit the ATM, then found a convenience store that had yesterday's Italian sub in the cooler. He stripped off the wilted lettuce for Herman and squirted mustard on the rest of the sub, and ate half of it down at the subway stop. He rewrapped the other half and left it on the edge of the trash bin. Some actual street person would find it and thank his lucky stars. Until he opened it. Ew-w, mustard.

He couldn't think on the rattling subway, but did sort out some things on the walk home. He had to be methodical. This trial would be a little over three days. Then roughly a month, and then a year. Then fifteen years, during which time it would be nice if the whole world was waiting. And he was, incidentally, famous and tenured.

After only three more demonstrations. They'd better be compelling.

One thing he had to check with this trial was just how much stuff the machine would take with it. A coin was interesting, but a camera and a watch and a turtle would give actual data.

He would put the turtle in a metal container and set it where the coin had been. But he'd attach a bigger metal container, his desk trash can, to the machine by a conducting wire. Put something heavy in it.

He was assuming, since the metal coin was transported and the wooden base was not, that conductors of electricity went and nonconductors didn't. But maybe it was because the coin was above the machine and the base was below. So check that out by putting something nonconductive on the top.

There was a note taped to the door, and for a wild moment he could hope it was from Kara. But it was just the landlord reminding him to shovel the walk. Now *that* would be a reason to travel into the future. Spring.

Herman had withdrawn into his shell, which was understandable. He had probably spent all his remembered life in a pet-store window. Then he was thrown into a cardboard prison and thrust into a backpack, to endure a long subway ride and then a swaying walk while the bitter cold slipped in. The turtle equivalent of being abducted by aliens.

Traveling through time would be nothing in comparison.

Matt put him in a big bowl with a jar lid of water and his wilted lettuce leaf, and set him under the desk lamp to warm.

He rummaged around the kitchen and found a metal loaf pan that could serve as Herman's time-travel vehicle. It was kind of sticky; he washed it for Herman and posterity. Someday it would be in the MIT Museum.

Should he top it off with foil? That would make a Faraday cage out of it, a complete volume enclosed by conductors. But that hadn't been necessary before. Anything sitting on metal connected to the outside of the machine ought to do it.

So the loaf pan went on top of the machine, with a bigger jar lid of water and five pellets of Baby Reptile Chow. He cut the cheap cell out of its blister pack. ONE HUNDRED HOURS OF CONTINUOUS OPERATION, it said. USE FOR SURVEILLANCE. Or voyeurism. Or to win a Nobel Prize. He turned it on and it worked. It went next to the loaf pan. Then the watch, sideways so metal was in contact with metal. A stub of pencil for the nonconductor—no, that looked too ad hoc. In the everything drawer he found a white plastic chess piece, a pawn.

Connecting the metal trash can was a slight problem. In the lab, he could just use alligator clips (continuing the reptile theme), but here he had to improvise. He used a computer power cord and lots of duct tape. The multimeter verified that they made a closed circuit. Something heavy to put in it? A gallon plastic jug; he filled it with water up to the rim. See how much evaporates.

Herman was drinking, his neck craned over the jar lid. Matt let him finish, then moved him to his new abode.

H Hour. He set the cheap cell camera on LOCK and placed it so that it looked at the clock radio. Then he set his own camera up to take his picture when he pushed the button.

"This is the sixth iteration," he said to the camera. "We expect it to be gone for about three days and eight hours." *We* being himself and Herman, he supposed.

He pushed the button at exactly noon. The machine faded nicely. The white pawn fell with a click to bounce off the wooden base.

Everything else had gone, including the heavy trash can.

He went into the kitchen and opened a beer quietly, aware that posterity was listening.

4

Matt spent all of Monday writing an account of
the thing he had to call a time machine. He could change
the name to something less fantastic before anybody else
read it. The disappearing machine? Not much better.

He wouldn't finish the paper, of course, until he had a
live turtle and video footage. Or a dead one and blankness,
whatever.

There wasn't much to say about the physics involved,
the disappearing or time-traveling mechanism, especially
since reproducing the machine didn't reproduce the effect.
It had to be some accidental feature of its construction.

But he was understandably reluctant to take it apart. In
all likelihood, he wouldn't find anything conclusive, and
when he put it back together, it might just be a photon calibrator again.

The report was only five pages long, and even he had to
admit that it wasn't very impressive. He could have set up
this iteration better. The machine was going to reappear at
8:16 Wednesday night in his shabby apartment. He could've
taken it back to the lab and had it appear on Professor

Marsh's desk at ten in the morning. Or in the middle of the rotunda in Building One, high noon, with hundreds of students as witnesses.

Then again, there was something to be said for keeping control over the conditions of the experiment. If he had done a public demonstration now, it probably wouldn't be *him* who pushed the button the next time. The machine was technically the property of MIT's Center for Theoretical Physics. They had only given him a degree and a job, both begrudgingly. He wasn't eager to turn over the science scoop of the century to them.

When he checked on his e-mail that afternoon, he found he had one less reason to be loyal to the Center and MIT. He'd been fired.

Technically, the funding for his appointment had not been renewed. So there would be no paycheck after January 1. Merry Christmas and Happy New Year.

The message had come from the Center's administrative assistant, not Professor Marsh. But it was Marsh who had done it, who hadn't renewed the funding.

Matt picked up the phone and put it back down. Go talk to him in person.

On the clattering ride down to Cambridge, he considered and rejected various strategies. He knew better than to appeal to the old man's mercy. He couldn't claim outstanding job performance; the job hadn't been that demanding recently. More puttering than math. He was reasonably well caught up on the literature, though most of his energy of late had gone into time-travel theory, of course.

Could he use that as a trump card? Instinct said no: Hire me back for my penny-ante job and I promise to rewrite the laws of physics. On the other hand, when he did want to publish his results, the connection with the Center and MIT would be valuable.

But not essential. He could take his evidence to Harvard, for instance. That made him smile. The rivalry between the

THE ACCIDENTAL TIME MACHINE   29

two schools went back to the nineteenth century. Maybe Marsh would be fired for firing him.

The sky was the color of aluminum. Snow piled up in waist-high drifts, but the sidewalks were clear. The students were so bundled up you couldn't tell their gender.

There was no wind as he approached the Green Building, which was so unusual it seemed ominous. Usually it whipped across the quad from the frozen Charles and chilled you to the core.

He showed his card to the scanner at the entrance to the Green Building, and it let him in. So he still existed, at least until the end of the month.

He got off the elevator on the sixth floor to a pleasant shock: Kara, standing in the foyer.

"Kara? Were you looking for me?"

"Matt!" She looked surprised. "Um . . . this is Strom Lewis."

Matt took his hand, dry and strong. He was younger and better-looking. "I graded your papers in 299. Marsh."

"That's right; I thought you looked familiar. I'll be working for him, starting next year." The elevator door started to close, and Kara caught it and slipped in. "Maybe I'll see you?"

"Maybe." Kara held up a hand in good-bye, and so did Matt.

Lose your job and your girl to the same punk kid. It just couldn't get much better.

Marsh wasn't in the laboratory. Matt went through to the man's office. He had a journal and a book open in front of him, making notes in a paper notebook. Matt knocked on the open door.

Marsh put a finger down to mark his place in the journal. "Matthew. What can I do for you?"

"Well, for starters, you could give me my job back. Then you could tell me what's going on."

"Nothing's going on." He set his pencil down but didn't

pick up his finger. "You've had the same job for four years. It's time for you to move on. For your own good."

"Move on where?"

"You could finish your dissertation," he said, "for *starters*. Then I could give you a good recommendation anywhere."

"You think that kid Lewis can do what I do?"

"Nobody's better than you as a technician, Matthew. But you can't be a lab tech all your life, not with your education."

He didn't have a good argument against that, since it was true. He enjoyed the work, but he couldn't deny that it was underemployment. "So I have to leave at the end of December?"

He shrugged. "You finished the calibrator. I don't have any short-term work for you. Might as well go on home and work on your dissertation." He picked up the pencil and turned his attention back to the journal.

Matt went back into the lab, suddenly a stranger there. He opened his drawer, but there was almost nothing of value there that didn't belong to MIT.

Except a pair of earrings. Kara had taken them off when they went skating on Boston Common a couple of weeks ago. Her skimpy outfit, otherwise perfect, hadn't had a pocket.

Might as well take them. Send her a note.

He went over to the campus pub, the Muddy Charles, and had a beer, and then another. That fortified him enough to walk the cold mile to the nearest liquor store. He got a bottle of cheap bourbon and a bottle of red vermouth. The road to Hell would be paved with Manhattans.

When he got home, he was slightly intimidated by the silent witness to history in the living room. He took a tray of ice and a glass into the bedroom and quietly made a big drink, and found a mystery novel he didn't remember reading. He took both into the bathroom and slid into a tub of hot water.

By the third chapter he remembered he'd read the book

before, and was pretty sure the murderer was not the beautiful ex-wife, but rather the lawyer who had hired the private eye. He grimly read on, though, rather than get out of the tub and try to find another book.

There's more than one way to read a book, though. You can make a template out of the edge of the page, holding it in such a way that it reveals only the first letter of each line of the page underneath. In this way you can search for hidden messages from God. On the third try he found the word "sQwat." Then the phone rang.

It was his mother. "You're in the bathroom again."

"Taking a bath. I should take a bath in the living room?"

"You weren't home earlier."

"No, I went down to school." Might as well. "I got an e-mail that my appointment isn't being renewed. So I went down to talk to my boss."

"What, you're being fired? What did you do?"

Well, my boss thinks I'm crazy because I see boxes disappear. "He said it was for my own good. Like I have too much education for the job. I should finish my dissertation and move up in the world."

"So what have I been telling you?"

"Okay, fine. Can you loan me about twenty grand for rent and groceries while I sit around and think?"

Wrong thing to say. There was a long pause and a sniff. "You know I would if I could. It's hard enough to make ends meet. . . ."

"Just kidding, Mother. I'm gonna start looking tomorrow. For a job."

"Have you been drinking? At three in the afternoon?"

He didn't say, "Haven't you?" He rattled the ice in the glass. "In fact, I am. It seemed like the right occasion."

"Well, you call me when you're sober."

"I *am* sober." Loud click. "But not for long," he said to the dead phone.

5

Tuesday disappeared, and so did part of Wednes-
day. By noon, he was sufficiently recovered to dress up and
go out for a decent lunch, two hamburgers and fries. He
looked through the MIT freebie newspaper, the *Tech*, for
job openings, and found two possibilities, one in Cambridge
and the other at the Large Hadron Collider in Geneva. Cam
bridge didn't answer the phone and Geneva had already
found someone.

He was carrying his notebook, so he went on down to the
MIT main library, plugged in, and started rereading the notes
for his dissertation on patterns of local asymmetries in gravity wave induction associated with two recent supernovae.

His data stank. The inductions were so weak they were
almost lost in the background noise. Saying they actually
existed was as much an act of faith as one of observation.

It felt like the cable on his personal elevator had snapped.
The set of mathematical models that could contain his wob-
bly data was so large as to make any one solution actually in-
defensible.

At some level, he'd known that for a long time. He'd

been hiding the truth from himself in the complexity and false elegance of the argument. Coming to it fresh after months away made it clear that he'd been building a house of cards.

He closed the notebook with a whispered expletive that made one person look up and two others lean forward to concentrate on their screens.

There was no way to refine the data or hope for technological advances that would reduce the blobbiness of it. The gravity wave that a supernova produced passed through the solar system once and was gone. It was not too bright to bet your career on a set of evanescent and unrepeatable data.

He could still do something with it, if only an analysis of why this approach was wrong. He could visualize trying to defend something that feeble in front of a thesis committee. The death of a thousand cutting remarks.

He wouldn't need it, though. Not as long as the machine and Herman came back tonight.

He saved a subway token and walked through the stinging wind to Central Square, where thirty dollars got him a dish of nuts and a nonalcoholic beer at a place where pretty naked women danced almost close enough to touch, Middle Eastern music whining and twanging. It disturbed him that their beauty and sexuality couldn't penetrate his dark mood. That girl's undulating waist a perfect hyperboloid of one sheet. Another one describing oscillating conic sections as she swung around a pole. The third one's posture reminding him that, topologically, we are all just a coiling cylinder connecting two holes, with certain elaborations on the outside of the cylinder.

He stayed only a half hour. On his way to the T he optimistically bought a half bottle of decent champagne. For celebration or consolation.

When he got home, he put it in the fridge and opened a

can of minestrone for dinner. While it heated, he went to check the e-mail.

There was a note from Kara, with only a question mark in the subject line. He opened it eagerly:

Dear Matt—I'm sorry you lost your position with Prof. Marsh, and hope I didn't accidentally cause that to happen. I described that photon project to Strom, and he went to talk to Prof. Marsh about it, and I guess he offered Strom your job. He likes Marsh and always got As from him.

I'm sorry. Kara.

Well, wasn't that just a kick in the balls. Actually, it was kind of a relief to be able to think he didn't lose the job purely out of incompetence, or from the old bastard reading his mind.

He allowed himself a wicked moment of imagining how Marsh would feel when he published his time-machine results.

Besides, it wasn't just Marsh, technically, who had given Strom those As. It was Matt himself who had graded the papers!

The minestrone started boiling. He took it off the stove and, after it had cooled, ate it straight out of the pot, staying out of range of the camera and posterity.

At seven, he sat down at the couch with a book, a biography of Isaac Newton. After a couple of pages, he stopped reading and just stared at the board where Herman, history's first chrononaut, was going to appear. He was about a minute early. At 8:15:03 the whole apparatus appeared, with a slight scraping sound.

It had moved. The chassis of the machine stood on the woodscrews that had secured it to the board, like four little metal feet. They were a couple of millimeters from the drill holes. He looked into the pan and Herman looked back, apparently unaffected by his sudden fame.

Why hadn't the machine moved before? Or did it just move so little that the screws nudged their way back into the holes?

He knew he hadn't touched it. Could the house have shifted that much in three days? Unlikely.

He belatedly looked at the clock. It said 12:01:21. The machine had only been gone about a minute, in its own frame of reference.

He checked the water in the jug. No evaporation. Herman apparently hadn't eaten or drunk anything, or pooped.

He found an old engineering ruler that he hadn't used since his sophomore year—he'd taken an engineering drawing course and switched his major from engineering to physics—and he set the millimeter end down next to one of the woodscrew feet. He took extreme close-ups from three angles, which he could later analyze for the precise distance and direction moved. Next time, it might move centimeters. Or across the room.

Or into another state.

He'd have to affix a note—"If found, please return to . . ."—with a substantial reward. Share the Nobel Prize.

Or wire the machine to a big metal box and go along with it.

He took the cell off the machine and hooked its I/O into his notebook, and went back to $T=0$. It showed his clock radio at 11:59. Off camera, a tinny version of his voice said, "This is the sixth iteration. We expect it to be gone for about three days and eight hours." The clock radio went to 12:00 and disappeared.

The screen went gray for about a minute, then the clock radio reappeared, showing 8:15. He could time it precisely later. He ran it back and scrutinized it with the screen brightness turned all the way up. It seemed to be a minute of uniform gray.

But three days had passed, and three nights. That there was no alternation between dark and light meant that it wasn't getting illumination from the ambient surround.

Where had it gone?

That Herman was still alive indicated that it hadn't gone into outer space. The jug of water hadn't boiled away or turned to a block of ice.

He scientifically dipped a finger into the jug. Room temperature, give or take a couple of degrees.

The next time, he ought to include an environmental monitor, something that recorded temperature and pressure. L.L.Bean probably had one.

Money, though. He could probably borrow one from MIT, a midnight requisition. Bring it back in a month.

Forty days, actually. How long would it seem to him, in his metal box?

There was no way to interrogate Herman about the subjective length of his voyage. That he hadn't eaten indicated it was a short time. Or it could have been three days of turtle terror—he couldn't eat because he was too upset.

Probably not. If he'd been upset, he would have been locked up tight in his shell, the way he was after the trip from the pet shop. Matt had looked in the pan only a few seconds after it reappeared, and Herman seemed unruffled. Though it was hard to tell. He might be having a profound existential crisis.

Matt looked into the pan again. Herman was gnawing on a pellet of Baby Reptile Chow.

He went for a beer and remembered the champagne. Opened it, poured a jelly glass full, and sat down to think.

If everything was simple and linear, then the next time, the machine would move about twelve millimeters, half an inch, and the gray period would be about twelve minutes long. But it would be dangerous to assume linearity.

The safest course, if he were going to put himself in that metal box, would be to take along enough food and water for forty days. How much would that be? He typed the question into his notebook.

The consensus seemed to be about a gallon of water a day, which seemed like a lot if you weren't staggering across a desert. Eight of those big five-gallon jugs. Then one thousand five hundred calories of food a day, which would be easier. A couple of boxes of energy bars. A bottle of bourbon to keep from going insane. Maybe two. And a really good book.

And what about air? The only data points he had were that Herman was still alive and the water jug hadn't evaporated. Presumably a small turtle could last a long time on the air inside a loaf pan. A human could last for hours on a proportional amount. Only hours. So the water would be moot.

In fact, he could do the experiment without any of that, assuming it would take only minutes. If the minutes dragged on into hours, he could always call it quits and disconnect the fuel cell.

If that didn't work, call 911.

He'd been visualizing himself inside a metal cube, a gargantuan loaf pan like a clean Dumpster. But any sufficiently old car would do. Anything made before the Fossil Fuel Users Tax would have a mostly metal shell.

Mostly might not do it, though. His Mazda, for instance, had only a spidery titanium frame sunk inside a plastic aeroform. Technically, that would be a Faraday cage. But he wanted to be wrapped in metal.

Denny Peposi. Dopey Denny, Matt's main connection for recreational drugs. He had a 1956 Ford Thunderbird in his garage. The radio only played recordings of appropriately ancient music, and there were yellowed magazines from 1956 scattered on the backseat. He drove it around the block once a week, and maybe once a year bought enough gasoline to take out a girl he wanted to impress. Otherwise, it just sat there, a perfect Faraday cage with seats of soft Mexican leather. And all the Elvis Presley you would ever want to hear. Or was it Buddy Holly and the Beetles back then?

He was sure he could talk Denny into letting him sit in it, and take a video of him. "Watch! I'm going to make this car disappear." And then reappear forty days later.

But *where* would it appear? Matt looked at the machine on his way to refill his jelly glass. It had moved northeast a millimeter. If it moved northeast far enough, it would be in Boston Harbor. Or the North Atlantic. Wise to take some precautions about that possibility. Matt swam like a brick.

Which is how Matt wound up, the next morning, in a bad part of Boston, going from pawn shop to pawn shop looking for a wetsuit and a snorkel. He finally found both, at a place full of shabby sports relics. They cost more than half his cash reserves, but the man agreed, with a puzzled look, that he would refund 75 percent if Matt brought them back unused before the end of January. "In case the diving trip falls through," he said. At a military surplus store he bought an emergency raft that inflated if you pulled a lanyard. He saved the receipt.

He also got a proper cable with alligator clip to neatly solder onto the machine's chassis, so it would look good in the pictures, and a used high-speed camera, so he would be able to review the moments of the car's next disappearance and reappearance in slow motion. Unless it reappeared in Boston Harbor, or off the coast of Spain.

6

Dopey Denny lived in a large three-story Victorian
in Back Bay. He swung open the door and gave Matt a big
hug. Three hundred pounds of dope dealer, understandably
stoned at nine in the evening. "Dr. Einstein, I presume?"
He was wearing a black robe with glittering astrological
symbols, tied with a silver rope. Barefoot in January.

"Hi, Denny." Matt looked over the big man's shoulder.
"Louise home?"

"Ah, no. No. She moved on. How you doin' with
what's-her-name?"

"Kara. She moved on, too."

"Ain't it a bitch. Want a drink?"

Came here to do science, not socialize, but why not?
"Sure. What you got?"

"Got it all." He took Matt by the elbow and dragged him
toward the kitchen. Matt hauled along the duffel bag with
all his time-machine stuff in it.

The kitchen was all chrome and tile and looked like no
one had ever cooked a meal in it. "I'm doin' Heineken with a
whisky chaser. Or is it whisky with a Heineken chaser?"

"You have one and I'll have the other." Matt took a seat at the kitchen table, a spare, elegant Swedish thing. There was a bottle of twenty-five-year-old Glenmorangie on it and one crystal glass. Denny produced another glass and got two Heinekens from a huge metal refrigerator that seemed to have nothing in it but beer and wine. He should use *that* for the time machine. It would be cold, but he wouldn't die of thirst.

Denny tried to twist the bottles open, then remembered that wouldn't work with the imported beer, and crashed through a drawer until he found an opener.

He put the beers down and poured Matt a generous amount of whisky, and himself a little more generous one. He sat down on the delicate chair with exaggerated caution. "So you say you need the T-Bird. But just to sit in it?"

"Basically, yeah." Matt took a sip of the whisky and one of the beer. "Then it should disappear, and then come back."

He nodded slowly. "Like those guys who made the Statue of Liberty disappear. Way back when."

"I don't know anything about that. This isn't magic . . . Well, hell, maybe it *is* magic. I don't know what the hell it is."

"Not gonna hurt the car."

"No way. It just goes, like, somewhere sideways in space. Hell, I'm gonna be *in* it. I wouldn't do that if there was any danger, would I?" Matt resisted the impulse to slug back the whole glass. That might communicate uncertainty.

Denny took a vial out of his shirt pocket and tapped out a small pile of white powder, then produced a little cocktail straw and sniffed it up. He shook all over, like a big dog. "Ah! Want some?"

"No, thanks. Haven't done it in years. Are you sure you can—"

"Sure, sure. It's not cocaine; it's a DD beta for alertness." He shook again, grinning. "God *damn*! Cuts to the chase."

This was just great. The sole witness to a scientific revolution stoned on an untried drug. Fortunately, all he had to do was push a button.

Which was all Matt had to do, as well. He took another sip from each reagent. "How long have you been taking it?"

"Got it last night. Right up your alley, man; work till dawn."

"Maybe later. After it's not a beta." He laughed. "You're a fucking wild man, Denny."

"Hey, it's a job. Somebody has to do it."

Matt unzipped the duffel bag and brought out the camera. "You know how to work this?"

"Yeah, sure. Point an' shoot."

"Right. But I want to make sure the time function's on, the clock down in the right-hand corner." He toggled the switch until CLOCK came up, and selected it. "See?"

Denny took the camera. "No sweat." He held it up and looked at Matt through the point-and-shoot viewfinder. "Just push this big button?"

"Right. It'll be on a tripod, set for video, already aimed. Just start it when I tell you to, and if I disappear, leave it running till I come back." Maybe in a taxi.

Denny looked at the back of the camera. "No picture?"

"No, use the viewfinder. That's to save power. Don't know how long till I come back." He heard his voice quaver. He really didn't know *whether* he'd be back.

He pushed the glass away. "Better not drink any more. Change in the bathroom?"

Denny waved an arm back the way they'd come. *"Mi casa, su casa."* Matt picked up the duffel and went down the hall.

The bathroom was Italian tile with gold-plated hardware and a shower curtain by Salvador Dalí. Ornately framed nude paintings. Matt unzipped the duffel and laid out his gear. Stripped and threw his clothes back into the bag. Wallet and keys and change in a plastic bag, which he would carry into the uncertain future.

The wetsuit was talcumed on the inside, and slid on easily. How would he explain it to Denny? Just that he didn't know what to expect. Denny would probably not be able to understand, under the best of conditions, the tensor calculus he'd used as a shot-in-the-dark guess for describing the thing's behavior. And these were not the best of conditions.

He opened the Chinese carryout box and looked at Herman, who stared back accusingly. He couldn't leave him at home, and couldn't leave him with his mother with no explanation. Herman probably had a better chance of surviving, hurtling into the unknown in a '56 Thunderbird, than risking Denny's pet-sitting abilities.

He put the jar of Baby Reptile Chow in the suit's blouse pocket and picked up the time machine along with the case of bottled water and the bright yellow square of emergency raft, and walked back into the kitchen.

"Holy shit," Denny said. "I'm swearing off the stuff." He blinked twice, slowly. "I could swear you were standing there in a SCUBA outfit."

"Just the wetsuit. I don't know what environment we're— *I'm* going into. Couldn't afford a space suit."

"You're going into outer fucking *space*?"

"No, no, nothing like that. The last time I used this machine, it moved. But less than a millimeter." He held up his thumb and forefinger.

"So not outer space. Guaranteed?"

"No. Not outer space." He hoped.

"Just the fucking ocean. You're going to take my T-Bird and drop it in the ocean?"

"No. It probably won't move more than an inch."

"But just in *case* you dump it in the ocean—"

"Or the Charles or the Harbor—look, Denny, I can't

swim. The probability is almost zero, but it scares me shitless."

That mollified him a little. "Yeah. Me, neither." He shrugged. "If it was the Charles or the Harbor, I guess we could haul it back up."

"Yeah. No problem—unless I *drowned*. Then I wouldn't be able to tell you where it was."

Denny nodded rapidly and stood up with surprising speed. "Let's do it."

Matt and Herman followed him through the kitchen and out into the garage. There it was: a 270-horsepower dinosaur gleaming under a dozen coats of Tahitian Red lacquer.

"It . . . it's beautiful," Matt said.

"New paint job. Be careful with it." He opened the door and snapped on the radio. It started playing "I'm Mr. Blue" by the Belmonts.

Matt unfolded the tripod and set up the camera so it would be pointed at him in the front seat. He put the machine and the rest of his gear on the passenger side and hooked up the alligator clip to the car's frame.

"Hey, and don't get any Chinese on the upholstery."

"It's not Chinese food. It's a turtle."

"Oh. Yeah. Of course."

"Almost forgot." He reached into the pocket with the Baby Reptile Chow and brought out a three-by-five card with Professor Marsh's name and phone number. "Anything goes wrong, call this guy. My boss."

"Professor Marsh, like in swamp?"

"Right." Matt started to close the door but left it open. If he wound up in water, he wanted to be able to jump out. "I'm ready if you are. Just point and shoot."

When Denny pushed the button, so did Matt. He was suddenly blind, immersed in opalescent gray. He heard Herman nervously scratching around in his box.

It was strange, but not unexpected. He had time to wonder

whether it would be a minute, ten minutes, forty days—and then all hell broke loose.

Bright daylight dazzled him and a Yellow Cab crashed into his open door, tearing it off and spinning into the on-coming traffic, where it was broadsided by the slow-crawling #1 bus.

He was in the middle of Massachusetts Avenue in Cambridge, outside of the Plough and Stars pub. Traffic was squirreling to a halt all around him, horns blaring. With a loud bang, the yellow raft decided to inflate itself. He grabbed Herman and scrunched out of the car, pursued by a wall of yellow plastic, his wetsuit rather incongruous under the present circumstances, morning rush hour with snow all around. A siren wailed and a large female police officer came bearing down on him with her ticket book flapping in the cold breeze.

"Officer," he said, "I can explain . . ." Or could he?

She sniffed at his breath. "Are you drunk?"

A male voice yelled, "Hands in the air. Put your god-damned hands in the air!" Matt did, and another policeman marched toward him holding a really large pistol at eye level with both hands.

"But I haven't done anything," he said inanely. Just dropped an antique car in the middle of Mass Ave during rush hour. With no tires; those were still in Denny's garage.

The man's pistol was homing in on Matt's nose. "Ran the plate," he said to the woman. "The car's stolen. Owner murdered."

"What?" Matt said. "Denny?"

"You have the right to remain silent," the woman said, her own gun pointed at Matt's heart. "Anything you say can and will be used against you in a court of law. You have the right to speak to an attorney, and to have an attorney present during any questioning. If you cannot afford a lawyer, one will be provided for you at government expense."

"But I didn't kill anybody." Including the Yellow Cab

driver, who was very much alive even though his nose was bleeding profusely as he stomped toward the three of them, yelling incoherently.

Never losing her point of aim, the woman reached up and took the Chinese carryout box and expertly thumbed it open with one hand.

She peered inside. "A turtle?"

"Well," Matt said, "it's a long story."

7

They allowed Matt to change out of the wetsuit and into gray prisoner's coveralls. Then they put him in a small room and handcuffed him to a chair. The room had a big mirror or one-way window, and a tear-off calendar on the table said it was February 2, consistent with a time jump of thirty-nine days, thirteen hours.

"What's with the handcuffs?" he asked the guard. "I'm not going anywhere."

"It's standard operating procedure when someone shows up in a wetsuit holding a pet turtle. We don't have any strait-jackets."

He left and was replaced with a Detective Reed, a small tough-looking man who smoked nonfilter cigarettes. Where did he get them, Matt wondered, and how come he could smoke on city property?

The detective sat down across from Matt and crushed out his cigarette stub in the ashtray, where it continued to smol-der. "You knew Dennis Peposi. You bought dope from him."

"I bought Ritalin, for concentration enhancement."

"I suppose you had a prescription and can produce

receipts." Matt shook his head. "When was the last time you saw him?"

"December 14, at exactly 9:38 P.M."

Reed wrote something down. "That's about the time he died. The day, anyhow."

"He was alive when I saw him. Drunk and stoned, but alive."

"Sometime around then, he was murdered. Presumably by the person who stole his million-dollar car."

"How did he die?"

"Suppose I ask the questions for a while? How well did you know Mr. Peposi?"

"Not too well. Met him through another student when I was an undergraduate at MIT. Maybe eight years ago."

"He was just your dealer?"

"We went to some parties now and then. He liked to show off the Thunderbird."

"You did hard drugs at these parties?"

"No—I knew he was involved with them, of course. He didn't make that kind of money selling Ritalin to students."

"When you last saw him, he was under the influence of drugs?"

"Yeah, but he almost always was, at night. He snorted something he said was a beta, a drug that was being tested."

"You had some, too?"

"No. No way in hell. Denny was crazy."

Reed nodded slowly at that and looked through a couple of pages on a clipboard. "They found a vial of white powder on his body. A stimulant of some sort. Along with the name and phone number of an MIT professor."

"Not related," Matt said quickly. "I gave him the phone number."

Reed nodded. "Yes; your fingerprints were all over the card. The professor said you used to work for him. You stole some valuable equipment and disappeared."

"Oh boy. It wasn't like that at all." Except that it was, come to think of it.

"Nobody's seen you in a month or more."

"Thirty-nine and a half days. I've been . . . Look, this is being recorded, right?" He nodded. "Let me tell you the whole story. From the very beginning."

The detective looked at his watch. "Give you ten minutes. It was a dark and stormy night?"

"Dark and snowy . . ."

In fact, it was over twenty minutes before Matt wound down. Detective Reed flipped through his notes and looked at the one-way mirror on the wall. "Harry? You wanta come in here?"

The door opened a moment later and an angular man in tweeds walked in. "Mr. Fuller, I am Lieutenant Sterman. Dr. Sterman."

"A psychiatrist," Matt said.

"Psychologist. Ph.D." He rolled a chair over quietly and sat down next to Detective Reed. "That was a very interesting story."

"All of it true."

"I'm sure you think so." He looked at Matt as an entomologist might look at a bug whose species was not quite familiar.

"We called Professor Marsh, as Detective Reed mentioned. He did verify that a laboratory assistant named Matthew Fuller had disappeared a couple of weeks before."

"That's good."

"He fired you for instability and drug dependence. Your name came up, in fact, when we asked him to explain why *his* name was in the pocket of a dead drug dealer—"

"He wasn't my *drug* dealer!"

"—and you've since become rather a legend in your department. Crazy Matt who lost it and killed his drug dealer

and ran away with his big antique car. They said you were
babbling about time travel then, too."

"Okay. How do you explain my materializing in the middle of Mass Avenue in this antique wheelless car?"

"Nobody saw you materialize," the detective said.
"The assumption is that you were being towed and fell off
the truck. There *was* a tow truck in front of you, which we're
trying to find. There was quite a traffic jam when you . . .
'materialized.' "

"What about the cabbie who hit the car door?"

"He's sure you fell off the truck."

"*Jesus!* And the wetsuit. What kind of crazy person would
be sitting in a towed car wearing a wetsuit in the middle of
winter?"

They both just looked at him.

"What about the camera? You must have taken it as evidence. It shows me and the car disappearing!"

Reed looked at his top page. "It was under your fat
friend. 'Beyond repair,' it says here."

"Oh, shit. Denny saw the car disappear and had a fucking heart attack! That's how he died, isn't it?"

"We don't know," Dr. Sterman said. "He'd been dead
for more than two weeks. Many causes of death were possible, I suppose—I'm not a pathologist—but the autopsy
indicated drug overdose."

"Well, *I* sure didn't drug him. He didn't need any help
for that."

"It's not that simple. When someone is as deeply connected with organized crime as Mr. Peposi was, any death
is suspicious. Especially drug-related."

"So go round up some Mafia guys. I'm just an innocent
time traveler. Or a crazy graduate student in a wetsuit. I
don't see how you can hold me for murder."

"We can book you for grand theft auto," Reed said, "and
meanwhile include you as a suspect in the murder investigation."

"Hey, I'll admit to taking the car! Denny loaned it to me. You must have gotten the crystal out of the camera. It'll show me and the car disappearing."

Reed actually smiled. "That would be a first. Using a video of you disappearing in a car to prove that you didn't take the car. But there's no evidence record of a data crystal."

"But I know it had one." Or *did* it? He'd had Denny use the optical viewfinder, to conserve power. "Maybe it rolled out when the camera broke."

"I'm sure they would have found it during the investigation. They're pretty thorough."

Matt wondered how thorough anybody would be, stuck in a room with a three-hundred-pound rotting corpse.

Dr. Sterman rose. "Ron, I have to get to a meeting. Let me know how this turns out." He bobbed his head at Matt. "Good day, Mr. Fuller."

"I'd hate to have a *bad* one." He watched the man leave. "So what now? I get one phone call?"

He slid a cell over. "Take two. You want to call a lawyer?"

"People like me don't have lawyers. I guess the court appoints me one?"

"When they set bail, later today."

"Better not be more than two hundred bucks." He punched in Kara's number, but she hung up without a word.

His mother wouldn't be any help. The only person he knew who knew lawyers was the guy he evidently killed by surprise. He called Professor Marsh and got sputtering incoherence. The police hadn't been too respectful when they first contacted him, after finding his name and number in the pocket of the huge rotting corpse of a drug dealer.

Detective Reed watched his discomfort with a neutral expression. He took the cell back. "I didn't take much physics in school, just basic physical science. They said that time travel wasn't possible, I remember. Paradoxes."

"Well, I'm here. Whether you believe me or not, a few

hours ago I was in Denny's garage and it was 9:38 on December 14.

"If this thing's a time machine, though, it's an utterly useless one. As long as it's one-way."

"Yeah, I get that. If you could take a newspaper back to December 14, just the business section, you could clean up on the stock market."

"And that's your paradox. It plays hell with cause and effect. Unless every time you use the machine, it starts a new universe—one where you're a rich guy."

"But then when you got up here, the second of February, wouldn't there be two of you?"

"Some say yes and some say no. Let's see whether I walk through the door there."

Somebody knocked on the door and they both jumped. But it was only a uniformed police officer, an attractive blond woman. "Lieutenant, they sent me up to get Matthew Fuller, if you're done with him."

"Yeah." He came around to unlock the handcuffs.

"I could tell you about Kurt Gödel and Albert Einstein."

"Close personal friends, I'm sure. Stand up and turn around, hands behind your back."

She put a pair of soft plastic cuffs on him. "Is he dangerous?"

"No. Just let me know if he suddenly disappears into thin air."

"I might, you know. I don't understand the process."

"I half believe you. Otherwise, I may see you at the arraignment, or afterward."

She touched him on the shoulder. "Come on, Matthew. Your room's ready."

His cellmate was a small man with a red face and white stubble, named Theo Hockney. He actually said, "What you in for?"

"Murder." Saying the word made his heart skip. "And grand theft auto. What actually happened, I borrowed a friend's car and he died right after I left."

"Now that's a bitch. I'm innocent, too." As they always said, the place was chock-full of innocent people. "I ran into a guy with my car. Hell, he jumped in front of me, crazy. So he commits suicide, and I wind up in the slammer."

"Did you know the guy?"

"Yeah, well, that's the problem. He was sort of my ex-brother-in-law. We weren't exactly pals. But you wanta kill someone, you don't go hunting him with no goddamned *car*. I mean, I can carry a gun. I got a permit and all. So I'm gonna kill this bastard with a *car*?"

"I see what you mean."

"Even though I should get a medal, the guy was such a prick."

"He married your sister?"

"Kind of. Slapped her around. You know? Big guy, got friends on the force."

"The police? That sucks."

"You bet it does." He went to the window and looked out at the gray day, parking lot piled up with dirty snow. "They're gonna nail my fuckin' ass to the wall."

Matthew didn't know what to say. He was overcome with a desire to escape from jail, especially this particular cell. "Can you . . . could you . . . prove it was an accident?"

"Yeah, I wish. There wasn't no witnesses. Just a god-damn security camera in a bank across the street. Two in the morning." He turned and gave Matt a look you might call murderous. "Why you so curious?"

"Sorry." Matt raised a placating hand. "Didn't mean to pry. I've never done this before, been in jail."

"What does *that* mean? Like I spend all my time here?"

The blond guard tapped on the bars and rescued him. "Matthew Fuller? Come with me. You have a lawyer conference."

"But I thought I didn't have a lawyer yet."

"I guess you do. This way." She kept her eye on the other prisoner until the door crashed closed.

"Hey!" he said. "I didn't tell him nothin'!" She ignored that and led Matthew, without cuffs, out of the confinement area and back up to an office across from the room where he'd been interrogated.

The man there looked like a lawyer, a successful one, all Armani and Rolex with a haircut that must have cost more than Matthew made in a month. He rose and shook hands from across the scarred table.

"Matthew, I am Calvin Langham, of Langham, Langham, and Cruise." He glanced at the officer, and she left. He sat back down, and so did Matthew.

He looked at him appraisingly. "You're innocent, aren't you?"

"I am, yes. Are you, what, going to represent me?"

"You wouldn't want me to. I'm a corporate lawyer." He leaned back and nodded. "This is peculiar. A little while ago a messenger brought to my firm an envelope with two cashier's checks and instructions. One check was for me, and it more than covered the expense of my coming across town. The other was one million dollars, to apply toward your bail. Which, I just found out, is exactly one million dollars. You don't look like a murderer and a car thief."

"I'm neither."

"When I showed the check to the judge, she accepted it, and said that after the arraignment today she would release you on your own recognizance, not to leave the Boston area. From her remarks, I take it she assumed the check was mob money."

"But I don't know anybody like that."

"Nobody?"

"I guess the man who died, Dennis Peposi—the cop who talked to me said he was connected to organized crime."

"Was he?"

"Probably, now that I think of it . . . He dealt drugs and had to get them from somewhere. I didn't think he was a Boy Scout, but I knew him for years, and he never dropped a hint about that kind of connection."

Langham shook his head. "Better watch your back. Maybe they bought your way out so they can get to you."

"But I don't know anything. Don't have anything."

"They don't know that. All they know is the police think you killed one of them. The mob."

"Jesus. I should stay in jail."

"Personally, I wouldn't advise that. It's a high-crime area." He took a folded-over piece of paper from a pocket and handed it to Matt. "The courier left a message. Don't read it aloud."

It said, *Get in the car and go.*

Who knew about the car? "This messenger. Did he look like me?"

"Somewhat. I didn't get a good look at him. When I opened the envelope and came back down to the receptionist's place, he was gone. She played back a security camera that showed the back of his head, and he was your size, long hair."

Matt wondered. Could he have come back from the future to rescue himself? Maybe in some future, he learns how to reverse and control the process, and comes back in a Gödelian closed loop—reappearing a week ago, making a million on the stock market, and then . . .

"What time did this guy show up at your office?"

"Not long after we opened. I'd say 9:30."

So he could leave before Matt got here. Just before. Which would short-circuit the paradox; they wouldn't both be in the here and now at the same time and space.

Or maybe it was just a Mafia trap. "How seriously would you take the mob thing?"

"Do you know anyone else with a million dollars?

Someone who would just drop it off and not hang around for an explanation?"

"No . . . no, I guess not. My department at MIT, but I'm not exactly a hero there. What do you think I should do?"

"I think, as I said, I would watch my back." Langham picked up his leather portfolio and stood, looking at his watch. "The arraignment will be pretty soon. The court will appoint you a lawyer, but that's pro forma; you probably won't even meet him or her. Just plead not guilty. The judge has your bail."

"I can just walk away from a murder charge?"

"They can't charge you with murder just because you were in the victim's car. Immobile car, I understand. You're pleading not guilty to grand theft auto."

"Which is true. I didn't steal the car."

"It's also irrelevant. You'll be free to go once you sign some papers." They shook hands and he left.

Matt spent a few minutes leafing through a worn copy of *Time*, catching up a little on what happened two weeks before, and the blond officer came back. "This is pretty quick," she said. "You know somebody?"

"Somebody knows me, evidently. The lawyer says a stranger made my bail."

"Before you even knew how much it was?" Matt shrugged. "Judge said she'd take you first."

The judge was a white-haired lady with a weary expression, sitting behind a desk piled with paper. She picked up a sheet. "This is an arraignment on the warrant initial presentment. Matthew Fuller, you are accused of grand theft auto, the vehicle in question being a . . . 1956? A 1956 Ford Thunderbird belonging to the late Dennis Peposi. How do you plead?"

"Not guilty. I—"

She brought a gavel down. "Your bail has been arranged. The trial date is tentatively set for March 1. You're free to go, but you cannot leave the Commonwealth of Massachusetts without first notifying this court." She looked up at him for the first time. "We're serious about that. You're a material witness in a homicide investigation. Don't leave town, or you might find yourself back here." She looked past him, at the man guarding the door. "Next."

The blond officer took him back to the room with the *Time* magazine and told him to wait. There were no stories about time travel in the magazine, its name notwithstanding.

She came back in a few minutes. "Here are your things." She put the wetsuit and snorkel on the table, and the plastic bag with his wallet and keys. "Those coveralls are city property. I'll leave you alone while you change."

Go out on the street in the dead of winter wearing a wetsuit and a smile? Evidently.

Cambridge is a college town, though, and Matthew looked young enough for his attire to be part of a fraternity prank or a lost drunken wager. People either stared or looked right through him as he hurried the two blocks down to the Gap. The wetsuit was cold, but its rubber bootlets gave him good traction on the ice.

Get in the car and go. He bought jeans and a warm flannel shirt, shoes and socks and a lined anorak. Where would the car be?

He went back to the police station and asked the sergeant at the front desk. The sergeant typed and moused around on an ancient computer.

"You can't have it yet. It's evidence, grand theft auto."

He evidently didn't know the gory details. "I don't want to take it. I just need some stuff from work that's on the front seat."

He stared at Matt for a long moment. What, did he expect a bribe? Matt started for his wallet.

"You go talk to Sergeant Roman." He scribbled on a yellow Post-it note. "He's in charge of the vehicle pound in Somerville; that's where it is. Maybe he'll let you take your stuff; maybe he won't."

"Thanks." Matt didn't recognize the address, but he could look it up.

He got on the Red Line but went past Somerville to his own stop. He walked home on the lookout for Mafia goons, but saw only a bundled-up jogger who might have been sexy underneath the shapeless coverall, and an old woman in an orange jumpsuit walking two tiny dogs.

He was shivering by the time he let himself in. The apartment was stifling hot, which for a change was welcome. He put the kettle on for tea and sipped a glass of warm red wine.

He spent the rest of the day and part of the next collecting and organizing every scrap of data about the device, and made a clear copy of his mathematical analysis of it all. He put it in a neat binder and boxed it up with the cheap cell that had traveled with the machine in the first experiment, and the crystal from the camera that had recorded its going and returning. Then a long description of what had happened from the time he knocked on Denny's door.

He addressed the box to Dr. Marsh and rode down to MIT so he could send it via campus mail. That would delay delivery for two or three days.

By the time Marsh opened it, Matt would be very elsewhere.

He went back to the apartment, figuring to get a good long sleep before he went to talk to Sergeant Roman. But a voice mail gave him a sense of urgency.

The voice didn't sound tough. There was no cheesy Italian accent. But it said, "I represent Mr. Peposi's employers, and we have some questions about his last hours. We'd like to meet with you at your convenience. Tonight. Please give me a call."

He gave a Charleston number. Some fine Italian families live there. Matthew decided it was time to be missing.

8

Sergeant Roman was a tall, thin black man with a shaved head and a dour expression.

"You stole this car and you want me to let you get into it and look around?"

"I *didn't* steal it. I—"

"Sorry. You're 'under indictment' for stealing this car, and you expect me to do that."

"It's not as if I could drive it away," he said.

"What do you mean?"

"I mean it doesn't have any *tires*."

"Doesn't have tires? Oh. That's the antique came in on the flatbed."

"That's probably it." Maybe he hadn't looked inside. "I have some stuff on the front seat, an experiment from school. I'm a graduate student at MIT."

"You got an ID, then."

Matt took it out of his wallet and passed it over. Roman scrutinized both sides. Please, please don't call to check it.

"You can't take any evidence out of the car."

"I don't want to remove it. Just make sure it's okay."

He handed back the card and gave Matt a sharp look. "I suppose. But I'm goin' with you."

Please do, Matt thought. An eyewitness. "Sure. Where is it?"

He pointed with his thumb. "Still on the flatbed."

They walked between two long rows of impounded cars to a flatbed trailer. The Thunderbird was under a canvas. The sergeant helped Matt peel it back. The canvas crackled and shed frost.

"Good God . . . what a paint job like that cost?"

"A bundle," Matt said. He clambered up onto the trailer and slid into the driver's seat through the hole that used to be a door. The Mexican seat leather was frozen stiff.

The machine was there, apparently untouched, the conducting cable still clamped to the doorframe. The inflatable raft was wadded up in the backseat. It probably had enough residual air to act as a life preserver.

His thumb hovered over the button. He looked back at Sergeant Roman. "You got the time?"

He checked his wrist. "About ten till—2:48."

"Okay. The fourth of February—14:48." He pushed RESET.

Just like the last time, he was suddenly blinded by gray. It probably wouldn't last long; he groped behind the seat and hauled the bundle of raft up into his lap and held on to it for dear life—if he materialized over water he'd have to dive out the door. It was going to be 465 days, May 15, about 4:00 in the afternoon—at least the water won't be freezing—

Tires screaming facing the wrong way on a superhighway a pickup truck spiraling toward him—Matthew slapped the button just before impact and everything went gray again.

He hoped nobody had been hurt. If somebody dies every time he pushes the button, maybe he'd better stop doing it!

This time would be about fifteen years. He braced himself for water, for traffic, for anything—

Except applause. He materialized in the middle of what looked like a football or soccer field, thousands of people on bleachers, cheering, jumping up and down. A tuba band started playing a triumphant march.

Beyond the bleachers, a solid crowd of people. Tens of thousands?

A fat man with a Santa Claus beard, wearing a sky-blue tuxedo, strode toward him. It was Professor Marsh!

"Welcome home, my boy," he said, reaching into the car to shake Matt's hand. "My boy"? Marsh had called him a lot of names, but never that one.

He took Matt's elbow. "Come with me. Your public awaits."

Somewhat dazed, Matt staggered along with Marsh toward a grandstand where several older people stood applauding. That tuba band below them must have had a hundred tubas, large and small. Matt had never seen a small tuba before.

There would probably be even stranger things, up here in the future.

They mounted the grandstand, and everyone sat down except for one of the women, who turned out to be the governor of Massachusetts. She had a few general and mildly confusing remarks before she introduced the other woman, the president of MIT, who praised Matt for his originality and daring, not mentioning that his last connection with MIT had been a disconnection.

By the time the director of the National Institute of Chronophysics had spoken, and introduced Professor Marsh—Nobel Prize–winning discoverer of the Marsh Effect—the pieces had started to fall into place.

The bastard who'd fired him had taken his notes, along with data from police and security cameras, and parlayed them into a Nobel Prize in Physics. He predicted where and when Matt was going to appear, which was in the middle of a block of tenements in Roxbury. The city had torn down the tenements and replaced them with the Matthew Fuller Sports Center.

So Marsh gets the Nobel Prize and the Marsh Effect, and Matt gets a soccer field named after him. There was a consolation, though: They hadn't been able to duplicate the Marsh Effect. They'd been waiting for him to come back with the machine.

He was sorely tempted to run back down the field—*his* field—and jump back into the car and push the button. Let them wait another couple of centuries.

But this might not be so bad. Marsh noted that Matt had been given a doctorate by MIT, and a professorship in the chronophysics department.

Maybe he'd get the girl, too. He scanned the bleachers for Kara—but of course she'd be over forty now, and might look quite different. There was a front row of seats occupied by people who must have been of some importance, but that might not include ex-girlfriends who had betrayed the guest of honor.

His throat suddenly tightened when he realized that his mother wasn't there.

People were applauding. Marsh had asked him up to say a few words.

He stood up and fainted.

9

The doctor said it was a combination of extreme fatigue and the succession of shocks. They kept him under observation for twenty-four hours anyhow. Candled his head and didn't find anything surprising.

He had a large single room on the top floor of MIT Medical. He could see the Green Building from his window. Way too many flowers; he had a sneezing fit and asked a nurse to take them out.

He was facing the corner of the Green Building from which students had conducted the Great Piano Drop his first year of graduate school. Three in the morning, they had pushed an ancient, out-of-tune player piano off the top, thirty floors up, along with a speaker system. It played a few distressing seconds of a complex Mozart tune on the way down.

Matt was out of bed and dressed when Marsh came to visit the next morning. Tweeds suited him better than a blue tuxedo. "Sorry about all that brouhaha," he said. "They've been anticipating your return for some time." He sat down heavily.

"Are you all right, sir?" His normally ruddy face was pale.

"Up too late. A man my age should know when to stop celebrating." He smiled broadly, teeth too perfect to be real. "But that was quite a day. You should have seen the car materialize, right then and right there."

"I'm surprised you could predict the time and place so accurately."

"I'll go over the math with you. Or have Dr. Lewis do it; he knows it better."

"That would be *Strom* Lewis?"

"Yes, of course. He was a student of yours when you were a TA, wasn't he?" And took his job and stole his girl, incidentally.

"Sure. How's he doing?"

"All right. Assistant professorship, tenure. Has a family, I believe."

"Oh. How nice."

Marsh paused. He was not completely clueless. "You outrank him, of course. Honorary full professor, and tenure is, um . . ." He waved it away with one hand. "You're the safest person in the department. After me, perhaps."

"So I'll be teaching . . . not chronophysics."

"No, no, not yet. You have some catching up to do. We have you penciled in for 8.225."

"Doesn't ring a bell."

"It's an introduction to old modern physics—'Physics of the Twentieth Century'—you know, Einstein, Oppenheimer, Feynman."

"Twentieth century?" Marsh nodded. "Jesus!"

"A lot has happened in physics since you disappeared," he said. "*Because* you disappeared. There are even aspects of Newtonian mechanics that have to be reconsidered. String theory's completely rewritten, and with it, quantum mechanics and relativity—moving toward a Grand Unified Theory, finally.

"These past fifteen years have seen a total revolution. People compare it to the 1920s, after Einstein's bombshell."

"So I have some studying to do."

"Quite a lot, I think." He reached into his bag and brought out two books, one at a time: *Aspects of Time Travel* and *Intermediate Chronophysics*, both by himself. "You might want to look through this one first." *Aspects.* "You'll want to bone up on rings and algebras and topology for *Intermediate*."

Rings and algebras? "What does set theory have to do with it? Topology?"

"I think you'll find it an interesting approach. But do read the general treatment first." He levered himself up out of the chair, wincing. "If you feel up to contributing, we'll be having a press conference at noon. The big conference room on the fourth floor of the Green Building."

"No harm in it. Not much to tell them."

"See you there about 11:30, then. Think I'll go have a little rest first." He shook hands and shuffled away.

Matt was halfway through the book's introduction when there was a tap on the door. "Mattie?" It was Kara, a little heavier, poised on the brink of middle age, still attractive in a short skirt and SPAMIT tee shirt—Stupid People at MIT, a select fraternity. Strom Lewis followed her in, not quite a young Turk anymore, salt-and-pepper in a short beard.

She giggled, hand in front of her mouth, then shrugged off her backpack and kissed him on the cheek. "You look so *young*!"

He couldn't immediately come up with a tactful reply— "You look so old" wouldn't be kind—so he just nodded.

"By God," Strom said. "Was it like . . . I mean, did no time pass at all?"

"Less than a minute each time, each transition," Matt said. "I was in Somerville yesterday, at the police department's stolen automobile pound."

"I'd forgotten about that," Strom said. "That must have been pretty unpleasant."

Did people know about the mysterious stranger with the

million bucks' bail? It had to be a matter of record. "What about when I came back for a few seconds on the expressway? Fifteen years ago. Was anybody hurt?"

They looked at each other. "There was a big pileup," Kara said. "I don't remember whether anyone was hurt or killed."

"Well, yeah," Strom said. "I've seen the cubes a hundred times. A pickup truck rolled, but I think the driver stayed inside—that's right; you can see an air bag. Other cars banging around. One was a police ghost car, fortunately, so we had your appearance time down to the thousandth of a second, and with five or six different GPS readings, we could position you within a fraction of a millimeter."

"So if I pushed the button now? Would I wind up in Arizona, or what?"

"Up by the New Hampshire border, I think, 177 years from now. Of course, no one's going to push the button until we have a duplicate made."

"Okay by me. Fifteen years is disorienting enough."

"Oh, I brought you some stuff," Kara said, and rummaged through her backpack. She brought out a stack of magazines and a thing like an old-fashioned iPod stick, but without wires. "Here." She pulled a little red dot off the machine and pressed it onto his cheekbone. "I put some old music on it, too, but it's mainly what young people are listening to. Your students' ages."

"Pure crap," Strom said.

"No, it's just different." She did a shrug and a moue that hadn't changed. "They look different, too."

"Brands," Matt said. "I've seen a few here."

"And other kinds of scars. Not so much at MIT. It can be pretty extreme on the street." She put the magazines on the rolling table by the bed. "You'll want to look through these."

Strom stood up. "Once you get settled, come on up to the office. Spend a few hours getting you up to speed on the math."

"Yeah . . . I'll Google around for a few days first, get my bearings." Have to ask. "Um . . . does anybody know who bailed me out?"

"Bailed you out?"

"The first time I came back, after forty days?"

"Of course," Strom said. "That's when you sent the preliminary results to Dr. Marsh."

"That's right. I was in jail for causing a pileup on Mass Ave. A lawyer showed up with my bail, which he got from some anonymous stranger."

Strom shook his head. "I don't know anything about that. Could it have been Marsh?"

"No way. He was . . . sort of angry with me."

"I remember," Kara said. "He got my number somehow and called me. He thought you'd stolen the machine and disappeared. Of course you'd just—"

"But I left him a duplicate! Slogged down here in the snow to put it together. It didn't travel through time, but it did supply one photon per chronon, which is what it was designed to do."

"He must not have found it."

"But I put it right where . . . I'll take it up with him later today." Could somebody have broken in and stolen it? Nobody would know of its importance.

Except perhaps a time traveler.

"Well, we'll see you over at the press conference," Strom said. "Come early. I heard Marsh talk to Maggie about the catering. It's going to be a real blowout."

"Sounds good. I'll see about checking out of here." He watched them go with mixed, not to say confused, feelings. Just a few days ago, they had destroyed his life. Now they were strangers and allies.

The suitcase in the closet was his, but most of the clothes hanging there were unfamiliar. Once they'd realized what had happened, the department had rented his old place, partly to keep it against his return and partly to see if there was any clue there to the machine's anomalous behavior.

Most of the clothes he'd left behind had been ten years old already, and not too clean. Another fifteen years wouldn't have helped.

It looked pretty warm out. He put on an unfamiliar tie and tweed jacket. Stroll through campus and check out the current crop of undergraduate girls. Brands and all.

The dispatcher at the main desk said that everything had been taken care of; he was free to go. An hour and a half before the press conference. Walk up to the Student Center and back, and get there just as the canapés come out.

He was headed for the revolving door when the emergency doors next to it whooshed open. Two men and a woman rushed in guiding a gurney.

It was Professor Marsh, mouth open and eyes closed. They pushed him into a waiting elevator.

Matt went back to the dispatcher. "Is that Professor Marsh?"

"Was, I think." He squinted at his computer screen. "Somebody found him in the Green Building, in his office. We had this team there for a big press conference; they got right to him. Too late, though."

"Damn."

"I saw him on TV last night," the dispatcher said. "Too much excitement, I guess. You knew him?"

"A long time ago, yeah."

"How old was he?"

"Sev—eighty-five or so. Closer to ninety."

"That's what I thought. Be a miracle if they can bring him back. Sorry."

"Me, too." Matt nodded. "Me, too." He turned and headed for the other exit, toward the Green Building. Might as well see what was happening.

10

It was Marsh's ascension into scientific sainthood and Matthew's fifteen minutes of fame. The cover of *Time* had Marsh brooding in a hyperrealistic painting by Fiona Wyeth—probably on file for years—against a ghostly background of clocks, where a wraithlike figure of Matt is stepping out of the mists of time.

The press had it all figured out. Matt wasn't much more than an experimental animal, even though it was his clumsiness that had started it all. It was Marsh's genius that had explained Matt's accidental time machine.

But Matt could see that the Marsh Effect didn't explain what happened in a definitive way. It really just described what the machine did. Then Marsh and others had tried, and were still trying, to twist physics around so that it allowed the machine to exist.

But it was as if physics had been a careful, elegant house of cards, then Marsh—or rather his earthly avatar, Matthew—had been a playful child who blundered into it and brought it down, not out of malice, but just by accident.

Now Matt, true to the analogy, sat in the middle of the

mess, picking up one card and then another, trying to make sense out of it.

He came to the office every morning at nine and spent part of the day working on time travel and the rest trying to put together his course on antique physics. He had more than three months before classes started; if he'd been assigned the course back in his TA days, and there were no time machines to complicate things, he could've assembled the course in a few weeks. But ignoring the Marsh Effect would be like trying to conduct a class around an elephant sitting in the front row.

Marsh had been right in his warning that Matt would have to bone up on topology and the manipulations of algebras and rings—mathematical tools he'd never needed before. So he was attempting a mental juggling act, trying to learn the old new math while preparing to teach the new old physics. It made his brain hurt.

And it wasn't as if he'd be allowed to sit uninterrupted and work. There were more than a thousand copies of his time machine in the world, and science demanded that he push the RESET button on all of them, in case the Marsh Effect was really the Matthew Effect. They couldn't just FedEx a machine from China, have him push the button, then mail it back after having failed to make it disappear. He had to hike down to a lab and sit in the middle of a circle of cameras and other instruments and push the button.

A few times, he agreed to duplicate the original physiological circumstances—stay up for thirty hours high on coffee and speed. He argued that the whole thing was more like superstition than science, and the response was basically: Okay, do you have a better idea?

Meanwhile, it wasn't only science that had changed drastically in the past sixteen years. Movies were either dumb static domestic comedies (during which the audience laughed insanely at things that didn't seem to be funny) or brutal bloodbaths from Japan and India. Popular music set his teeth on edge, harmonic discord and machine-gun percussion or syrupy, inane love ballads. Popular books seemed to be written for either slow children or English Ph.D.s.

Women his age had been children when he left. Of course *they* liked the music and books and movies and thought the height of fashion was symmetrical cheek brands—not only on the cheeks of the face, he was given to understand. The women who were his contemporaries were either like Kara, middle-aged and married, or middle-aged and not interested in men.

His mother was in a rest home, lost to Alzheimer's Disease. He visited her several times, but she didn't recognize him.

He did have a little notoriety by virtue of being an artifact from the past, but sixteen years didn't exactly make him a caveman. More like an old-fashioned geek who hadn't kept up with stuff.

He went to his twenty-fifth high-school reunion and left early, deeply rattled.

About that time he started to fantasize about pushing the RESET button again. The world would be truly alien, 177.5 years in the future, but he wouldn't be trying to fit in. He would be a genuine curiosity, like a nineteenth-century scientist appearing today. Who wouldn't be expected to do any real physics. And the big questions would presumably be answered. He might even be able to understand the answers.

The time machine was very much under lock and key, with a twenty-four-hour armed guard. But if anybody could get to it, Matt should be able to.

That stayed in the back of his mind, the ultimate escape fantasy, while he did his damnedest to adjust to this not-so-brave, not-so-new world.

Ironically, Kara and Strom, whose betrayal had pushed him into pushing the button, became his best friends and mentors. He often went to their place for dinner, to hang around and play with their son, Peter. At nine years old, he was close to being Matt's equal in social sophistication.

He tried to date. It wasn't hard to find women his age who were interested in him, either as famous semiscientist or social freak from the past. But neither characterization was a good starting point for a relationship. His foolish aversion to facial brands didn't help, either, eliminating half the pool of young women a priori.

Male friends were even harder to make. He wasn't interested in sports, the one cultural fixation that hadn't changed at all, as far as he could see, and that was the one place where men assumed they could make an easy connection. When somebody said, "How about them Sox?" he would mumble something and look at his feet.

Under normal circumstances, his natural pool of friends would be the graduate students and young professors in his own department. But he didn't know enough about post-time-machine physics to chat about their work, and his unearned full professorship was an obvious obstacle.

A couple of times he resorted to "dates" from escort services, but that was so disastrous that not even the sex was very much fun. It was like taking a department-store manikin to dinner and a show, and then home to a perfect body with nothing inside but lubricant.

Then one night after dinner, Peter put to bed and Strom off in the study, Kara led him out to the front porch, where they sat together on a swing with glasses of wine. She was just close enough that they barely touched.

"I'm sorry about what I did," she said quietly. "I should've stayed with you."

Matt didn't know what to say. "Water over the bridge," he tried. "I mean under."

"I don't know. Does it have to be?"

"Kara . . ."

"I'm desperately unhappy," she said without inflection. "Strom bores me to tears."

He patted her hand. "You wouldn't've been any better off with me. One chronophysicist is about as boring as the next one."

She smiled up at him. "See? Strom would never say that. And you're anything but boring."

This couldn't be happening. The full moon hanging over the horizon romantically, crickets chirping. Her wonderful smell. Her husky voice: "But I'm too old for you now."

"No! Kara . . . you're beautiful. You're still the most beautiful—"

"We should talk. Strom's taking Peter up to Maine on Friday, to his parents' country place. He knows I can't go because I'm allergic to horses. Let's spend the weekend together . . . and talk." She moved her hand, with his, to between her thighs.

"I shouldn't."

"Just one weekend."

"If we were caught . . ."

"We won't be." She squeezed his hand. "Please, Matt."

That was awkward. A couple of months before, he'd been madly in love with her, or with someone who could have been her younger sister. Just shy of forty, she was still sexy as hell, and still the same person he had fallen in love with.

It wouldn't hurt his wounded masculinity to get back at Strom. But Peter was in the equation, too, and it could be devastating to the kid.

And make Matt look like a fool, as well as a home-wrecker.

She kissed him softly, and then deeply. "Please? Your place at 6:00 on Friday?" She moved his hand to her breast, and then her own hand somewhat lower.

Of course he said yes and, before the subway was halfway home, regretted having said it. He never watched soap operas on the cube, but he was pretty sure he'd just signed up for chapter n-minus-1. And they never had a happy ending. If they had a happy ending, they'd have to go off the air.

A mature man would have called Kara the next day and said he got carried away, sorry, there's no way that it could work. Let's admit we made a mistake and stay good friends.

Instead, Matt figured he had just two days to get to the machine and escape into the future.

His first plan was direct passionate action: buy a gun at one of the Southie pawnshops, go disarm the guard, and take the machine. It wouldn't be stealing, really; it was his machine. *Stealing* would be when he crawled into a Dumpster and pushed the button, using it as a getaway car, and showing up in the future with tons of exotic garbage.

A less dramatic opportunity presented itself. The chronophysics department wanted to run the machine through a positron scanner three times—alone, and then with a person touching it, and then with Matt touching it. Careful not to push the RESET button, of course.

Once he was inside the claustrophobic tube, he'd just find a piece of metal, clip it with the alligator clip, and push the button. Off to the twenty-third century.

It would look like an accident. Poor Matt, sacrificed to science.

This time he wouldn't need any protective gear. Marsh had calculated where he would wind up next, to within a few dozen meters. It was up by where Route 95 crosses into New Hampshire, pretty far from the ocean. Pretty near to the tax-free liquor warehouse. Have to take a credit card.

What, really, ought he to take up into the future? His first thought was old coins. But they'd probably have him take all of the metal out of his pockets for the positron scan.

Rare documents, small ones. He went down to Charles Street and maxed out two credit cards buying a note Lincoln had scrawled to Grant and a letter from Gabriel García Márquez, in the last year of his life, to Pablo "El Ced"

Marino when he was an unknown poet, forty years before his Nobel Prize.

Of course he might wind up in a future that cared nothing for history or literature. That would be trouble, no matter what.

There was also the small matter of 177.5 years' interest on those two credit cards. Maybe they'd go out of business.

It was bound to work one way or another. In some future he was going to come back to that law firm sixteen years ago and leave a million-dollar check to bail himself out.

He spent a day worrying. How could you plan for a trip like this? There was no Baedecker for the future. Science fiction had a really bad record, world peace and personal dirigibles. For lack of anything else positive to do, he bought a really good Swiss Army knife with twenty-one functions, in case they didn't make him empty his pockets.

Of course, he might be vaulting into a radioactive hell. Or a wasteland rendered sterile by nanotechnology or biological warfare.

He couldn't un-push the button.

But he *could* press it again, and again. Two thousand years. Then 24,709 and three hundred thousand. The fifth push would be 3,440,509 years, long enough for anything to quiet down.

It would also be a kind of suicide. If there were still people that far in the future, he would be more distant to them than a Cro-Magnon man would be to the here and now.

Did you make your computer chips out of flint back then?

He went to the old-time theater on Brattle Street and watched three twentieth-century movies in a row. A soft-porn romance, a Western, and a once-daring epic about a war in Southeast Asia. It kept his mind off everything, though he emerged with a seriously sore butt and didn't care if he never saw popcorn again.

He might not.

He got a few hours of imperfect sleep and went down to the Green Building early.

The first time traveler, Herman, inhabited a deluxe terrarium in the lobby. He had grown to helmet size, and slept through Matt's tapping on the glass to say good-bye.

The only things alive now that might still be alive when he came back were some young Galápagos turtles in zoos here and there. He would look them up and talk to them about the old days. I knew your cousin Herman.

He'd never been to the seventh floor before. It had a slightly shabby atmosphere. Perhaps positrons were out of fashion.

"Dr. Fuller," a young Asian man said, walking toward him with his hand out. It still startled him when people called him that, but he'd stopped protesting.

He'd never get a real doctorate now. Maybe another honorary one, for being Guy from the Past.

"Joe Sung," he said, shaking hands. "You're up next. Maybe ten minutes."

"Okay." The positron scanner was in the next room, visible through a big window.

It was all white plastic. Would there be anything metal inside to contact with the alligator clip?

He should have looked up the machine's design. It probably did have metal all through it, and so would act as a kind of semiopen Faraday cage, and go up into the future with him.

If not, not. The time machine would disappear for about nine generations, to be recovered near the antique ruins of the liquor warehouse on the New Hampshire border. Matt would be fired, perhaps jailed. Though there probably wasn't yet a law against sending stuff into the future.

Sung had said something. "Pardon me?"

"Just have a seat out here. I'll come to get you." He paused with his hand on the doorknob. "You'll be in the machine for more than an hour. You might want to use the washroom."

"Thanks." Matt went across the hall to the men's room and sat there thinking. Reluctantly, he decided he'd better not do it. There will be other opportunities.

Or would there be? The rent-a-cop who normally stood outside the door on the ninth floor was not here. When the machine went back to its usual place, he would be. How to get by him? Flash the Swiss Army knife?

He went back to the anteroom and flipped through a copy of *National Geographic* backward. The clam farms of Samoa. Our Friend the Dung Beetle. Surprising Pittsburgh.

"Okay." Sung came out with a pallid young man, the control for the experiment. He looked a little shaky.

"Don't open your eyes in there," he said. "It's kind of close quarters."

"Thanks." Matt watched him stagger toward the elevator.

"I monitored him while he was being scanned. Nothing unusual. 'Scuse me."

Sung headed for the men's room.

Matt slipped into the room with the positron scanner. The machine was right there, on the end of the platform that went in and out. He snatched it and ran into the corridor and stabbed the elevator button.

The door opened immediately. The pale guy was still there. "What . . . what's happening?"

"Have to, um, take it down to recalibrate it."

"Mm," he said. "Don't open your eyes in there, man."

"Yeah, I'll be careful."

When they got to the ground floor, Matt went for the door with unseemly haste. He had maybe a minute. There were Dumpsters behind Starbucks and Au Bon Pain.

But there was also a cab. It pulled up to the curb in front of the Green Building and the passenger got out. Then the driver got out, too, to help with the luggage.

Matt dove in. "Hey," the driver said. "I've got another fare."

Matt clipped the alligator clip to the exposed frame in the open door. But there was a plastic dome over the RESET button.

"Look, buddy, you've got to get out." The cabdriver was large and menacing. "Let's don't have any trouble."

Matt pulled out his Swiss Army knife and broke a thumb-nail getting the blade out.

"Man . . . like you're gonna scare me with that thing."

He popped the plastic dome off. "Don't have to." He pushed the button and everything went gray.

11

Matt tumbled into the front seat and groped for the steering wheel, in case he wound up in traffic again. But when the world reappeared, it was all forest.

He still had the plastic dome in his hand. He pressed it into place over the RESET button, and it locked in with a loud click.

The engine was humming. He turned it off and got out of the driver's side door and looked around. A deer bounded away, white tail flashing.

Something smelled funny. After a moment he realized it was a lack of pollution. He was just smelling the planet.

Where was everybody? They supposedly could predict within tens of meters where he was going to appear—and predict when, within minutes or even seconds. Where was the welcoming committee?

That didn't bode well.

The cab still had tires, after a fashion. The rubber had disappeared, or rather stayed behind, and left four wheels of steel-mesh foam, squashed slightly out of round.

He switched it on and put it in gear and carefully maneuvered around the trees and brush. He was supposed to be a couple of hundred meters east of Highway 95. Well, it felt like afternoon, so he steered eastward, away from the sun.

The road appeared with no warning, bumpy, broken asphalt with grass and even small trees growing through it. That was not a good sign, either.

Maybe it didn't mean the end of civilization. Maybe America had finally outgrown the car.

But still. Where was everybody?

Maybe the calculations had been off, and he was where he looked like he was, the middle of nowhere. He started driving south, in the breakdown lane. It had less brush, for some reason.

Hungry, he popped open the glove compartment and found a Baby Ruth, half a bag of red-hot peanuts, a bottle of water, and an old-fashioned snub-nosed revolver. There was also a half-empty box of .357 Magnum cartridges.

He put the gun back and ate the Baby Ruth, saving the peanuts for dinner. Maybe the next time he saw a deer he should shoot it. Then skin it and dress it out with his Swiss Army knife, sure.

It gave him a cold chill when he realized he might have to do just that, or whatever inelegant approximation of butchering he might be capable of. He stopped and did a more thorough search of the glove box. No matches or lighter.

Deer sushi, how appetizing.

The taxi had a quarter charge; the gauge said its fuel cells were good for another seventy-seven miles. It shouldn't be more than fifty miles back to Cambridge. If their calculations had been right.

What if it was more than fifty miles? More than 177 years?

A few miles down the road, he came upon an abandoned car. He stopped and, obscurely frightened, took the pistol with him when he got out.

There was no sign of violence, but the car had been totally stripped, no tires or seats. The hood was open, and the fuel cells were gone.

The plastic body was a dull pink. He had a feeling that it had started out red but had been out in the sun and rain and snow for decades.

Was it possible that the world had ended? Some ultimate weapon had given the Earth back to nature?

Not all at once. Somebody survived to steal. Or salvage.

The trunk of the car had been forced open, and was empty, not even a spare. That reminded him to check the taxi's trunk.

It did have a spare, and a small toolbox, which might prove handy. A shoulder bag that had the driver's wallet with about $800, reading glasses, pills, and a small notebook, dark at first. He held it up to the sun, and after a few seconds it showed an index full of moving porn.

He flipped through it for a minute and was becoming aroused, but then there was a girl who looked just like Kara, as a twenty-one-year-old, and a sudden access of sadness wilted his desire.

What was he thinking? He could have just said no to her invitation. Or he could have said *yes*. He was crazy to leave everything behind and leap into the unknown.

He threw the bag into the backseat and drove on.

The abandoned cars came more frequently; soon he was never out of sight of one or two. They all seemed to be in about the same shape.

Didn't this used to be mostly pasture and farmland? How long would it take for such land to return to forest? He remembered as a child being taken to a forest outside of Paris, which had been the site of a vicious battle in World War I. The gunfire and artillery had been so intense that no tree had been left standing, except for one battered sapling. A hundred and fifty years later, it had become a huge oak darkly looming in a forest of lesser but uniformly large trees.

That there were no large trees interrupting the highway and shoulders indicated that somebody used it. Or maybe the ground under the road had been treated to discourage growth.

He went around a long, slow bend and saw, a couple of hundred meters away, a man on a horse, riding with a child on his lap. They saw Matt and bolted into the woods.

Matt leaned out the window. "Wait!" he shouted. "I won't harm you!" He stopped at the place where they had left and listened. Nothing. "I won't hurt you," he shouted again. "I just want to talk. I need information."

He listened for fifteen minutes or so. Then he drove on, until he fell asleep at the wheel and crunched into some brush.

Time to call it quits for the night. He didn't want to drive with lights on: too conspicuous and a waste of power. He ate the peanuts with a few small sips of water.

He got a greasy blanket out of the trunk and wrapped up in it and tried to find a comfortable position for sleeping. When it got dark, a skylight appeared in the cab's roof. The stars were unnaturally bright, crowding the sky. There were noises in the woods that probably were animals. He locked the doors and kept the revolver by his side.

He woke at dawn, suddenly, to loud birdsong. There were six deer, four of them fawns, grazing nearby. When he opened the door, the two adults looked at him for a moment, then they all bounced into the woods.

When he finished peeing, he heard a quiet sound of water over rocks. He took the car keys and pistol and water bottle to investigate, and just off the road found a trickle of waterfall. He filled the bottle and drank deeply, and refilled it. The water tasted wonderful, and if it was polluted, well, it wasn't as if he had any choice.

When he returned to the taxi, he had a strong feeling that he was being watched.

"Hello? Anybody here?" No response. He got into the car and continued on.

After a few miles, the forest began to thin in a systematic way, the largest trees left standing, but ones up to about a foot in diameter were chopped down roughly at waist height. Harvested for firewood, or maybe building.

As he kept moving in the direction of Boston, the edge of thick forest moved farther and farther from the road, until finally there was no forest at all, just a rank confusion of weeds, with a few large, old trees.

When the gauge said he had twenty-two miles left, he came to a farm, or at least a ruined side road that led to a cultivated area. But the turnoff was marked with a sign that had a stylized assault rifle between the words KEEP and OUT. So he drove on.

There were a half dozen such roads, all with the same sign. That was a little encouraging—at least the neighborhood was organized enough to support the work of a sign painter.

Perhaps a gunsmith as well.

He saw the tollbooth coming for about a mile. By then eight lanes of abandoned superhighway were apparent, with only the two lanes in the middle clear. All of the toll stations but one were blocked with rubble and brush.

His watch said 7:01. Did they do Daylight Savings Time here? He stuck the pistol in his belt, but then decided to conceal it a bit and stuck it between his butt and the seat back, hidden but easily accessible.

As he approached, a man in uniform stepped out into the middle of the road. He had a weapon slung over his shoulder. As Matt drew closer, he unslung the weapon and held it across his chest, port arms. It was an ancient Kalashnikov.

He was standing by a sign painted by an amateur:

BOSTON CITIE LIMMITS / PAY TOLE ONE DOLAR. Matt dug into his pocket and found a two-dollar coin.

The man took the coin and looked at both sides. "Old. How you make that old car work?"

"Found some fuel cells. Have to recharge them."

"Hah. You will that." The man put the coin in his pocket. There was a purse on a string around his neck. Holding the Kalashnikov awkwardly between his elbow and side, he counted out four quarters and handed them to Matt. They were light as aluminum washers. One side was covered in small print, alternating "25" and "Boston"; the other side had IN GOD WE TRUST in one semicircle and JESUS SAVES underneath, framing a smiling Jesus wearing a crown of bloody thorns. There was no year on the shiny coin, but it couldn't have been very old; the picture and type were just printed on, not stamped.

The guard relaxed and slung the rifle over his shoulder again, and Matt stifled a sigh of relief. "You headin' a Boston?"

"Cambridge, actually. MIT."

The man nodded. "They might could charge ya' up. Sometimes they do real magic there."

"They do. Thanks." Matt eased the taxi forward and the man went back to his book. It was a Bible, bristling with bookmarks.

This was going to be an interesting environment for an atheistic nonpracticing Jew. He remembered when, as a third-grader, he'd begged his parents to let him go to a Methodist summer camp with all his friends. Of course it became a big family joke, our boy the Methodist. Not so funny now.

Of course the tollbooth guy was not necessarily typical. But the coins were a bad sign, too.

He made his way south down the interstate, which was bumpy but relatively free from vegetation. The monorail next to it had bird's nests on the maglev rail. This had been a green corridor ever since they'd moved to the Boston area, the interstate and monorail high above manicured parkland, a bicycle and running path connecting Boston with Lowell through a lovingly maintained arboretum corridor. Now it was scraggly forest.

He wasn't going to make it to Cambridge. When he got to the monorail terminal, a sign pointing down Route 3 said CAMBRIDGE 18, and his gauge said twelve.

While on the elevated highway, he'd seen a few farms, but no sign of urban civilization on the ground. Now there was thick forest on both sides of the road, which was once again overgrown with weeds.

No saplings, though, and no small trees anywhere near the road. Low limbs had been hacked off, too. Every now and then a fresh stump. For firewood, maybe for building.

He didn't encounter any traffic until he was nearing Arlington, he estimated a little before eight. He passed a horse-drawn cart loaded with carrots and turnips, and then a dairy cart, its cargo area enclosed and dripping. The drivers both stared at him as he passed, neither answering his hello.

Ice without machines? Well, they used to cut big blocks from the lakes in winter and keep it in icehouses through summer, insulated by sawdust. Maybe they were doing that again.

Church bells chimed eight. Matt's watch said 8:05.

In town, there were people walking along the sidewalk or maneuvering bicycles among the potholes. Most of the storefronts were boarded up or had collapsed long ago. A Bible store was opening up.

It didn't look as if men's clothing had changed very much. He could walk around in what he had on, jeans and a short-sleeved shirt, without anybody giving him a second look.

When the gauge hit 1.0 mile, it started chiming for his attention (a POWER LOW light had been flashing for miles). He turned right at a sign toward Spy Pond and coasted downhill. The motor whined to a stop about a block from the small lake.

His mother's old place would have been just across the water. There was an apartment building there now, most of its windows boarded up.

He got the taxi driver's shoulder bag out of the back-seat and put all his worldly goods in it: time machine, pistol, ammunition, water bottle, two rare documents, the driver's wallet and porn notebook. They might be worth a lot or nothing. The Bible store probably didn't have much porn.

The toolbox was bulky, about fifteen pounds, but it might be valuable. He rolled the blanket into a tight cylinder and tucked it under his arm. He could walk to MIT in two hours this way, maybe three.

A group that looked like a family was fishing at the end of the parking lot. They'd evidently dispatched the youngest, a boy, to go find out about the taxi driver. He ran about halfway, then slowed to a jog, a walk, a shuffle. He took off his cap to reveal an amateur haircut.

He was about ten, wearing clothes that were clean but seemed more patch than original cloth.

"Mister? You fishin'?"

"No. I was just driving to MIT and ran out of gas."

"Gas?" That anachronism evidently hadn't survived.

"My car's fuel cells ran down."

He nodded slowly at that. "My pa wondered about the car. Where you got it. If they was more."

Matt looked up at the group, and they were all watching the transaction. The father waved in a friendly way. "Well, let me go talk to him." Pump him for information. He waved back and followed the boy.

The man had a broad-brimmed black hat and was dressed all in black, maybe fifty years old. His wife was younger, in a shapeless black shift that fell from neck to ankles, with no ornamentation other than a silver cross. The man had a similar one, both evidently snipped out of sheet metal.

"He's headed to MIT," the boy said.

The father shook hands conventionally and said his name was Mose. "So that 'splains the car." He looked up the street. "They got lots of old stuff there. That one looks 'most new."

Matt nodded noncommittally. "How the fishing?"

"Couple a little ones." Mose looked down at the transparent toolbox. "Got a extra rod, but the reel's broke. You fix it, you could try your luck."

Matt set the box and bag down. "I'll take a look at it. No guarantees."

"Abraham?" The boy ran off to get it.

An opportunity to find out something about the now and here. "You all live in Arlington?"

"Past few months. Prob'ly go back in the city 'fore it gets cold." He didn't have anything like a New England accent.

"Native Bostonian?"

"Aye. Grandfolks come up from the Carolinas. You?"

"Mostly Cambridge. And Ohio," he added without thinking.

"Ohio the *state*?"

"It was some long walk," he improvised. "My father wanted me to go to MIT."

Abraham brought over the rod and reel. "She won't let go a the line," he said, and demonstrated by jerking it taut twice.

"Let me see." Matt took the contraption and sat down on the ground. Pulled the toolbox over, as if he knew what he was doing, and found a set of small screwdrivers. The smallest Phillips head fit the recessed screws that held the reel together.

"Helps to have the right tools," the man said ruefully. Help even more if one knew what one was doing, Matt thought, but he kept the thought to himself.

It was an elegantly compact system of wheels and pawls and a cam, controlled by a button on top. He studied it, pulling gently on the line while doing this and that. The cam seemed stuck in an odd position, so he pressed it gently. Suddenly, a click, and the line pulled loose. "Here, this is it." He held it up to Mose and showed him the part that had come unstuck.

"The drag?"

"Whatever you call it." He loosened it with an external dial, gave it a drop of oil, and tightened it partway.

"So you workin' at MIT?"

"Used to." Take a chance. "You know anything about chronophysics?"

He laughed. "Didn't have school past readin' and numbers. Not much in numbers—that's what you do?"

"Used to. See whether I can get my old job back."

Mose jerked his head in the direction of the cab. "You can get that old thing to work, they *better* give you a job."

Matt screwed the housing down tight and handed it up. "Give that a try."

Mose stirred up a jar full of dirt and pulled out a wriggling worm, and threaded it onto the hook at the end of the line. He did a couple of arcane tests, the worm dropping and stopping, then grunted okay.

Matt followed him to the water. With a practiced flip of the rod, Mose sent the bait out in a satisfyingly long arc. It splashed about twenty-five yards out, and he handed the rod to Matt.

"Uh . . . what do I do? I've only fished with cane poles." About two hundred years ago.

Mose picked up his own rod and demonstrated. "You feel the fish bite, wait a second, an' set the hook." He gave it a little twitch. "Not too hard. Then reel 'er in." He rotated the handle on the side, clockwise, and the line came back. Matt imitated him.

"So what do you do in this kronny stuff?"

"Chronophysics? Well, I'm actually kind of a handyman. I build . . . devices for experiments and fix them when they don't work."

"Plenty of that around. If MIT doesn't take you back?" Indirectly asking, "What did you do to get fired?"

"Mose . . ." he looked around. "Can you keep a secret?"

He transferred the rod to his left hand and crossed his heart. "Swear to Jesus."

"I'm . . . well, I'm sort of an experiment, myself. I've been asleep for almost two hundred years." Mose just looked at him. "What year is it now?"

"Seventy-one."

"Seventy-one years from what?"

Mose winced. "Don't talk like that," he whispered.

"Look, I *mean* it. I don't know anything about this world. You're way in my future."

"That's why you talk so funny."

"Yeah."

"I thought it was maybe Ohio."

"No, it's the way *everybody* used to talk. Thanks to TV, I suppose."

"I've heard of that. We don't have it anymore, praise Jesus. Sometimes you see piles of them, all burnt, left over from the Day of Return." He looked around. "That's what happened seventy-one years ago. Jesus came back, just as was prophesized."

Matt had a strong urge to set the pole down and go south as fast as possible. Find someone at MIT who would tell him what was going on.

"You shouldn't let on you don't know," he continued quietly. "Some folks aren't reasonable. And there used to be Deniers."

"Used to be."

He nodded and reeled in some line. "Still are, 'way west, in Gomorrah. Or so it's said. Nothing in the Bible about that, just the old Gomorrah."

"California?"

"I heard it called that. Or Hollywood," he said slowly, savoring the three syllables. "Decent folks say Gomorrah."

"No doubters out here, no Deniers?"

"Not since I was a boy." He looked troubled, staring out to where his line met the water. "It was a bad time. Best not to talk of that either, except in family."

"There's a lot people don't talk about," Matt said.

"It wasn't that way in your day?"

"Not so much—wait!" The end of his rod twitched twice and, before he had time to react, bent sharply.

"Got one!" Mose said. "Steady, now." The fish swam left and right as Matt reeled it in, and a couple of times it sped straight away, overcoming the drag, but in a minute Matt had it close to shore. Abraham waded out with a hand net, and used it with both hands to lift the fish out of the water. It was as big as an adult's forearm, and lively.

"It's a blessed one," the boy called excitedly. He almost tripped, splashing through the water.

"Beginner's luck," Matt said.

"Oh, it ain't luck," Mose said. "It's fortune, for us, but it ain't luck."

The fish was thick and glittering black and had a precise silver cross on each gill plate. "You don't know about these."

"Never seen such a thing," Matt said.

"Don't get one ever' day. Ruth!" He called to the woman, who was sitting at a picnic table reading the Bible. "It's a blessed one!"

She hurried over, her eyes down. "Oh, my," she said, and took fish and net over to a thick plank by the water's edge. She held it down, still flopping, on the wood, and with a thick-bladed knife pressed down hard behind the gills and decapitated it. She kissed the cross on each gill plate and threw the head back into the shallows.

It wriggled away.

Abraham had brought a bucket of water. Ruth used a thin-bladed knife to slit the belly of the fish, and threw away a small mass of red-and-silver entrails. Then, with thumb and finger, she peeled the fish like a fruit.

"Almost all meat," Mose said.

So it was. A bioengineered food machine. "You don't catch them often?"

"This kind, maybe twice a week, praise God. This is a good sign for you."

"Well. Good." Matt was watching Ruth clean the fish. It didn't seem to have any bones; basically a rectangular slab of meat. She rinsed it off and sliced it into eight thick steaks, which she arranged in a shallow bowl and covered with a red sauce from a Mason jar.

"Barbecue," Mose said, pronouncing it "Bobby Q." "Let's get the fire goin'."

"Good coals, Moses," Ruth said. "We don't need a big old fire."

He rolled his eyes. "Good coals." He led Matt to the barbecue pit, by the picnic tables. Abraham and the other two children, younger girls, had rounded up fuel—dry grass and thin sticks—and were arranging it in neat piles. From well-used plastic bags they sorted out larger sticks and a few large chunks of wood, some carbonized from earlier use.

"The girls sniff around and pick up wood in the morning," he said. "Gets harder to find."

"You move into the city for heat? Later on."

"Yeah, they got solar. Crowded, though." He made a pile of the light grass and arranged a cone of twigs, teepee style, over it, then took a firestarting thing out of his pocket, like a fat nail file with a metal stick hanging from a chain. Striking the stick against the file made bright blue sparks. The grass started to smolder, and he blew it into flame. The twigs began to crackle, and with intense concentration he added slightly larger twigs in tripod threes, still blowing gently on the flame, with his hand cupped behind it.

Surely that action went back to the Stone Age. But the firestarter went back only to the twentieth or twenty-first century, as did the Mason jar with the "Bobby Q" sauce. To pour on the bioengineered fish.

"Where'd you get the spark maker?"

"Always had it," Mose said, not looking up. "Took it outa my daddy's pocket when he died."

He built a loose house around the small blaze with twigs about as thick as his thumbs. "You did well, girls," he told them, and they nodded gravely.

"This area must be pretty well picked over," Matt said. "Lot of people live out here?"

"When it's warm, yeah, gettin' out of the city. Churches here expect almost two thousand today, plus some people go into town for the day. Maybe twenty-two hundred in Arlington, till October, November."

"You know how many people live in Boston, the Boston area?"

"Huh-uh. *Feels* like a million in the winter."

"No heat out here?"

"Only what you make." He arranged the rest of the wood around the blaze and sat back. "How did it used to be?"

Matt pointed at the apartment building. "My mother used to live right here, on the lake, year-round. In the wintertime her place was usually so hot I couldn't stand it."

"She had electricity?"

"And a fireplace, too, for special occasions. That was in the 2050s."

He shook his head. "No good with numbers."

Matt added and subtracted in his head. "That would have been about 130 years before Jesus came back."

"Long time." His face pinched in concentration. "My gran'ther was born about twenty years before, B.S.C. So his grandfather . . ." He tried to do it on his fingers but shook his head again and let his breath out in a puff.

"Well, if you count twenty-five years per generation, that would be *his* grandfather's father."

Mose looked up, his eyes shining. "And you were around back then."

"Yeah." Something suddenly drained out of Matt. Energy, hope.

Mose saw it. "Will you get back?"

He cleared his throat. "I . . . I don't know. I think so." Someone had to make his bail 293 years ago.

Ruth came over carrying the fish and two metal grates, which looked like refrigerator shelves. She peered at the fire. "Ready in about ten minutes, Moses?"

"Ready when it's ready, woman." She shrugged and set the fish down on the table.

He placed a few small sticks in with the larger ones and blew gently until they were blazing. "If you don't get back, stuck here, you want to join a church. I mean you have to. What were you back then?"

"You mean religion?" Mose nodded, not looking at him. *Ex–Reform Jew atheist* would probably be a bad answer. "Guess I'm sort of a Methodist. Church wasn't so . . . central to our lives."

"As it was written," he said. "And so you were laid down low. *We* were, humanity." Matt couldn't think of a safe response to that. "Meth-o-dist," Mose said softly. "That was like the old Catholics?"

"They split off from the Catholics long before I was born." They were something else in between, he vaguely knew from his childhood friends. Lutherans or something.

"Hope they don't give you trouble about that at MIT. They shouldn't, since you were born before the Second Coming and then sort of hop-frogged over it. But those religious people are unreasonable sometimes, you know what I'm sayin'?"

"I should be careful what I say around them."

"Say and do. Really careful."

"I will, Mose. Thank you."

"They're scientific, so they might give you some room. Like any reasonable person would. But they're all priests, too, or most of them."

The fire was going well now, hot enough that both men moved a little away from it. "Let it burn down a bit."

"So . . . there aren't any Methodists anymore?"

"Not around here. Down south they still have Church-o'- Christs and Baptists and what all. Here we're just Christians."

"Everyone?"

"Oh yes." He said that a little too quickly. "You would be about twenty-two?"

"I'm older than I look. Twenty-seven—or two hundred-some, if you count from date of birth."

"They might make you spend some time in service."

"In the military?"

"Military? No, just in service to the Lord. I was in service from eighteen to twenty, which is usual. But if you're in school a grown-up, they wait till you're out."

"What do you do in service?"

"Whatever you're best at. You'd probably be a mechanic or some scientist's assistant." He laughed, shaking his head. "Might just make you a scientist and give *you* an assistant. You probably have enough school to be a scientist."

"Old-fashioned stuff, though. Science goes out of date."

"Maybe so. I never heard of your chronochemistry. Maybe they don't do it anymore."

"Chronophysics, but you're right. That would be a . . . a shame." Not to say a goddamn kick in the balls.

Matt was wondering what would be the best way to approach MIT. Probably best not to walk in and say, "Hi! I'm the chrononaut you've all been waiting for." The fact that there had been nobody waiting for him up at the New Hampshire border spoke volumes. He should try to sneak in and get the lay of the land before he identified himself. It might save him from being ridiculed, or burnt at the stake.

Abraham had come to whisper something to his father. "Ask him," Mose said.

He came over. "Father said I could ask you could we look in the car."

"Sure. I'll go over with you, unlock it." Matt stood up and fished in his pocket for the thick bunch of keys on the taxi driver's ring. Mostly plastic electronic keys, with a few old metal ones. One of the plastic ones said MIT-SUBISHI. He clicked on it as they approached the car and the key blinked red twice. Of course, out of power. The doors unlocked one last time, with a slow thunk.

The two girls had tagged along, and now they all piled into the cab and bounced around. The musty old thing was probably the newest car in the state, or the East Coast. Let them play, though; there was no way they could do any harm.

"What's this, mister?" Abraham had found a .357 Magnum cartridge on the floor.

"Here, I'll take it." Matt reached for it.

"Is that a bullet?" Mose said, behind him.

Matt paused. A cartridge, actually. "Looks like." He passed it to Mose.

The black man pushed it around on his palm. "Never seen one like this. Not a rifle?"

Could they have peeked into his bag? "It's for a handgun." He didn't look in the bag's direction. "You have rifles but not pistols?"

"Not since my father's time. They're illegal." He looked through the car window. "You be careful, Abraham." He glanced at Matt. "No pistol in there?"

"Not that I know of. I haven't looked all through it."

"Children, go back to the fire." They protested. "Abraham, see if the coals are ready."

The kids moped away from their forbidden toy. "You weren't surprised," Mose said. "At this." He handed Matt the cartridge.

"No. Plenty of guns back in my time."

He nodded. "Be careful. They're big trouble here."

"Thanks. I have a lot to learn."

Abraham was calling that the fire was ready.

Lunch was polite but strained. They gave profuse thanks to both God and Matthew for the fish, but the adults were obviously glad to see him go. Mose asked him to lock the car, but the key didn't work; not enough power. They gave it a thorough search and didn't find any contraband or anything useful.

A bike path still ran by the lake to the subway stop he'd last used to bring his mother wine and groceries. Mose warned him away from the subway, home to "tunnel rats," vagabonds who lived there year-round. It was relatively cool in the summer, and survivable in the winter, but a haven for the lawless, and unsafe even for them.

Matt said good-bye and walked up the hill to Mass Ave. He'd never walked from here to MIT, but it couldn't be more than six or seven miles. He'd biked it a couple of times.

It was pretty grim. The street was a ruin of frost heaves, unmaintained for decades. Shop fronts were decrepit, signs faded out, painted over. There were brick-and-board tables along the sidewalk where people sold food and drink or had stacks of worn clothes and junk for sale or trade. Matt got a questionable glass of homemade beer, warm and sour, for a quarter. One fourth of his contemporary money.

When he felt he wasn't being watched, he ducked into a door and fished a single hundred from the taxi driver's wallet. He didn't want to flash a thick roll, but sooner or later he'd come to a bank—or whatever or whoever served as one—and wanted to find out whether the old money was worth anything more than the paper it was printed on.

He wished he'd been able to talk more with Mose. The pistol cartridge had shut that door, with the accurate implication that Matt was lying and dangerous.

Walking down the sidewalk, he drew less attention than he would have back in his own time—wrinkled, slept-in clothes of an odd style, lugging a knapsack and a toolkit. A lot of people were similarly attired and burdened, a mobile population without Laundromats.

There was an actual bank, of sorts, where Arlington became Somerville. It had once been a savings and loan establishment. Now there was a card in the cracked window that said FAMILY BANK • DEPOSITS PROTECTED • LOANS MADE TO PERMENT RESADENTS. The best spelling he'd seen so far.

The place had a big walk-in safe, standing open, flanked by young men armed with assault rifles. It probably had a worthless electronic lock.

Even with the big window and open door, it was kind of gloomy inside. There was a man wearing a shabby coat and tie sitting at a broad table in the middle of the lobby, a tall filing cabinet behind him. In front of him, bowls of coins and a sawed-off shotgun.

"Good afternoon," he said. "I don't know you."

"Just passing through. I wondered what this was worth." He took the hundred-dollar bill from his shirt pocket and unfolded it and laid it in front of the man.

The banker picked up a white plastic thing that resembled Mose's fishing reel, but when he cranked the handle it made an intense spot of white light. He scrutinized the bill with a magnifying glass, then held the light behind it, looking at the structure of imbedded wires. He rubbed the president's face with his thumb and it faintly said "hundred."

"It's well preserved," he said. "Where'd you find it?"

"In a trunk," he said, true enough. "What's it worth?"

He rubbed his chin. "I could give you fifty for it."

"Thanks," Matt said, reaching for the bill. "I may be back."

The banker snatched it away. "Just a second." He cranked the light up again, and studied both sides, then sniffed it.

"Twenty seventy-four . . . maybe I could give you seventy. Seventy-five if you have more."

"That's the only one I've got. I'll take seventy-five for it."

The man pretended to consider it. "All right." He pulled out a fat wallet and extracted three faintly glowing twenties, then scooped three heavy five-dollar coins from a bowl. Matt put the coins in his pocket and held up the bills to the dim light. He couldn't identify the portrait. They were soft and worn but looked like real currency.

"Come by if you find another one of those."

"I might." First see what he could get in Boston proper.

When he got to Porter Square he had to make a decision: keep going down Mass Ave where it turned, or continue straight on through what used to be a bad neighborhood. On a bike, from here it was a ten-minute cruise to campus. He'd never walked it, but it was probably half the distance of going down Mass Ave through Harvard Square.

Carrying the bag and toolbox was wearing him down, and the neighborhood didn't look that foreboding in the afternoon light.

Besides, he did have a gun, though the idea of using it gave him a sudden thrill of dread. His total experience with firearms was a forbidden friend's BB gun at the age of twelve, and he hadn't even been able to hit the target.

Well, he didn't intend to shoot it. But it could be a powerful psychological weapon. Unless his adversary had one as well.

Mose hadn't ever seen a pistol, yet the idea of it was obviously potent and frightening. Matt felt its considerable weight and strode on down through the slums.

Actually, once he was in the neighborhood, it didn't seem any more run-down than what he'd just come from. No street merchants and fewer people. No pets, he suddenly realized; there ought to be dogs barking and cats lazing in the sun. An unaffordable luxury, he supposed, when you couldn't just pop down to the grocery for pet food.

Every now and then a bicycle would rattle past, and twice mule-drawn carts. The mules had to eat; their existence implied a certain level of civilization, organization, since there were no pastures around where they could freely forage.

Of course they might not be completely natural. The anomaly of the bioengineered Christian fish was no anomaly, actually; this culture was going to be a mixture of high technology and low. He had to keep his eyes and mind open.

Inman Square was reassuring, a couple of blocks of vendors' tables and a small crowd milling. There was a table full of books, but they were all Bibles, hymnals, and tracts. He bought a small New Testament, well thumbed and full of underlined passages, for nine dollars. Protective coloration and research. It would be smart to start learning something about Jesus.

A tea shop was open, so he sat down there to rest and watch the crowd. The teas on the menu were mostly herbal, probably homegrown or gathered locally. A cup of "Chinese tea" went for twenty bucks, the same as "real coffey." He settled for a fifty-cent spearmint infusion.

So imports were expensive, even next to a huge port. It occurred to him that he hadn't heard or seen a single airplane. At three in the afternoon the sky was a deep, unbroken blue. Had he ever seen a Boston sky without haze?

Nobody in the marketplace was wearing new-looking clothes. Maybe people didn't dress up for going to the market. Maybe there *weren't* any new clothes, or they were only for special occasions. Most of the women were dressed modestly, like Ruth, though some teenaged girls wore jeans or short skirts, startlingly seductive. That might be cultural; a sixteen-year-old was by definition a child, and so couldn't be an object of desire.

Other men didn't stare when they walked by. It would be prudent to follow that example.

He still had more than a mile to go, and he wanted to get

to MIT well before offices closed. So rather than tarry for a second cup, he shouldered the bag and continued down the street. Where he saw a sign that stopped him in his tracks:

MASS. INST. OF THEOSOPHY, ONE MILE. It was over the MIT dome logo. What was theosophy? Had it existed in his time? He needed to Google.

"You need help, mister?" It was one of the gorgeous teenaged girls. He realized he was standing staring at the sign, and probably looked lost.

"What . . . uh, what's theosophy?"

"It's *science*," she said with careful emphasis. "The science of God. Are you a pilgrim?"

"No, I guess not. Just a traveler."

She opened her mouth to say something, then just nodded. "Good journey, then. God b'with you." She bounced away, running to catch up with another girl.

The science of God. He'd better study that book.

Even more than that, he needed a history book. Something huge had happened. How long ago? Was it one thing, like a cataclysm, or was it a slow evolution?

The Massachusetts Institute of Theosophy? What did they do there? He would never fit in. Matthew Fuller, professor of atheism. You will be amused by his quaint theosophy.

Or maybe they still did do science and engineering, but had to make it appear closer to religion, for some social reason. Like this Second Coming.

Soon he was walking among tall buildings that in his day had been more or less independent research establishments associated with the Institute. People like Professor Marsh would often split their time, teaching at MIT a few days a week while maintaining lab space down the street at Biotech or Allied Chemical. MIT's charter had forbidden some kinds of work, like weapons research, but it couldn't control what happened slightly off campus.

Those tall, proud buildings were tenements now, with clothes flapping on lines, kids playing in the dignified court-yards. Scrawny vegetable gardens where there used to be elaborate flower beds and fantastic topiary.

But the fact that people could grow vegetables out in the open and not have their crops pilfered demonstrated a reassuring degree of social order. Along with the absence of actual starvation.

No telling where MIT's administration would be nowadays. Building One would have enough natural light, assuming no electricity, so maybe it would still be there. He angled across campus toward the Infinite Corridor.

He wasn't sure of the history behind it, but the oldest buildings in the Infinite Corridor dated back to 1916. By the middle of the twentieth century they comprised a linked chain of consistent design that shared a corridor about a quarter-kilometer long—not quite infinite, but a hike. It was precisely straight; twice a year students could prop the doors open and the setting sun would send a beam down 850 feet of suddenly not-dingy corridor.

Maybe they still did that, but sacrificed virgins. They used to joke that that was one thing you *couldn't* do at MIT, for lack of raw material. That might have changed. Depending on the theosophical attitude toward sex.

The campus wasn't crowded, but it wouldn't have been in August back in his time, either. The classrooms had been individually air-conditioned, to keep bills down, and the halls and unused rooms were ovens when it got into the nineties. It was close to that now. He walked up the stairs to the Infinite Corridor door and braced for a wall of heat.

It was dim and stuffy at this end, offices with closed doors. Plenty of light farther down, where there were class-rooms with corridor windows and the dome's skylight. It felt odd, walking down these halls, now yellowing whitewash instead of Institute Green, the woodwork centuries older, with amateur-looking repairs. Broken windows patched with plywood squares that didn't look new.

The few students walked slowly and quietly, which was beyond odd. With the gloom at the periphery and overhead, and a whiff of mildew rather than the persistent subliminal tang of chemicals and machines, the place had the air of a monastery. Which it might now be.

In the rotunda windows, stained-glass panels that identified the Stations of the Cross, whatever that meant. On inspection, it was obvious that the windows had been moved here from some other source, probably a church. The panels were too small for their spaces and had to be framed in plywood, painted flat black for contrast.

Matt had noticed one improvement over the world of his last materialization, 2074, in that facial scarring was no longer the height of fashion. But it wasn't completely gone; he'd seen a few scarred people walking the corridor, mostly older men. A few of the women had faint scar lines on their cheeks.

In fact, within the Infinite Corridor you could almost generalize that the older a man looked, the more scarred his face would be, and the scars weren't particularly artistic. Parallel gouges on the cheeks and foreheads. Perhaps it was a fad that had recently petered out, possibly one with religious significance, and possibly more than meets the eye. God knew (presumably) what was under their robes.

Room 101 was General Administration, but the door was closed and locked. Of course; it was Sunday.

Beside the door was a handwritten list of curriculum changes for the Bachelor of Divinity degree. You now had to take Signs and Wonders 101 and 102 (instead of just Signs and Wonders 10) and Advanced Christian Ethics 111 and 112 simultaneously with two iterations of Preaching Workshop. Instead of Life Transformation, freshmen who could demonstrate their qualifications could opt for Interpretive Glossolalia.

A large man with one scar straight across his forehead came up. His cassock was blue and belted and he carried a heavy staff. He didn't need a badge or a gun.

"You have business here, sir?"

"No, sir. I was just looking around."

"The office will open tomorrow about ten. Until then, people who are not students or faculty ought not to be here."

Matt didn't protest that he *was* faculty, a genuine fake full professor. Instead, he meekly thanked the man and went out the front way.

It was still the impressive, sweeping colonnade, with marble steps down to the street. The steps were extremely rounded, worn down from millions of feet hurrying or trudging to class.

He had to find a place to stay and something to eat. And a bath and change of clothes; he was starting to smell like someone who had worn the same thing for a couple of centuries.

At the base of the stairs, next to what used to be a bus stop, a woman was selling clothes. A table displayed neat stacks of old shirts and trousers, and there was a rack of black academic robes, some less shabby than others.

He started looking through those, protective coloration.

"You'll need an MIT ID to buy a robe," she warned.

"Oh. Thank you." He had one, of course, but the date on it might raise an eyebrow. He picked out a pair of sturdy jeans and a gray tee shirt with an MIT logo. That apparently didn't require an ID.

It came to twenty-one dollars. She made change from an open box of bills and coins. No credit-card reader.

"I'm looking for a place to stay," he said. "Not too expensive."

"You're in the wrong place for that. You might get a room for fifty or sixty dollars up in Central Square. Magazine Street. Up Mass Ave a half mile or so."

"Thanks. I'll go check it." In his time that had been a kind of artsy neighborhood. High crime rate but "interesting," full of transients and foreigners. He was both now.

He started up Mass Ave, and the smell of cooking stopped him in the second block. At an outdoor table he got a bowl of beans and potatoes cooked with onions and garlic, washed down with cool, thin barley wine, for five bucks. While he ate, a disheveled woman with one blind eye plucked a harp and sang. The last piece was a haunting blues, a vaguely religious song about unrequited love. He put a quarter in her cup as he left.

Most of the storefronts along Mass Ave were open, people selling pills, stationery, furniture, rugs. A large bookstore had textbooks of a general nature as well as religious texts. He leafed through a few mathematics ones and, unsurprisingly, they all started out with an inspirational chapter before getting down to geometry or calculus. But it was reassuring that students of theosophy still had to put up with the basics.

There were no physics textbooks, though. The light from the skylight was growing dim before he found things like Newtonian physics covered in the metaphysics section.

Thermophysics and basic electricity and magnetism. But no obvious treatments of relativity or quantum mechanics. Let alone chronophysics.

He'd have to come back later. He bought a text, *Metaphysics and the Natural World*, and headed on up to Magazine Street.

Dusk was closing in when he found a place with a card saying ROOMS AND BATH in the window. An old lady who smelled rancid took $40 and gave him a wooden coin that would pay for a bath once the sun came up. For an extra dollar he got a candle with two matches, an admonition not to burn the place down, and directions to the outhouse.

The third-floor room was small, with just a bed, table, and chair. Moonlight came through a high window. He blew out the candle and sank gratefully into the soft bed.

12

Matt was half-awake, lying in a pleasant torpor, when church bells started banging next door. He dressed and went downstairs to a notice that said bath and breakfast would be available after church. On Monday? Not a good sign.

The outhouse was a little more hospitable with daylight filtering in; in the candlelight he'd been sure there were bugs everywhere, just out of sight. Instead of a roll of toilet paper, there were neat squares torn from church newsletters, which made the experience more pleasant than he'd expected. It also bespoke a certain level of civilization, he realized. In primitive cultures there were less sanitary expedients.

He went around front with the idea of going for a walk, but hesitated. There was nobody else in sight. No traffic up on Mass Ave. Maybe everyone was in church at this hour; maybe being anywhere else was illegal.

Back in the parlor, he stood still and listened. No one else up and around. An invitation to snoop.

The house was old, twentieth century or even earlier. It

had electrical outlets in the walls, but nothing was plugged into them. Two Bibles, but no other books except a scrapbook of recipes in the kitchen.

The large Bible, fairly new, had a supplement tabbed "Revelations S.C." and a pictorial section, "The Second Coming Illustrated." It showed Jesus healing an entire intensive-care ward, Jesus standing in Times Square in front of a mountain of loaves of bread, Jesus in the Oval Office with a presidential-looking white-haired guy, Jesus hovering in midair with a glowing halo over his crown of thorns.

There were two possible explanations. One was that Jesus had returned to Earth in the brown-haired, blue-eyed visage that was familiar to Matt's youth. The only other explanation was that it was a hoax.

Matt's natural impulse was to go with the second one and start asking who and why and how. But first . . .

Was it possible that he had been completely wrong all his adult life? God and Jesus and all were real?

If that were true, then everything else fell apart. The rationalistic universe that he so completely believed in was an elaborate artifice that God maintained for His own reasons. Or some such circular assertion, neither provable nor disprovable. Literally sophomoric—he'd last heard someone seriously present such an argument back in those beery, youthful midnight bull sessions.

Actually, there had been one more recent time, the two well-dressed lads who'd knocked on his door and tried to infect him with enthusiasm for their faith. One of them had earnestly argued that Matt's rationalism was just one belief system among others, and one that didn't explain everything. It didn't explain their own unshakable faith, for instance.

But it did, Matt said, as part of abnormal psychology. That was pretty much the end of the conversation. But he could have gone on to point out that rationalism doesn't require "belief," only observation. The real, measurable world doesn't care what you believe.

He looked at the pictures again. A guy levitating with a halo. A pile of bread. An ICU ward full of actors and a president who was going along with the game. No actual miracles necessary.

Did the whole world believe this? He desperately needed to find someone who didn't. Or a history book— *any* book that wasn't a Bible.

The front door clicked, and he guiltily closed the book, then opened it again. The landlady walked into the parlor pulling a brush through her hair.

She nodded at him. "As good as church, I suppose. Won't put you to sleep like the good rev." She held the door to the kitchen open. "Bread and coffee."

The coffee was some burned herb, but the flatbread was crumbly and good, served with butter and a dab of strawberry jam. The landlady showed him the bucket of water steaming on the stove and said there were soap and "cloths" out back.

He lugged the bucket out onto the porch. There was a bathing area, about a square meter of slatted floor with head-high modesty screens on three sides. Another bucket, rinse water, and some gray tatters of towel. A cube of harsh soap that smelled of bacon.

It was good to be somewhat clean, though the soap turned his hair into a fright wig and left him smelling like breakfast. Back in the small room he changed into his new old clothes. He rented the room for another night, and the landlady gave him a padlock so he could leave his things behind in the room's strongbox while he explored.

What should he leave behind? She probably had another key. It would be inconvenient if she started snooping around and sent the machine into the future. He wiggled at the plastic dome over the RESET button, and it was secure enough that removing it would be an act of deliberate vandalism.

The pistol and ammunition were a problem, but maybe it would be wise not to carry them into MIT.

He wound up leaving it all, except his wallet and the taxi driver's money. The two rare documents could wait until after he'd learned more.

He'd have to learn a *lot* more before he decided what to do with the porn notebook. Its technology might make it extremely valuable. Its contents might put him away for the rest of his life, which could be short.

Mass Ave was sunny and pleasant, the clop and creak of horse and mule traffic, a slight barnyard smell overlaid with sea breeze from the harbor. He took a hundred-dollar bill into a bank and got a response similar to yesterday's—are there more where this came from?—but the clerk initially offered him $100 and wound up paying $125. It would be smart to shop around.

He walked slowly down to Building One, getting his story together. His various possible stories, depending on what he could uncover. It wouldn't do to just walk into the dean's office and say, "Hey, I'm Matthew Fuller, the time traveler you've been waiting for." That nobody *had* been waiting evidenced a profound discontinuity with the past. The time and place of his projected arrival must have been widely known.

Or would they have been? Professor Marsh hadn't been all that generous with the information Matt had given him about the time machine, back in 2058. Had Matt ever seen the actual time and place published? He couldn't recall.

He went into Building One and walked past the administration offices, on down the Infinite Corridor toward the library, or at least the building that had once housed the science and humanities library.

The walls of the corridor were disturbingly bare. They used to be covered in a riot of posters and announcements, MIT-approved or not. Of course, it would have been bustling with students, too, Monday morning. There were only eight other people in the whole quarter-kilometer of hall.

He didn't want to be the only person in the whole library. Kill an hour doing something else.

Halfway down the corridor, at the rotunda with the stained-glass Stations of the Cross, double doors led to the outside, what used to be the quad.

It was still a large quadrangle, not as well kept, the grass brown or bare dirt in places. A woman in head-to-ankles black was taking advantage of the morning cool to push a mechanical mowing machine. Matt had seen pictures of them. He wanted to go investigate, see whether this one was a museum piece or newly constructed, but it might not be smart to approach a single young woman that way. Or even look at her too hard. He averted his gaze and walked on toward the river.

That was different. Both banks of the Charles were solidly packed with ramshackle houseboats, most of them just moored rafts that obviously weren't going anywhere except, eventually, straight down. Student housing in the twenty-third century, apparently; most of the people in evidence were young men, and a few women, all dressed in black. The men and women were separated.

The places weren't drab; it was a riot of disorganized color. Walls of bright green next to orange and red, with cartoon figures stenciled or spray painted on. No obscenities, unsurprisingly; paragraphs of scripture in neat block printing. In some places, collages of scrap metal and glass clattered and tinkled in the breeze. Someone was quietly practicing intervals on a violin. That would've been grounds for murder, or at least musical defenestration, in the MIT dorms of Matt's youth.

There was a faint aroma of fish frying, and people were fishing from some of the houseboats, idly watching lines or, in one case, throwing out a circular net. Matt wondered how often they caught the bioengineered Christ fishes, or whether those even swam in this river, open to the sea.

Well, he could wonder till the cows came home, though if they were bioengineered, they probably just stayed at home. He had to nail down some data. He angled across the frost-heave ruin of Memorial Drive toward the library.

The glass wall that faced Mem Drive was broken in several places, but those sections had been carefully repaired with glued stacks of clear glass bottles. The automated security system had been replaced by a guard with a wooden staff. He was sitting outside the door and looked amiable.

Matt didn't lie. "I don't have a card."

"Are you carrying any books?"

"No."

"Don't bring any out, then." Matt went on inside.

There were low stacks of books all around, and trays of books spine up in rows between irregular arrangements of tables and chairs. The books on shelves were behind glass, locked away, and the glass was frosted so that the titles were illegible. The trays held well-thumbed paperbacks that didn't seem to be in any order.

There was no console for finding books. What did libraries do before there were computers? There must be a list somewhere. Look up a book and ask someone to get it for you.

Maybe he could figure it out. Meanwhile, be inconspicuous. He started sorting through the paperbacks, which seemed as limited in range and sophistication as the assortment he'd seen in the bookstore.

Then he found a slender volume simply titled *American History*. He sank into a soft chair by the window and opened it to the first page.

"On the first day of the first year, Jesus Christ appeared in the Oval Office of the president of the United States."

On the facing page there was a photograph identical to the one in the Bible on Magazine Street.

The text dismissed all previous history with "Men and women had lived in the United States for centuries in a condition of sin, forgivable because of ignorance."

Some few had refused to accept the reality of their senses and what their hearts told them about the Second Coming and so there was the One Year War, followed by the Adjustment. It didn't say how long the Adjustment had been, or whether it was over.

It seems that President Billy Cabot, the one in the picture, had already been touched by God, which is why Jesus chose his office for His appearance. Cabot became First Bishop, and proceeded to simplify the government in ways that were part divine inspiration and part the stewardship of Jesus.

Looking at a map, it was easy to read between the lines. The One Year War had produced an entity that still called itself the United States of America, but it comprised only the Eastern Seaboard states south of Maine and Vermont, with obvious lacunae. The eastern third of New York was blacked out, as was a large part of Maryland and Virginia, bordering Washington. Metropolitan Atlanta and Miami. What had happened to them? The book had no index and little organization; it rambled along like a disjointed conversation. Well, the author was Bishop Billy Cabot, as told to Halleluja Cabot, presumably his daughter.

As a military history, the book was of questionable value. The Army of the Lord chose its battles well, evidently, and never lost. It apparently didn't bother to fight for 80 percent of the fifty-one states, though.

What kind of battles were they? He couldn't imagine tanks rumbling down Broadway, but New York City was in the blacked-out portion. Was it destroyed?

Maybe it was all metaphor. The "war" was not military at all, but some kind of propaganda war for this new version of Christianity Which could be almost as scary as a fighting war.

He could walk up to Maine, which would only take a few days, a week, and ask his questions there. If he was allowed to cross the border into that heathen state. If there was anyone left there to talk to. What if Christ had nukes?

There was a thing about the all-seeing Spirit and His Avenging Angels that sounded a lot like satellite surveillance and low-orbit killer satellites. But how could he reconcile that with the horse-and-buggy technology around him?

He got up and searched through all the rest of the paperbacks. No politics, economics, world history. There were three other copies of Cabot's *American History*, but no rivals.

"What is it you are seeking?" An older man had come up behind him, quiet on bare feet. He had on the black robe, white hair to his shoulders, and a pair of vertical scars on each cheek.

"Just . . . something to read. I'm not sure." The man nodded slowly, not blinking or changing expression.

Silently waiting for input. It was a robot, like the McWaiters in Matt's world. Ask it for a burger and fries.

"Is there a world history text?"

"Only for scholars. What level of scholarship are you?"

"Full professor," he said firmly.

"At what institution? I don't recognize you."

"I . . . I'm freelance. I don't have an institution right now."

It stared at Matt, perhaps trying to process that idea. "You were at the Admissions Office yesterday, though it was Sunday."

What to say? "That's right."

It didn't move. "But no one could be in the office. It would be a sin."

"I wasn't looking for anybody," he extemporized. "I was just checking the course changes on the wall."

It nodded gravely. "I understand." It turned and walked away silently.

A world where they put scars on robots and give them a large database but low intelligence. Where there wasn't enough electricity to put lights in a library.

Matt sat down and looked at the history book without reading it. What was the deal here? There was electricity and artificial intelligence for robots. There was an industrial base adequate for mass-producing Bibles and history books with color pictures. But most of the world was living in the nineteenth century, if that.

Worse than that. It was a modern world overlaid with a nineteenth-century costume—this building still had elevators, but no way to make them go up and down. The McRobot was evidence of generally available computing power, but there were no data stations in the MIT library.

Another robot approached, robes and scars but bald. A short female behind it.

Not robots. They moved like people. The man smelled like old sweat. He introduced himself as Father Hogarty.

"You're a visiting scholar," he said, and offered Matt a black robe.

"Thank you." Not knowing what else to do, Matt put it on over his clothes.

"This is your graduate assistant, Martha." She was nervous and pretty, a blonde in her early twenties. One almost invisible scar on her cheek. "Hello, Dr. Fuller."

Matt shook her hand. "Hello, Martha." What the hell was going on? "Are you in physics?"

She looked confused. "I'm a graduate assistant."

"She's born again," the man said. That explained everything.

"You know my name," Matt said.

The old man nodded. "The library searched you and sent a messenger. He told me that you were the full professor we were waiting for. Even though you have no marks of scholarship." He touched the scars on his cheeks. He had four prominent ones. "You are in the Data Base." Matt could hear the capitals. "But your office number is wrong. It says you are in Building 54."

Matt nodded. "The Green Building."

"A green building? Where would that be?"

"There's a bluish green one behind Building 17," Martha said. "I had Prayer Variations there."

"It's not the color. It was named after a guy named Green." The tallest building on campus, hard to miss. "Maybe it's gone?"

They looked at each other. "Where would a building go?" Martha said.

"Not like it moved," Matt said. "It maybe got old and was taken down."

The old man nodded. "That happens. But how long ago? I would remember."

Matt took a deep breath and plunged in. "I was born more than two hundred years before the Second Coming. I'm a time traveler who used to be a professor here. Back when it was the Massachusetts Institute of Technology."

They both flinched, and the woman covered her ears. "Bad word," the other said.

"You can't say tech—" They both shrank away. "It used to be the *name* of this place."

"This place was evil once." Hogarty stood up straight and put his hand on the young woman's shoulder.

"What is a time traveler?" she asked. "We all move through time."

"But I *jump*," Matt said. "Day before yesterday, I was back in 2074. That was 106 years before the Second Coming."

Hogarty laughed nervously. "If this is a joke, I don't understand it."

"The Nobel Prize for physics in 2072 went to the man who claimed he discovered time travel."

"A noble prize?" the man said. "Physics?"

"It's part of metaphysics," the woman said.

"I know that. How do you get a prize for it, though? What does it have to do with time?"

"It's all *about* time," Matt said, "and space. And energy and mass and quantum states and the weak interaction force. You're scholars?"

The man touched his scars again. "Of course."

"Didn't you ever study any of that?"

"It's like you're talking Chinese," he said. "Quan tong states and interacting forces? What does that have to do with Jesus?"

Matt felt behind him, found a chair, and sat down. "Um . . . Jesus is part of God?"

"They're both part of the Trinity," he said. "They share attributes."

Matt pressed on. "And God is everything?"

The man said, "In a way," and the woman said, "Everything good."

"So there are *parts* of everything that can be weighed and measured, rather than taken on faith. That's what I'm a scholar of."

Hogarty was thinking so hard you could hear the gears grinding. "But that's for craftsmen and tradespeople. What is scholarly about things you can weigh and measure?"

"It's because of the times he comes from," Martha said. "The measurable world was very important to them." She pursed her lips, then said it: "The T word. That's what it was about."

"Be good, Martha," he warned.

"We shouldn't be afraid of saying things," she said. "Words aren't magic."

"You don't know, child." He appealed to Matthew. "Young people."

Matt didn't want to go there. "Why do you think measurable things aren't scholarly, scholastic, whatever? The real world."

Hogarty smiled, on comfortable ground. "You're joking again. That's the Devil's big weapon."

"The illusion that this world is real," Martha supplied. "But not everybody thinks that way."

"Martha . . ."

"God made this world, not the Devil. In six days? The actual world itself isn't evil."

"She's an independent thinker," the man said, not quite through clenched teeth. "An excellent graduate assistant for you." Church bells were chiming outside. "Noontime. I have to meditate and break fast. Martha, you will see to the professor's needs?"

"Of course, Father."

"Professor, I'll come by your office Wednesday morning sometime. There will be a faculty meeting in the afternoon."

"My office?"

"Martha will find you one. Tomorrow, then." He left with the haste of someone really looking forward to meditation.

"So . . . how are you going to find me an office?"

"They gave me a list. But four of them are small. I know the one you want."

"Okay. So who are 'they'? How come they knew I'd need an office?"

"The administration. I had a note this morning saying I'd be assigned to you, and to expect you soon. Then Father Hogarty came by and said you were here in the library."

"But the administration, they knew about me yesterday?"

She nodded. "Somebody knew you'd need an office. Maybe they knew your building was gone."

All that from the casual encounter with the guard in Building One? It occurred to Matt that it had probably been a robot, too, and he'd been scanned and identified.

So who knew what around here? He was in a database

as a scholar, even though he was last employed 177 years ago.

Did that mean someone was expecting him?

He followed Martha up three flights of stairs to a dim corridor. She gave him a brass key. "This is a nice bright one." She pushed the door open with a creak.

Well, it was bright enough. It should have been in the shadow of the Green Building, but instead he looked down on the roofs of low wooden structures. No sign of the building or its venerable Brancusi sculpture.

But just a couple of days ago, he'd snatched the time machine there and commandeered a cab and come here.

"Professor? Don't you like it?"

"It's fine, Martha. I was just looking at where my old office used to be. The Green Building."

She looked out the window. "It's not one of those?"

"No, a lot bigger. You don't have any pictures of what it used to look like here?"

"Of course not. Nothing before Jesus."

"Because it's a sin?"

"No," she explained patiently, "because it was before."

"All the pictures from before just disappeared?"

"Oh, no. We have Rembrandt and Leonardo and all those men. I like Vermeer best; there are two of his downtown."

Not very religious, a reassuring characteristic. "No photographs, though—nothing from my own time?"

"That all disappeared when Jesus came back."

"What, it just went *poof* into thin air?"

"That's as it is written. Angels took it all away. I wasn't there, of course."

Like Billy Cabot's Avenging Angels? "I have a lot to learn," Matt said, "before I can think of teaching anybody anything."

"I can help with everyday things," Martha said. "Father Hogarty said you won't be teaching this semester."

"Glad to hear it." There was an old metal desk to the left of the window. Matt went through the drawers and found a small stack of paper, two pencils, a dip pen, and a bottle of ink. Next to it, a cylinder of cloth obviously used as a pen-wipe was rolled up around a small knife and two extra pen points.

She picked up the two points and held them up to the light. "Somebody hasn't been too careful. I'll bring you a potato."

"All right. Why a potato?"

"It keeps the points from getting rusty. You stick them into a potato when you're done for the day." She had the amused patience of a graduate assistant telling the professor how to turn on his new computer. "You didn't have pens like this."

"Actually, I've only read about them. Ours carried their own ink around."

"I've seen those. The dean has one, his pen-stick. May I show you how this works?"

"Please."

She pulled out the old desk chair, which was on wheels that didn't roll, and sat down carefully. She treated the ink bottle with care approaching reverence, holding it tightly while the top unscrewed with a rusty squeak. She showed him how to dip the pen partway and remove the excess ink by sliding the nib left and right along the rim of the ink bottle. Then along the top of a piece of paper, she wrote, "Jesus died to save us from our sins" in a careful hand. Matt remembered the tollbooth's crudely lettered BOSTON CITIE LIMMITS / PAY TOLE ONE DOLAR and wondered how rare her talent was.

She stood up and handed him the pen. "Would you like to try it, Professor?"

Not really. He sat down and tried to duplicate her motions. In block letters, he printed THE QUICK BROWN FO, and ran out of ink. The letters were wavering and blobby.

"A brown fo," she read. "Is that like an enemy?" He completed the line, dipping the pen twice. "It sounds like the start of a parable, or a fable. The fox is quick and gets away?"

"It's just a nonsense line. It uses every letter of the alphabet."

"Oh, like, 'Jesus up on high rules few vexed crazy queers today.' " She laughed behind her hand. "The sister who taught me that in school was reprimanded. So I memorized it."

"As you told Hogarty. Words aren't magic."

"Only some of them, in the right order." She took the pen from him and wiped it with the cloth. "Always—" Someone knocked on the door. "That would be your midday."

She opened the door and a male student handed her a wooden tray covered with a black cloth. "Thank you, Simon." She set it on a small table by the door.

"Professors don't eat with the students. I took the liberty of giving the kitchen this room number, but you might prefer to have it sent to your quarters."

A long way to Magazine Street, he thought. "We'll go find your quarters this afternoon," she said. "I'll be out of class at three. May I meet you here?"

"Sure, that'd be fine. Thanks." She slipped quietly out the door.

Under the black cloth, a small loaf of bread and a wedge of crumbly cheese, like an old cheddar. A plate of dried apple slices on a string. Raisins in a cup, plumped with sweet wine. Ceramic flasks of water and red wine. It wasn't Twinkies and speed, but it would do.

In fact, he had become ravenous, and though it was fine, he could have eaten twice as much. He kept the water and wine bottles and the ceramic cup that matched them, and set the rest on the floor in the hall.

There wasn't much else in the room. A filing cabinet that

was empty except for the bottom drawer, which held a
rolled-up black leather bag. He'd seen people carrying them
in the corridor; it was evidently a standard item. He'd use it
to move his stuff here from the rented room; less conspicuous than the taxi driver's plastic shoulder bag.

He sat down and practiced writing with the pen for a
while. One of the nibs was flexible, and his writing with it
went all over the place. The blunt one Martha had used
worked best.

It wouldn't be too smart to put his speculations down,
where they could be read by others. He wrote random stuff
for about a half hour and then his hand began to stiffen up.
He dutifully made sure all the nibs were clean, waiting for
their potato, and went downstairs to have a walk and look
around.

The quadrangle that used to front the Green Building
was still there, sporting oversized rusted bolts that had
once held down the Brancusi *Flying Wing*. Too secular, he
supposed, or maybe it had just worn down.

The silence of the place was eerie. It had always been
relatively quiet, shielded from the Mem Drive traffic noise,
but when the weather was as nice as this, there ought to be
lots of students playing pickup football or Frisbee circles.
Not a soul in sight now.

But then a bell chimed for end of classes, evidently, and
there were dozens, then hundreds, of students surging out
into the sunshine. They were very quiet, but then back in
his day they hadn't exactly been a horde of rabble.

He walked along with them, trying to blend in, but he did
notice an occasional furtive glance. Maybe his evident se-
niority and lack of scars.

They walked among the low wooden buildings, a combination of dorms and meeting halls, to a large central
building that smelled of cooking. Matt turned around and
passed back through the crowd, observing.

In his time, about half the students would have been

Asian. In this crowd there wasn't a single one, and few black people. Was that the result of gradual change, or had there been a sudden purge? If he could find a reliable history of MIT, he could infer a lot about the missing history of the world. Even an unreliable history would hint at things.

He saw the back of a large sign a block away and angled toward it. It was at the easternmost entrance to the old campus, and it used to be a welcome sign with a map.

It still was, though the disciplines invoked were different. Anointed Preaching, Satanic Nature, Blood Covenant. What was a blood covenant and how many courses could they offer in it? Finally he found Natural Philosophy and Metaphysics, a part of the Mechanical and Mathematical Studies wing in Building 7, not far from his office. It might be a good idea to visit it now, incognito.

The walls on the Green Building had been a kind of inspiration, displays about the history of science, mostly physics, with replicas of old experiments along with old photographs. The walls in Building 7 were inspirational, too: reproductions of dignified paintings of Jesus and various saints. No cluttered bulletin boards, no stacks of returned papers—certainly no cartoons or provocative articles taped to doors, which used to be a professor's declaration of individuality.

Perhaps Theosophy didn't encourage individuality. He thought of Father Hogarty's impatience with Martha.

He went into an empty classroom—none of them were in use at this hour—and sat down in the chair behind the teacher's desk, fighting a tide of helplessness and panic. He was *not* trapped here. He knew that ultimately he would find his way back, at least to the offices of Langham, Langham, and Cruise, in 2058.

He might have to go farther into the future, though, before finding that kind of rabbit hole. Maybe he should push the button now, before he got into trouble with these religious nuts. But there was no guarantee that the world 2094 years in the future would be safer or more sensible.

This place should have been comfortably familiar. He had spent most of his life in classrooms, and for many of his years had aspired to be right here, in front of a room full of young people pursuing knowledge. It smelled right; it felt almost right. But on the wall behind him there should be a clock. Not a picture of Jesus smiling benevolently.

Well, he'd spent many an hour staring at those clocks, praying for time to pass more quickly. Maybe kids were just more literal about that now.

He checked his watch. There wasn't quite enough time to walk up to Magazine Street and back, but maybe he didn't have to walk. He'd seen horses with carts parked across the street from Building 1, where there used to be a cab stand.

He went up to the office and retrieved the black bag, then went down and engaged the lead cart of four waiting there. The driver wanted eight dollars each way, but allowed himself to be bargained down to thirteen for a round trip.

It was stifling hot in the sun, but the cab had a leather canopy and moved just fast enough to generate a cooling breeze. It made the trip in a leisurely ten minutes, about what it would have taken in Matt's time, crawling through traffic and waiting for lights.

The landlady wasn't there. Nothing seemed to have been disturbed in the strongbox, so he transferred his stuff to the black bag and was back in his office by 2:30.

Waiting for Martha, he leafed through *Metaphysics and the Natural World*, which was full of biblical citations, but in between them did do a fair job of outlining Newtonian mechanics and basic electricity and magnetism, presupposing a knowledge of elementary calculus and trigonometry. The section on what caused the sun and stars to shine was ingenious, the heat generated by gravitational compression and the constant infall of meteorites. It allowed for the Sun to be about six thousand years old, and close to burning out, which of course would happen on Judgment Day.

Martha knocked on the door just as bells were chiming for change of classes. "Shall we go find your quarters, Professor?"

"Sure." He got up and shouldered the bag.

She held out her hand. "Let me take that for you."

"No, that's all right." The revolver's heft was pretty obvious.

"But I'm your graduate assistant." It was almost a whine.

"Look, Martha. I was a graduate assistant myself not so—"

"What? *Men* were graduate assistants back then?"

"Sure. About half and half."

She shook her head, openmouthed. "But what . . . what did you *do*?"

"Helped my professor out. Mostly math and electronics—that's working with electrical machines. I gave tests and graded papers."

"I can't do anything like that," she said. "I'm not supposed to. That's for scholars."

"So what does a graduate assistant do here?"

"I'm a graduate," she explained. "And I'm your assistant."

"Oh. Okay. But humor me on this: I carry the bag."

She shook her head. "But you'd look like a scholar, not a professor."

"Humor me, Martha."

Her mouth went into a tight line. "If Father Hogarty sees us, will you tell him it was your idea?"

"Absolutely."

He followed her down the stairs and across the quadrangle, the same route he'd taken after lunch, but they kept going on past the dining hall. It was obvious when they entered professors' territory: the residences were smaller, individual cottages, and instead of browning lawns they were fronted with carefully raked gravel and luxurious potted plants.

"Number 21." The door was framed by two bushes covered in velvety purple flowers. She unlocked it and handed the key to Matt.

The single room smelled oddly of orange peel, some cleaning fluid, he supposed, and reflected on how far away the nearest orange tree must be. Which implied a thousand-mile chain of interstate commerce.

It looked comfortable. A large bed and bentwood rocking chair. An open rolltop desk with a padded office chair. On the desktop, an inkwell and a potato with two pen nibs stuck into it. What passed for a word processor in this place and time.

She handed him a folded-over piece of paper. "My schedule, Professor. I have Faith Enhancement twice a day, and directed reading in Alien Faiths three times a week. If you need me in those times, step outside and ring the bell in the yard. Another graduate assistant will go find me."

He looked at the schedule, then his watch. She was due at Faith Enhancement in twenty minutes. "Well, you go on. I'll settle in here. Then what, dinner?"

"At six. I'll take you over there."

She hurried off and he poked around the room. A covered chamber pot under the bed, how convenient. A small closet held stacks of sheets and blankets and a wooden box of candles, along with a red metal box that held matches, handmade and presumably dangerous. A cupboard held a loaf of bread, some hard cheese, and corked bottles of wine and water.

There was one window, with a gauze curtain, and a skylight. So he could read, after and before certain hours, without squandering candles and matches.

Next to the door a strongbox was bolted to the wall. Its padlock used the same key as the door. He unloaded the black bag into it. He held the porn notebook up to the window, but there wasn't enough light to activate it. Having to go out into the sun would make its utility as an adjunct to masturbation questionable.

A single shelf for books had a Bible and a prayer book, along with a water carafe and glass. He poured a glass and longed for coffee, and realized that the dull ache at the base of his skull was caffeine withdrawal. He stifled a strong urge to go back to that place on Inman Square and squander $20 for a cup of "real coffey." It would be better to invest it in aspirin and learn to do without.

He sat in the rocker and leafed through the natural science book. He could teach this stuff, second nature, but would he be able to stomach all the religion that kept cropping up?

Out of an obscure impulse, he went to the desk and took out a sheet of paper and duplicated an exercise that had been part of the final exam in undergraduate modern physics: derive the Special Theory of Relativity from first principles—there is no uniquely favored frame of reference and the speed of light is constant in any frame of reference. It took him two pages of scratching out blind alleys, but he wound up in the right place, with equations describing the distortion of measurements when one frame of reference regards another one that's in motion relative to it.

Time dilation. Saint Albert, you should see me now!

He allowed himself a few moments of fantasy. What would happen if he worked through these equations in front of a classroom here? God does not favor any one position; everything is relative.

Martha came back just before six, to escort him to the faculty dining hall. He was nervous about it, ready for an inquisition. Could he be convincingly polite about religion? Would he have to lie outright, and pretend to believe? Would being honest lead to ostracism, loss of tenure, or burning at the stake? Polite silence was probably the best strategy, and intense observation.

The faculty dining hall was a block away from the student one, with its separate kitchen and, according to Martha, much superior food. (She had a friend who worked there, and occasionally snacked on leftovers.) She handed him over to Father Hogarty and went off to the student trough.

They sat at a table with six others, two of them addressed as "Father" and the rest professors. The Fathers were older, and all had horizontal scars on the forehead; the professors only had cheek scars.

They all treated Matthew with a kind of gravity that had nothing of deference in it. It took him a while to realize that most of them thought he was mad. Divine madness, perhaps, but still crazy. They were conspicuously incurious about the past he claimed to have come from.

It seemed odd that not even one wanted to quiz him about the past—as if they had time travelers drop by for dinner all the time—but then he realized the obvious. Their uniform lack of interest was prearranged; they'd been warned to keep the conversation on safe grounds.

So a lot of it was talk about students and subjects unrelated to Matt's experience, which was a relief. He could just respond with conventional politeness and safe generalizations.

Hogarty and a younger man, Professor Mulholland, did mention Matt's future at MIT. The new semester would start in a couple of weeks. He would monitor various natural philosophy classes with the intention of teaching next year. Mulholland would lend him copies of all the course outlines, and he could have Martha copy out the ones he was interested in teaching.

The meal was good, a thick stew of beef and vegetables with dumplings, and included wine with an MIT label, a weird scuppernong flavor that wasn't bad. It was a 67, four years old.

Martha was waiting for him outside, totally absorbed in reading the Bible under a guttering torch. When he approached, he saw it was actually the Koran; she slapped it shut with a guilty start.

"I brought you some toilet things," she said. "I don't know what you have." It was a wooden box with soap wrapped in a cloth, a handmade toothbrush, a jar of tooth powder, and a straight razor with a sharpening block. Maybe he'd grow a beard. "Do you know where the men's necessary is?"

"No, in fact." He'd used the one across from his office, but that had been a while ago, and "necessary" did describe it. She led him down an unmarked path to two buildings that had remarkably unambiguous pictures as to which was which. How Puritan were these people?

There were oil lamps in sconces dimly illuminating the place. A row of open toilets, two of which were occupied by men sitting with their robes pulled up, talking quietly. There was an obvious urinal, a thick pipe sunk diagonally in the ground, filled with gravel. He used it and went to a basin between two of the lights, with a mirror and a large water urn with a faucet. He brushed his teeth and put off the issue of the beard.

Martha was waiting for him, and they walked together back toward his cottage. "They told me you're going to see the dean tomorrow."

"Ten o'clock," Matt said. "Do you know him?"

"Not to speak to. He's very old and wise."

"I guess a dean has to be," he said lamely. "He's the overall dean? I mean, there's no one over him?"

"No one but Jesus. He's the Dean of Theosophy."

Matt thought of his own Dean of Science, Harry Kendall, dead now more than a century. A fellow Jewish atheist, how he'd roll his eyes at being under Jesus.

"I still have only a vague idea of what theosophy is." He knew the word was adopted, or invented, by an obscure sect in the nineteenth or twentieth century, but there was no obvious connection to that, since it was dead as a doornail before he was born.

"You'll find the way, Professor," she said cheerfully. "Or the way will find you."

He was getting a little annoyed at that assumption, but kept his peace for the time being. "Did you grow up here, Martha?"

"Not in Cambridge, no. Newton, south of here. My family sent me into Boston to find work, but I became a student instead."

"Were they unhappy about that?"

"They pretended not to be. It would be sacrilegious." That was interesting. "Where were you from, back in the past?"

"Ohio. Dayton."

She nodded and pursed her lips. "I wonder if people still live there."

"Why wouldn't they?"

She looked left and right. "The Midland Plague," she whispered. "We're not supposed to talk about it."

"A plague?"

"Most people younger than me don't even know it happened. Maybe it's just a rumor."

"People don't come from there anymore?"

"No. You're the first I've ever met."

They walked in silence for a block. "Ohio . . . was it part of the war? The One Year War?"

"Right at the end," she said. "The infidels dropped a bomb from the sky. But it didn't kill the faithful. So they used to say. They stopped teaching it before I was in school."

Another isolated puzzle piece. They came to his cottage. She produced a key, opened the door, and followed him inside. She lit two candles from the one she was carrying. "What time do you want to be awakened?"

"Don't worry about it. I'll be up in plenty of time for the meeting."

"All right." She opened the closet and took out a rolled-up pallet and a pillow, and set them up neatly in a dark corner. She knelt and put her hands together and prayed silently for a minute.

Matt didn't know what to say or do. She was sleeping here?

She stood up and stretched and then pulled the robe up over her head. She wasn't wearing anything underneath. She folded the robe up neatly into thirds, then over once, and slid it carefully under the pallet, on the pillow end. Then she slipped between the sheets.

"Good night, Professor."

"Um . . . call me Matt?"

She giggled. "Don't be silly, Professor."

her inside. She lit candles from the only fire was early ...

"You must be you going to be awakened?"...

"Don't stay there. I'll be unhappy to get time on the meeting.

"Will it all?" She opened the closet and took out a rolled up mattress and pillow, and set them up neatly in a little room... She lit up and put her things together and stayed steadily on it finally.

She didn't know what to say, or to do. She was sleeping now?

She was limp and exhausted and she reached the robe up over her head. She wasn't wearing anything underneath. She folded the robe so neatly and then think, then over once and laid it carefully on the pallet, on the pillow, and then she slipped between the sheets.

"Good night, Princess."

"Me. You call me Marie—"

She giggled. "Don't be silly, Professor."

13

Martha walked him to Dean Eagan's office the next morning, wearing the usual shapeless robe. His memory and imagination supplied the shape underneath it, though, and he found it hard to concentrate on the meeting with the dean.

He felt scruffy, too, having washed up with a cloth and cold water, not shaving. He was not going to try the straight razor just before an important meeting.

If he let his beard grow out, he would be the only professor on campus so adorned. "Why doesn't anyone wear a beard?" he asked Martha.

She touched the scar on her cheek. "Nobody could tell your rank."

"Maybe I could get away with it. Not having any real rank other than 'professor from the past.'"

She reached up demurely and rubbed the stubble on his chin. "Maybe. It looks nice."

When they stepped into the anteroom of the dean's office, he smelled coffee for the first time since he'd left the past. He tried not to salivate.

Martha took a seat there, and the dean's secretary, a beautiful woman with long black hair and no mark of academic rank, escorted him in.

It was a corner office, flooded with light. The walls that weren't windows were crowded with paintings, some religious, but mostly portraits of deans, ending with Dean Eagan. Not a book in sight.

The dean was an old man, but vigorous. He came around the desk with a sure stride, helped slightly by an ebony cane, and shook Matt's hand. When they sat down, the secretary brought over a tray with an elegant silver coffee service and delicate porcelain cups. The sugar was in irregular brown lumps, and the cream was thick and real.

She left after pouring the coffee, and the dean studied Matt for an uncomfortable moment. His eyes sparkled with intelligence.

"Matthew . . . Fuller. Is there a foolproof way for you to convince me that you are what you say you are?"

"A traveler from the past."

He nodded. "From this Institute, when it was . . . before Theosophy."

Matt clumsily sorted through his robe to the jeans underneath, and pulled out his wallet. His MIT ID was five years old, but it did still resemble him. And it was three-dimensional, a white-light hologram.

The dean looked at it and tried to stick his finger into the holo. He looked on the back, shook it, tapped it on his desk, then handed it back. "These were common then?"

"Every student and employee had one." Matt had three, in fact, with different names, which he had done just to prove he could hack the system. "I was just a graduate assistant." The dean's eyebrows went up. "It meant something different then, a kind of apprenticeship. I think like scholars, now."

He took a sip of coffee and tried not to make a face. It was acrid and flat.

"All the way from Georgia," the dean said. Matt decided to hold out for Colombian.

"So how did you do this, traveling through time?"

"There was a machine," he said, not lying, "in the Green Building. That used to be near where the dining areas are now."

"They did natural philosophy there?"

"Yes, physics. I used to work there, in the Center for Theoretical Physics."

"Before Theosophy."

"The term didn't exist then. To the best of my knowledge."

"To teach here, though, you can learn Theosophy. It's not as if you weren't a Christian—a Methodist, I believe?—so you're halfway there."

"That's right," he said slowly. They'd talked to Moses. "I can learn quickly. My graduate assistant, Martha, said I wouldn't be teaching until next year."

He nodded, a faraway look in his eyes. "What was it like, traveling through time? Did you see the future going by?"

"I wish I had. It was all just a gray blur, which seemed to last only a minute or so."

"You were in a car?"

"That seemed sensible. We didn't know where I might end up."

"We sent a team out to Arlington, to tow it in." It took a moment for the meaning of "team" to sink in. Horses. "Do you think you could get it to work?"

"I don't know. Can you generate electricity and store it in a fuel cell?"

"You'll have to ask the people in mechanical studies. I've seen them make sparks with electricity that they carried in a box."

"That would be a start." He choked down some more coffee to be polite. "If it's something like a chemical battery, in theory it could work." Though it might take months to get enough charge to go a few miles, he wouldn't mind having a getaway vehicle that was also a Faraday cage.

"Can you travel back? Go back to the . . . earlier MIT?"

"Some say yes, and some say no. If I were back in my own time, maybe I could build a machine that went the other direction. People were working on it when I left. But you can see the logical problem in going backward."

The dean's brow furrowed. "You would meet yourself? Be in two places at the same time?"

"That's one manifestation of it. But the larger philosophical problem is that it blows apart cause and effect. You could use the time machine to go back and murder the person who invented the time machine."

"But . . . that would be a sin."

"I don't mean you would actually *do* it."

"No, of course. Theoretical possibility." He laughed. "Sorry. I used to be a Father. So you would be using the machine to make the machine not exist in the first place."

"Exactly."

"But then . . ." He rubbed his chin and concentrated. "There doesn't have to be a paradox. Time just starts over, and goes on as if the machine had never existed. Assuming the time traveler would have to disappear once his time machine stopped existing."

Pretty damned good. "That's right, sir. And the 'loop,' as we call it, of time and space when and where the machine existed—that loop itself ceases to exist."

"So where does it go?"

Matt shrugged. "Limbo? Nobody can say."

"Interesting." He poured himself some more coffee, and Matt declined a refill. "How could one tell . . . how can *you* tell that you aren't in one of those closed-off loops? Suppose you do invent a reverse time machine, and you go back and smash the machine that sent you here. The fact that you obviously exist—does that mean you didn't do it?

Aren't going to do it? If you were in one of those closed-off loops, doomed to Limbo, how could you tell?"

"Well, you could jump forward again, and"—a thread of ice water down his spine—"you'd wind up in a future where your time machine had never been invented."

Dean Eagan put his fingers together in a steeple and smiled. "Like this one."

After the interview, Matt went for a walk to clear his head. Could he be in a Gödelian strange loop? It wouldn't have to be he himself who went back and destroyed the time machine. Anyone capable of traveling into the past could do it, and deposit him in this odd future. A future where he was an anomaly, because the time machine had never been invented and Professor Marsh never stole the Nobel Prize from him.

But thinking about interference from the future made him wonder about the machine's infuriating singularity. Thousands of copies had been made, and none of them worked; in essence, none of them had the vital, untraceable mistake that turned a graviton/photon calibrator into a time machine.

What if it hadn't been anything Matt did? What if somebody from the future had come back and modified the machine, so as to make his own present possible? And then someone else from *his* present—or future—came back and destroyed the machine, because his own history required that it not exist? There could be an infinity of closed strange loops like this one.

Or the straightforward explanation could be true. Occam's Razor. There was a conservative Christian revolution, and when they got into power, they systematically destroyed history in order to rewrite it. The Chinese had done that in ancient times, he remembered from an undergradu ate history class—they defeated the kingdom that would become Vietnam in a war, and made the possession of historical documents a crime punishable by death.

But those *were* ancient times, before universal literacy and printing made books ubiquitous. Somewhere there had to be an old book stashed away, overlooked by the Angels.

He had walked over Longfellow Bridge, which used to carry the Red Line into Boston. At the end of the bridge, he carefully made his way down a rusting spiral stairway to Charles Street.

This is where he had planned to start looking for a buyer for his rare letters from García Márquez and Lincoln. It used to be a street full of antique stores, a couple of them specializing in old documents. Would that commerce have gone underground when history was abolished and rewritten? Maybe the Angels would have gone after them first. The people with actual evidence.

There were more open shops and markets here than he'd seen in the suburbs. More fresh produce, though Arlington and Somerville were closer to the farms. They must get better prices in town, or maybe the city subsidizes them.

The place where he'd bought the Lincoln note to Grant was long closed and boarded up. On the next block, the shop that had sold him the García Márquez letter was still an antique shop, but only in that everything in it was old. It was more like a Salvation Army or Goodwill store in his time—very-used stuff being sold to people who would use it some more.

There was a dusty plastic bookcase with two shelves of Bibles and hymnals and a yellowed old booklet about Boston Baked Beans. There was no date on it, but it might have been pre-S.C.

In his time such a store would have been full of old questionable appliances—the question being, "If this still works, why is it here?"—but the main motif in this one was cast-off clothing, hanging on racks or neatly folded in stacks, according to size. Most of it was pretty threadbare, but he was tempted, since he had only one change of clothes. In this warm weather, he should emulate his graduate assistant and wear the robe with nothing underneath. He was contemplating that memory when a middle-aged male clerk came up, tubby and sweating.

"May I be of service, Professor? I do have an assortment of robes in the back, though none are as fine as yours."

He hadn't thought anything of it, but the robe Father Hogarty had bestowed on him was new. How rare was that now?

"Actually, I'm looking for scholarly materials, old things with writing in them."

He drew back. "Not forbidden books."

"No, of course not. I mean things like old letters. Written before Christ appeared."

He scratched his head. "I do have a box of old letters, but they're probably not that old. I'll bring them up to the light."

Matt looked through the coats, thinking of the winter ahead, but of course MIT might provide. He had an appointment tomorrow with the bursar, who would evidently haggle with him over terms of compensation, which took food and shelter into account, so possibly clothing as well. I'll trade you two Saturdays of one-on-one physics tutoring for long underwear and a winter coat.

The clerk came huffing back with a microwave oven full of loose paper. So some old appliances were still of use.

He cleared off part of a shirt table and began laying out the letters. They seemed all to be post–Second Coming, formal notes of congratulation or condolence. The handwriting was mostly childish script or block printing, not surprising if paper had been a luxury for generations. The wording of the notes was formal and unimaginative, probably copied from an Emily Post type guide.

Matt looked at about a hundred of them, and there was

nothing really interesting. His feet were getting tired, standing. He stacked the letters all back in the microwave and clicked the door shut.

The clerk came up to him with a large padded plastiglass envelope held to his chest. "I do have a curiosity you might want to look at. A holy relic." He opened the envelope and carefully worked out what looked like an ordinary Bible, and handed it carefully to Matt. "Signed by Jesus Himself."

"Really." He opened it, and on the front page was a dark "X," deeply indented, as if someone had leaned into a ball-point pen, with JESUS HIS MARK in parentheses.

Matt didn't know quite how to react. "How much would this be worth, do you think?" he asked the clerk.

"Oh, at least five hundred dollars. I'm not sure I would sell it, though. It makes me feel good just to have it here, and I think it brings luck."

"Selling it might be unlucky," Matt said, handing it back. "But couldn't anybody do this? How do you know it's authentic?"

"Oh, my father was there when Jesus signed it. Down in Washington."

That was interesting. Matt's stomach growled audibly. "Thank you for showing it to me. I'll be back later, probably buy some winter clothes."

"God bless."

Matt nodded gravely. Got to find a ballpoint pen somewhere.

Aromas from the food vendors were tempting, but Martha had told him that a tray would be delivered to his office unless he asked otherwise, so he climbed up the rusty stairs and hurried back onto campus, an appetite-building half hour. This time it was bread and a sausage and a fresh cucumber, all welcome. He wrote a note asking for salt and pepper.

He put the tray and note outside the door and sat down with the natural philosophy book and a piece of paper, and started a rough outline of a physics course that stopped short of special relativity. It was frustrating, but he did map out a thirteen-week schedule. He would never be able to fake the introductory bit about how the workings of nature reflect the handiwork of God, but he could probably ask one of the Fathers to step in for that part. Split the day's salary with you?

At 3:30 he went back to Building 1 for his appointment with the bursar, a fat little man with a scowl and a squint and the improbable name Father Gouger. He said that in addition to room and board, Matt would be given an allowance for clothing and books. Paper and ink and pen points had to be ordered in advance from Supply. Above that, he'd be paid fifty dollars for every class he taught. The price of two and a half cups of "real coffey." A good thing he was shaking the habit, and the coffee was lousy, anyhow.

MIT offered him a hundred dollars a week stipend while he wasn't teaching. Not unreasonable, Matt thought, since all his basic needs were taken care of, but on general principles he asked for two hundred, and eventually settled on $127.50.

To his surprise, Gouger counted out that amount and handed it to him, saying henceforth it would be delivered to his office with the noon meal every Monday.

He went out onto Mass Ave and took his newfound fortune to the nearest tavern, which had a faded sign that identified it as the Brain Drain. He got a mug of beer and a small glass of spirits and retreated to the darkest corner, away from four young men arguing over free will and destiny.

His own destiny was unsure and complex in a way the boys wouldn't be able to understand. He knew that on 2 February 2058, someone had appeared from *somewhere* to set him free—free enough to go to 2059 for a second or two, then zip to 2074 to celebrate Professor Marsh's genius.

But where was that benefactor now? Matt might be caught in a strange closed loop of space-time that contacted another strange closed loop at the moment he stole the cab—and that might be two other strange closed loops away from the one where the shadowy benefactor showed up with the million-dollar check.

There was a jar of pickled eggs on the bar. Maybe that was the model. Each egg was a closed three-dimensional solid touching other closed three-dimensional solids, unaware that it was floating in a larger universe of vinegar. Unaware of the bartender with his fork, ready to change any egg's destiny.

The liquor had an astringent green-apple taste, not unpleasant. The beer was even somewhat cool, having come up from the basement.

But he should be thinking, not drinking. He moved the shot glass a symbolic foot away.

One thing linking this egg with the one he'd come from was the fact that the library had scanned him and identified him as a full professor. A 177-year-old personnel record? Well, he'd neither quit nor died. Maybe there was no cell on the spreadsheet for "fired because he stole a taxi and escaped into the future."

There was a larger question about causality; about how he should act. Assume that it *had* been he who came back with the bail money. Since that had already happened—arguably, he couldn't be sitting in this bar if it hadn't happened—then it was going to happen no matter what he chose to do in the here and now.

That was A. Here was B: There was no way he was going to invent a time machine into the past with the resources of the Massachusetts Institute of Theosophy.

Therefore C: He had to be jumping into the future at

least one more time, to a place and time where such a machine could be built.

Built by him? He hadn't really built the one he was using now.

So somebody else would do the actual inventing—and maybe do the rescuing as well. Whatever, it wasn't likely that he was going to stay here and make a career in theosophy. So it would be wise not to stray too far from the machine and keep an eye out for large metal containers. There weren't a lot of cars and Dumpsters around.

Dean Eagan had said a team was bringing in the taxi. Better find out where it was going to be parked. Carry the time machine with him all the time? That could be awkward.

Another possibility was not exactly honest. He could follow his late, unlamented father's motto: "Shut up and play the cards you're dealt." He could settle in here, teaching natural philosophy and doing research—and he could "discover" special and general relativity. Quantum mechanics.

And maybe get burned at the stake. It would be smart to tread carefully.

He sipped the applejack and followed that train of thought a little distance. To be honest, it was unlikely that he was ever going to make a significant breakthrough in the direction of his research back at the real MIT. The gravity-wave stuff looked like a dead end. Here, he had a chance to reinvent physics and perhaps give these people a chance to rediscover what they'd lost.

But the lesson of Giordano Bruno was hard to ignore. He'd tried to teach medieval Europe that their small Catholic God was inadequate in the face of the majesty of the actual universe. Matt didn't know much about him, but remembered an image from a cube biopic he'd seen as a teenage protoscientist; Bruno dragged up from the Inquisitors' dungeon and tied to the stake by chest and legs with rough rope, his arms free, over a pile of dry brambles and sticks. They brought the torch forward, and the priest presented him with a crucifix. He knocked it away scornfully and watched with a stony, heroic expression as they put the torch to the pile.

Matt didn't think he was quite up to that. He moved his drinks up to the bar and bought one of the eggs and nibbled on it thoughtfully. He resisted the temptation to have another beer, and walked through the cooling afternoon sun back to his cottage.

He opened the strongbox and considered his worldly possessions. If he were to start carrying the time machine around with him, it would be in the expectation of having to use it with little or no warning. What else should he carry, planning to disappear suddenly into the future?

The gun. But no need for the whole box of ammunition; just the six cartridges that it carried fully loaded. It was just a noisemaker to him. He couldn't imagine a scenario where he would shoot all six bullets and then have time to reload, and not be killed during the pause.

The money, of course, and the two rare documents. They might still be worthless 2094 years from now, or they might be priceless.

But the notebook with its store of pornography was questionable. In some futures it might also be a priceless asset. In others, presumably like here, it might be a serious crime to possess one.

Or maybe not like here. The attitude toward nudity was evidently relaxed, and to his knowledge there was nothing in the Bible about pornography. Thou shalt not look at graven images of professional sex workers in improbable geometries?

Besides, it would be hard to turn on the thing accidentally, especially in a culture almost innocent of modern machinery. It was childproof, which also meant "ignorant-adult-proof."

He put it all in the black leather bag and hefted it, less than ten pounds. Other professors didn't carry their own bags, perhaps, but he was the man from the past, and ought to be allowed an eccentricity or two. For legitimacy, he put the New Testament Bible and the natural philosophy text in there, along with a pencil and several sheets of paper, folded over and slipped into the Bible.

Four rapid knocks on the door. "Come in?"

It was Martha, out of breath from running. "Professor! I just got word from Father Hogarty! You're going to see Jesus!"

"See . . . Jesus?"

"Right now—ten minutes from now!" She actually grabbed his arm and pulled. "Faculty chapel!"

He started to pick up the bag, but she snatched it away from him. "I'll take that. Let's go!"

When Jesus calls, Matt reflected, you might as well pick up the phone. "Okay. Lead on."

14

The Faculty Chapel was in Christ Hall, a big "old modern" building that used to house art exhibits in the old days. The part for general worship was roomy and bright, even at this late hour, but the Faculty Chapel was a side room, lit with flickering oil lamps. The homey smell of corn oil burning reminded Matt of the popcorn in theater foyers, and the attendant feeling of expectation.

There were two church pews with cushions for kneeling. Father Hogarty was the only one there, kneeling in quiet prayer. When Matt and Martha came in, he unfolded painfully and offered Matt his hand.

"This will be a wondrous time for you, my son. I envy you. The first is always the best."

"You talk with Jesus often, Father?"

"Only when he needs to tell me something. Perhaps once every two years."

"So how—"

"Please, please, take my place. He'll only come to you alone. We'll wait outside." With Martha's help, he pulled closed a door that must have been eight inches of solid oak.

Matt knelt where Hogarty had been and self-consciously put his hands together in an attitude of prayer, not sure what to expect. Belatedly, it occurred to him to be afraid.

Jesus cleared his throat. "Welcome to my house, Matthew."

He looked just like the pictures, which was no surprise. Handsome, thirtyish white guy with shoulder-length hair and a short beard, both neatly trimmed. White robe with a belt of rough rope. It made Matt think uncomfortably of Giordano Bruno.

"I've been expecting you," the image said. It was definitely a holographic projection. "Ever since I saw you appear up in New Hampshire."

"You were expecting me?"

"I see everything. But yes, you appeared less than two meters from where you were expected, and within about nine seconds of when."

"So you knew I was coming. But nobody here did?"

He smiled. "I'm God, Matthew, or at least one aspect of Him. That you don't believe in Him doesn't alter the reality of His existence. Nor of His omniscience."

"If you're omniscient, tell me what I'm going to do next."

"You have free will. But I suspect you're going to throw something at me, which will pass through, exposing me as a hologram."

Matthew loosened his grip on the piece of chalk he had taken out of his pocket, ready to throw. "You claim not to be a hologram?"

"I don't make any claims." Jesus picked up a paper clip and tossed it at Matthew. It bounced off his chest. "Maybe you need to see me as a hologram. I'm all things to all men."

Matthew's brain was spinning with trying to explain the paper clip. "Could you walk out into the sunlight? That's what I really need to see."

There was a sudden sharp pain in his chest, and he

couldn't breathe. He tried to rise, but some force held him down.

"Don't be petty, Matthew. God doesn't do your bidding, and He certainly doesn't serve unbelief."

"Okay," he croaked. "Let . . . me . . . breathe?"

"Gladly." Air seeped back into his lungs.

Nothing supernatural. A pressor field that thumped him over the heart, then squeezed his chest. Same thing that tossed the paper clip.

It could kill him faster than being burned at the stake.

"Thank you . . . Jesus."

"You do believe in me, then?"

"Of course I do. This world belongs to you." With his breath, he was getting back his equilibrium. "But I'm curious . . . what happened between my time and yours, here? I can't find an actual history."

Jesus smiled indulgently. "There is no history. This is a world without end. Without beginning, so without history."

Like a closed strange Gödelian loop. If he used the machine, which had never been invented, to jump out of this world, after affecting it. It *would* always be, without beginning or end.

"But I've read about the One Year War and the Adjustment. Those must have been real."

"There's only one book you have to believe." Matt felt a gentle pressure on his ribs. "Everything else is in error."

"I understand," he said quickly. "But you allow those other histories to exist."

"For moral instruction. Don't mistake it for literal truth."

Without moving his arm, Matt flicked the chalk toward the image. When it was inches away, it suddenly spun up toward the ceiling.

An invisible slap spun Matt's head sideways so hard his neck cartilage popped. "Stop trying to prove that I'm not real. I'm more real than you are, here."

"I know you're *real*," Matt said, rubbing his neck, "but I was just trying to find out whether you were *material* as well. I take it that you aren't. That if I walked over and tried to touch you—"

"You would die."

"I'm sure that's true, and I wouldn't try it in a million years. But I suspect that if I did try, my hand would be pushed away by a pressor field. We had those in my time, you know. They used them for security in the Museum of Fine Arts in Boston." He swallowed hard, but continued. "And if the pressor field wasn't turned on, my hand would go straight through your holographic image."

"If that's what you have to believe. As I say, it's a manifestation of free will. When you come to judgment, your apostasy will be weighed along with all your other sins. Weighed against your good works; your service to God and man."

The closest Matt had ever come to serving God was passing the plate at his aunt Naomi's Seder table, which he never attended willingly. If you asked him, he would say the only connection between free will and religion in his life was the fact that he hadn't set foot in a synagogue since he turned eighteen.

But he had to admit that this apparition was totally believable in a world that didn't even have words for hologram and pressor. And since they evidently had total control over education and research, there was no way that was going to change.

Unless he did it.

After half a minute of silence, Jesus spoke. "You should now ask, 'How may I serve you, my Lord?' "

"All right. What do you want me to do? Since you can obviously hurt me at any whim. Kill me, I suppose. I'll do whatever you want." He almost said, "within reason," but that would be meaningless.

"Bring the time machine here in one hour. I want you to destroy it in front of me." Jesus flickered and disappeared.

Well, that was interesting. Jesus didn't know the time machine was right here in Matt's bag. So he was all-seeing except when there was a roof in the way.

Matt put his shoulder to the heavy door and pushed out into the light, dazed and dazzled.

Father Hogarty and Martha were waiting expectantly. "You saw Him?" she said.

"Uh . . . yes. Yes, I did."

"What did he ask you to do?" Father Hogarty's eyes were bright.

"You were listening?"

"No, no. Whenever He talks to someone here, He asks him to do something. To prove his faith, usually." He touched his face. "Every mark of rank I have, past the first, was at his request. Did he require that of you?"

"No, not yet. Father, does he always appear here?"

"Yes, of course."

"In the chapel? Not in the other parts of the church here?"

He nodded. "Only the Elect may see him. And you," he added quickly.

That made sense. The room was wired for the pressor field and the holograph projector.

"But *He* sees all," Hogarty continued. "He knew you had come before you arrived here. He told me."

"He mentioned that," Matt said. "He saw me appear when I came from the past, up in New Hampshire." He didn't *appear* there because he couldn't. But any spy satellite could home in and read the taxi's license plate.

"If not a mark, what did he require of you?"

"Nothing yet. He'll see me later."

The old man studied him. "Matthew, don't be afraid of the pain. It is fleeting, but the joy of service is eternal."

It took him a moment to decode that. "He didn't say anything about getting a scar. That will come later, I suppose."

Hogarty and Martha both touched their cheek scars. "The first one doesn't require a command. Only a calling. We can take care of that anytime." He stepped toward the chapel door. "I will pray for guidance."

They watched him ease the heavy door shut. "Let's go back to the cottage, Martha. I have to take care of some stuff."

He thought furiously. He had one hour. If that room was wired up for a pressor generator, it would topologically be an enclosed volume of wires, and work as a Faraday cage. So he could go back in one hour, but instead of smashing the machine, he'd press the RESET button and carry the chapel with him up into the forty-fifth century. See whether Jesus came with him.

Or he could smash the machine and stay here, where at least some parts of the world were still familiar.

No. Whoever the man behind the curtain was, he was dangerous. That had to be the last time Matt would risk setting foot in that chapel.

"What was Jesus like?" Martha asked as they hurried across campus.

"Scary," Matthew said. "I mean, he looked like all the pictures. But he can hurt you. Do anything he wants."

"Why would He hurt you?"

"Power. Making sure I feared him."

"Why would He do that? Everyone knows He's all-powerful."

"Yeah, well, we have to talk about that." They got to the cottage and Matthew checked his watch. "We have about fifty minutes." He unlocked the door and went straight to the cupboard. "Give me the bag, please." He put the cheese and bread in it, and a stoppered bottle of water. An unopened bottle of MIT wine.

"Professor? What are you *doing*?"

"This will all be clear later, Martha," he said, knowing it wouldn't be. "I have to run downtown, down to the bank, but you can stay here."

"No, I'll come with you." She took the bag back. "But I don't understand."

"I don't quite have it all figured out myself," he said. "We used to call it 'flying by the seat of your pants.' "

"Well, that sounds . . . it doesn't sound nice."

He led her out of the door and locked it behind them. "We used to have flying machines, all right? 'Flying by the seat of your pants' meant propelling one of those machines by instinct."

"All right. Now I'm *totally* confused."

"I'm just not sure what's going to happen next. I think . . . well, I know. I can't stay here. I'll have to leave. Jump into the next future."

"That's what Jesus said to you?"

"Yeah. In a way. So I have to be prepared. I don't know what it's going to be like a couple of thousand years from now, in New Mexico, so I—"

"That's a place? One of the Godless states?"

"Right. That's where they calculated I'd wind up next."

After a few moments of silence, she said, "I can't go with you."

"I wouldn't want you to."

"No, I mean I *should*. But I'm afraid."

"You couldn't come back. Being a graduate assistant doesn't require throwing your life away."

"I think I would have to," she said slowly, "if your life were in danger."

Matt laughed. "I hereby relieve you of the responsibility."

"You can't, Professor. I swore to God and Jesus that I would stay by you, and serve you."

"Well, I don't know about God, but the Jesus I saw and

talked to was no more holy than that bird there." He pointed at a mockingbird that was scolding something. "Less. It was just a product of technology"—she winced at the word—"that was old when I was born. A holographic projection; a moving hologram."

"Holy gram?"

He wrestled with the robe and extracted his wallet and showed her the MIT card with the three-dimensional picture. "Like this, but moving and talking."

She stared at it and, like the dean, tried to push a finger into the card.

"Somewhere there's an actor made up to look like the historical Jesus. He watches me on a camera—you know what a camera is?"

"Sure. My Bible has pictures in it."

"Well, he watches from a distant location and makes appropriate responses to what his audience does and says."

"But that doesn't make any sense," she said, hurt and reluctance in her voice. "Why wouldn't they just use the actor?"

"He'd be vulnerable. This Jesus can't be stabbed or shot or crucified. And he can do things that look like miracles."

"How do you know they aren't miracles?"

"Because I know how they're done. I mean, I couldn't duplicate them without help, but the science behind them is clear enough, simple enough."

"They could still be miracles, though. Even though you could do some science that looked the same. Like turning water into wine; you could do something like that with a powder. I saw that when I was a child."

"Phenolphthalein. Big deal." They were walking up Charity, approaching Mass Ave. The intersection was a hopeless knot of people and animals and carts, so they cut diagonally across what used to be a parking lot, and was now a crowded, crazy quilt of merchants displaying their wares on makeshift tables or arranged on blankets.

"Look. Do you know Occam's Razor?"

"I do. Basically it says the simplest explanation is usually the right one."

"So there you are. You don't need to invoke miracles."

She looked genuinely perplexed. "But you have someone who looks like Jesus, who says He is Jesus, and He performs miracles—I would say that Occam's Razor says that He *is* Jesus."

"Oh . . . Jesus." The bank was half a block away, and there was a line out onto the sidewalk. Matt really had to pee, and they were passing a public toilet. "Look, I'd love to continue this argument, but nature calls."

"Nature what?"

"I mean . . ." He gestured toward the toilet door.

"Oh, you have to go do. I'll get us a place in that line."

The latrine was dark, just a small skylight, but it had pretty good ventilation, and didn't quite reek.

It had a piss-tube like the ones at MIT. He went through the complicated business of holding his robe out of the way and unzipping his jeans one-handed, and gratefully let fly.

"What's that?" someone said in the murk. He could see two men sitting on toilets, and one was pointing at his dick. "He's not *cut*!"

Well, that was beyond irony. The only Jew in Boston, and he was attracting attention because his parents had been New Reform and didn't believe in circumcision.

"Can you explain that?" said a voice with the gravel of authority.

"I'm sorry," Matt said inanely. "Where I come from—"

"He's a spy from Gomorrah!" came a high-pitched voice. "Got to be!"

"No! I'm a professor at MIT!"

"You wait until I'm finished here," said the authority voice. "I'm a policeman. We can talk to MIT."

"Okay—I'll wait outside," Matt almost caught himself in the zipper, fleeing.

"Wait! I command you to wait! In the name of the Lord!"

Matt ran clumsily down the street, clomping in sandals, and was breathing hard when he came up to Martha, a couple of yards from the bank entrance. "Give me . . . the bag," he wheezed, and pulled at it.

She resisted instinctively. "Professor? What—" A black-robed policeman with a staff had covered half the distance from the latrine.

"The safe. Have to—" He pulled it free and staggered through the door.

The clerk in front of the vault looked up with a quizzical smile. Matt strode up and reached into the bag and put the pistol straight into his face. *"Drop it!"* he yelled to the guard by the vault door, "or I'll shoot him, I swear to God!"

The lone guard had a pump shotgun. He set it on the floor and stood with his hands up. Outside, someone yelled, "Stop that man! He's a heathen spy!"

"Up!" Matt shouted. "Up! Into the vault!"

"All right," the clerk said, almost falling over backward as he stood. Matt jammed the pistol's muzzle into the man's temple and started walking him toward the big enclosure, the largest Faraday cage on the block.

Martha ran to his side. "Professor?"

"Stay away, Martha. Everything inside the vault is going to go."

Once he was inside the metal walls, he shoved the clerk back out, and kept the gun on him while he reached into the bag for the time machine. "Get out, Martha!"

There was a loud *bang* and a bullet whined, ricocheting around inside the vault. The cop from the latrine was at the door, holding his staff like a rifle.

Martha stood in front of Matt with her arms spread wide. "Put that down! He's a holy man!"

Everybody else, now including Matt, was flat on the floor as the cop swung left and right, trying to get a clear shot past Martha. He fired, and a bullet spanged off the floor and a couple of walls.

Matt ignored his own gun and pressed the alligator clip to the metal floor and pried the protective plastic dome off. "Jesus fucking"—he mashed the RESET button—

15

"—Christ!"

"Oh, my," Martha whispered. "It really works?"

"This is New Mexico?" Matt snapped the protective plastic dome back over the RESET button and stepped through the open door onto a manicured lawn. He turned to Martha, who stood staring. "It's supposed to be desert."

There was a white house that looked pretty much like a suburban rambler, though it wasn't obvious what it was made of. The lawn was enclosed in a metal fence about shoulder high. On the other side of the fence, a nearly identical house, light beige, then a pale blue one, and so on, curving away in both directions. Behind them, a forest too regular to be natural.

The back door of the house slid open, and a man and woman of about middle age stepped out and looked at them warily, hands on hips. They were both wearing only shorts and sandals and were deeply tanned or of mixed race. Matthew assumed the latter, given a couple of millennia of intermarriage.

"How you do that?" the man said. His accent was odd but clear.

"Pushed a button," Matt said. "It's a long story."

"Well, you'll have to move it," the woman said.

"Spoils the view," the man said. "And it *is* our property."

Matt looked over his shoulder. Twenty, thirty tons of bank vault? It wasn't going anywhere.

"Where are we?" Martha said.

"East Los Angeles," the woman said. "You aren't dressed for it."

"I'll say." Matt was stifling. He set the time machine down and pulled the rough robe over his head. He was wearing jeans and an MIT tee shirt.

"I can't . . ." Martha said. Her face was turning bright red.

"We'll find you something modest," Matt said. "How far is town?"

"Los Angeles City?" the man said. "About four hundred kays."

"Ah." So they had landed close to the predicted place in New Mexico. It had just been annexed to Los Angeles, and suburbanified. "But if you just wanted to buy some women's clothing?"

"Buy?" the woman frowned.

Matt gestured at the vault. "Money is one thing we have."

She looked at her husband. "Money?"

He smiled at her. "You didn't pay attention in school, Em. That's what they had before bee shits."

"Oh, I remember. Like dollars."

"Bee . . . shits?" Matt said.

The man rubbed his chin thoughtfully. "Where you from they still use money?"

"The past. We're from the past."

"Oh . . . key. From like when?"

"I started in the 2050s. Picked her up a couple of hundred years later."

They just looked at him. Then Em broke into a broad grin. "It's a movie! We're in a movie, Arl!"

He nodded slowly. "Not supposed to say anything about it," he murmured sotto voce. "That's your time-travel machine?"

"Yes, it is," Matt said, then realized the man was looking at the incongruous bank vault. Concrete dust was still sifting from its sides. He hoped no one had been hurt when it disappeared; it probably was holding the ceiling up.

"Mind if we take a look?"

"No, I don't mind." Martha took a breath as if to speak; he silenced her with a look. See how this plays out. He put the actual time machine back into the bag and shouldered it.

The man and woman walked toward the vault door with exaggerated casualness, but then hesitated at the opening. "This thing won't take off with us in it?"

"I'm sure it won't, no. Not a chance." Matt followed them in, Martha behind him. The four of them stood blinking in the semidarkness.

This part of the vault was mostly deposit boxes. They would be forced open eventually, but Martha found something more interesting—money bags.

"Look at this, Professor!" They were stacked like small flour sacks in a corner, four of them stenciled $2.5K IN Q and $10K IN D. Matt took out his Swiss Army knife and figured out which blade was an actual knife.

He cut the bag on top and quarters came cascading out. They watched it with mild interest. "That's what money used to look like," Arl said. "Heavy stuff to carry around." Matt scooped up a handful of aluminum quarters. Heavy?

"Can you imagine bee shits made out of metal?" Arl shook his head and smiled.

"So what's a bee shit?" Matt said, thinking the answer should be "honey."

Arl pulled a roll of bills out of his pocket and fanned

them. Several different denominations, different colors. They all had the word BARTER ornately printed all over both sides. "A barter chit," Arl said.

"Can I see?" Matt reached out, and Arl jerked the roll back protectively.

"He doesn't know," Em said. "They're not like your old-fashioned money. They're coded to the owner."

"I don't understand."

"It's like if you had a fish and I wanted it, but all that I had that you wanted was an apple. The fish is obviously worth more, so we bargain over how many B chits you get along with the apple. Say it's five. I hand you the five, and when we're both touching it, it knows it belongs to you. Until you pass it on to someone else."

"How does it know?" Martha asked.

"Everybody's DNA is different, you know? It just reads your DNA," she said slowly, as if speaking to a child. She winked at Arl. Part of the movie.

Martha looked totally lost. "What's DNA, Professor?"

"It's in most of the cells in our bodies. I'll explain. But it's like fingerprints; everybody has a unique pattern." He turned to the woman. "What, it analyzes the oils on your skin, your fingers?"

"How should I know?" she said defensively. "It's just DNA."

Matt gave a handful of coins to Arl. "These have to be worth something. Aren't there coin collectors?"

He laughed. "You can find someone who collects almost anything. I don't know anybody myself. You probably have to go all the way to LA."

"Maybe we could barter you something," the woman said innocently. "Take a hundred or so in case some collector shows up."

"We could take a whole bag," Arl said. "You're not going to be carrying them around."

That made Matt a little suspicious. Why would he want

ten thousand one-dollar coins if they were worthless? "What would you want to exchange?"

He shrugged. "Come look at our stuff?"

They stepped outside, and Arl asked whether Matt wanted to close the door. "I think it's safe here on our property. But you know people."

"No; I don't have the key." He wasn't sure the heavy thing would close anyway. "Nothing in there but worthless old money." Arl nodded with lips pursed, perhaps calculating.

He wiped his thumb across the door plate—interesting that they locked up to go out into the backyard—and held it open for them.

"Stuff" it was. Most of the house was one huge warehouse room. Motorcycles and bicycles seemed to be specialties. Above a neat row of parked motorcycles hung a row of bicycles dangling from hooks, all looking new and shiny. Three walls were full of paintings and holos and one was a floor-to-ceiling bookcase with hundreds of books, maybe a thousand. Martha stared at them; probably more books than she had ever seen outside of a library.

On the floor were obvious things like lawn mowers and vacuums, lamps, and fans, and many things whose functions were not obvious.

A door slid open as Arl approached it, and he stood in the doorway to let the others through.

This was a kitchen and pantry. Except for one wall with a window that looked out on the front lawn and street, every wall was covered with hanging pots and pans and utensils, and shelves of foodstuffs. There were hanging baskets of onions, potatoes, and fruit. A refrigerator and huge freezer, both with transparent doors.

Martha stared wildly around the room. "I've worked in the MIT kitchen, but I've never seen anything like this. You could feed a hundred people."

"We must *get* almost a hundred people when Arl sets up the grill out front. He's famous for his chicken."

He clapped his hands together and grinned. "You could've counted almost a hundred last Sadday. They were all over the front lawn with their stuff."

"What do they bring?" Matthew asked.

"Most of them straight barter for food and drink. Like you bring seven pieces of chicken; I cook six and keep one. Two whole chickens for a bottle of good wine." He looked at Martha with interest. "What's an MIT kitchen?"

"Massachusetts Institute of Theosophy."

"Oh, wow—I should've known from your outfits. That's in the old Christ Dominion?"

"I suppose. We call it the World of Christ."

"They let you *out*?"

"Well, we sort of escaped," Matt said.

"I guess you did," Arl said. "How long ago was that?"

"Couple of thousand years."

Arl nodded slowly, brow furrowing.

"It's still there?" Martha said. "MIT?"

"Who knows? Nobody's tried to cross the Mississippi since forever. They've got killer satellites waiting day and night with lasers. You don't want to fly within a hundred kays. Was it that way back in your time?"

"I was only there for a few days." He looked at Martha. "Do you know?"

"I don't know what a killer satellite is," she said in a small voice. "History says that the Lord's Avenging Angels can smite invaders from their place in Heaven, above the sky. I've seen a moving picture of it happening, in the Museum of Theosophy, and some melted metal from a flying machine."

"Could they still work, after a couple of thousand years?"

"Sure," Arl said. "I've seen it on the news. Every now and then, they try to fly a robot plane over there. Pow, every time."

"Hard to see how an automatic system could keep going

for more than two thousand years. They must be replacing or repairing the satellites, or at least their sensors and lasers."

Arl looked puzzled. "What do you mean? Machines repair themselves all the time."

That gave Matt pause. "Not really old ones."

"Well, I guess they've replaced the old ones with self-repairing ones. More than a thousand years ago, they could do that."

Matt suddenly realized how far into the future he'd actually come. He'd been lulled by the similarities between these people and the ones at home; much less strange than Martha's people. It was even easier to understand their speech.

"Seems funny that we can understand each other," He put the thought to words. "If we'd gone backward two thousand years instead of forward, we couldn't. It must be the cube."

"Sure," Arl said. "We see movies all the way back to the twentieth century, and understand most of it. Though people did funny things back then."

"We still watch Shakespeare," Em said. "But he's hard to follow."

"He was for us, too." Matt followed Em's gaze and saw that Martha was silently crying, tears rolling down her cheeks. He put his hand on her shoulder.

"I'm sorry," she sobbed. "I'm so lost."

Em took her hand and patted it. "You'll get used to it, sweetheart."

"But I *won't*! This is Gomorrah, isn't it? This is Hollywood."

"Huh-uh," Arl said, shifting nervously. "I don't know about Gum-gumorrow, but Hollywood's over in LA."

"We've been there three times," Em said. "Rides and all."

"But you don't live in God and Jesus."

"Well, we're not religious ourselves," Em said, still patting, "but there are those who are." She looked anxiously at Arl. "The Reynoldses, down the street?"

"Yeah, they're Christers. Always off to church." He scratched his chin. "Bunch of Muslims, downtown, and Unitarians and B'hai all over the place. Not like it was in the East, though, in your time."

Em gave her a tissue. "Thank you. What about now, in the East? People still live and worship over there?"

"Not many left, I don't think," Arl said. He looked at Em, then back at Matt. "This isn't really a movie, is it?"

"Never said it was," Matt said. "We are what we say we are, scholars from the past. I guess we should find a university."

"None nearby. Have to go to Santa Fe or Phoenix. Maybe just go on to LA. That's the biggest."

"Too far to walk. How do you get there, fly?"

Arl paused. "That's what you would do, in your day?"

"That or drive. Cheaper to fly."

"You'd take the train now, for the same reason. Flying's ten, maybe twenty times as much, even for a good barterer."

"What, you even haggle for airfare?"

"Bargain for it, yeah. You didn't?"

"No, the government set the prices."

He laughed. "And that's it? Boy, they'd love that!"

"They do set a price in B chits," Em said, "but not even half the people pay it. People who don't have any choice or are so rich they don't care. Everybody else, you show up with your luggage and something to barter with. By law, they have to show which seats are available, and you bargain with the agent."

"If there's no competition for the seat," Arl said, "you can fly anywhere for almost nothing. But you never know."

"Sounds like a clumsy way of doing business," Matt said. "Everything takes so long."

"But so what? It's time well spent. If you just pay and

get on the plane, the flyport wins and you lose. Wait 'em out and you can fly for less than cost." He grinned. "Worth an extra day, for the satisfaction." Em nodded enthusiastically.

Of course, Matthew knew people like that, who would go through hoops for any bargain, but a whole culture? A culture predicated on haggling?

Matt's stomach growled audibly. He hadn't had a thing to eat since that pickled egg two thousand years ago.

"Oh, you poor things," Em said. "I didn't offer you anything to eat or drink."

"We don't have any B chits," Matt said, not sure whether he was joking.

Martha looked into the bag. "We have bread and cheese."

"And that's not all," Matthew said, reaching into the bag and bringing out the wine bottle with appropriate reverence. "Two-thousand-year-old wine."

Arl stared at it, struck momentarily dumb. "MIT 67?"

"Bottled at the Massachusetts Institute of Theosophy sixty-seven years after the Second Coming."

"That . . . could be worth something."

"I should think so. Probably the only bottle of it in the world. Do you collect wine?"

"Only in a small way. But I know people who really are serious about it. I could broker an auction for fif   twenty percent."

"Ten."

"Oh, all right. Fifteen." He took the bottle carefully. "If I may." He walked around the dining room table to a small raised platform. A mirrored holo image of himself shimmered in the air.

"This is a straight American auction for B-chit valuta," he said in an announcer's voice. "Categories food and wine, antiquities, and curiosities. Minimum bid ten thousand. It is now 1310 LA time; the auction will be over at 1410.

"This is a bottle of wine produced more than two thousand years ago, in M.E. 2247, at the Massachusetts Institute of Theosophy, in their year 67." He turned to Matt. "What variety is it?"

"Scuppernong?"

"Of the rare scuppernong variety. The bidding starts now." He set the bottle down on the platform.

He stepped down and "BC 10,000" floated in green characters where he had been standing. Then "BC 10,100" and the number flickered and quickly increased to 12,000, with a chime and a red question mark blinking.

"Question?" Arl said. An old bearded man appeared, wearing a skirt, or kilt, with what looked like a tuxedo jacket and a diagonal sash full of medals. Floating next to him, the identification "Miki Ikiman, Curator, LA Museum of Consumables."

"Not to question your veracity, Arl Beekins, but what outside authority will vouch for this bottle's antiquity?"

"I have the man who acquired it here. A time traveler from that period."

The finger pointed at Matthew. "That is him?"

"Yes. When were you born, Matt?"

"March 4, 2030. Modern Era."

"Not very," the curator said dryly. "Are you willing to make the purchase contingent on verifying the bottle's age?"

"Absolutely," Arl said.

"I'll stay in for a while, then," the curator said, and disappeared, replaced by the floating number. Every time a new bid came in, it was topped by a number ending in the digits 37.

"That 37 is the LA museum system's traditional code number," Arl said. "Everybody local knows who they're bidding against."

"He didn't question the idea that a time traveler brought it?"

"No. What, did you think . . . oh, you thought you were the first."

"What, does it happen all the time?"

"No, just a few times. Ten or twelve, to my knowledge. We don't know how to do it ourselves."

"Did any of them come back from your future?" Martha asked. "Traveling back in time?"

"Not that I know of," he said. "I thought that was impossible."

Martha started to cloud up again.

"We don't know," Matt said quickly. "I think I have evidence of at least one."

"The ones we know about kept going forward."

"Except the Chinese fellow," Em said, "a couple of hundred years ago."

"That's right; he stayed. But he didn't have a *machine* as such." The chime and question mark again. "Question?"

An attractive woman of indeterminate age, wearing something gauzy, more like smoke than cloth, appeared and looked at Matt with a frown.

"I am Los Angeles," she said. "You are the real Matthew Fuller? The assistant to the physicist Jonathan Marsh?"

"That's right."

"The historical record says you stole that machine from Professor Marsh."

"History has it exactly wrong, then," Matt said. "I invented the machine, and Marsh stole it from me."

She brushed that away with a delicate wave. "I'm not concerned with crimes two thousand years cold. I would like to talk with you for a while, though. Perhaps a business proposition."

"You're Los Angeles, the city?"

"The county, you would say. I'm the intelligence that animates it and controls it. The spirit of Los Angeles. Perhaps you could come see me after the auction."

"I'll be glad to. May I bring my assistant?"

"Please do." She gave Martha a quizzical look. "You should find something to wear. That makes me feel like sweating, and I'm not even human." To Matt: "I'll send a conveyance as soon as the auction is over." She disappeared.

"Does that happen often?"

"Only at tax time. She can argue forever, in everybody's house at once."

Em touched Martha's elbow. "Let me find you something to wear, dear."

"But this *is* what I wear. I haven't worn anything else since I was seventeen."

"It's a different world, Martha," Matt said. "Let's save the robe for when you get back home."

"You could afford a few hundred outfits," Arl said. The auction had reached 21,037. "You want to look nice for the city. Show her what you have, Em."

"All right," she said, crossing her arms in front of her. "If I don't have to show my chest." Curious, Matt thought, that she could show her everything to him, getting ready for bed, but wouldn't match the older woman's degree of exposure. She probably hadn't been in as many topless bars as Matt.

Arl went to the refrigerator and began taking out cheese and fruit. He pushed some buttons on a thing the size of a toaster; it hummed for a minute and produced eight round slices of what smelled like fresh bread.

"Are you two connecting?" he said. "Or whatever they call doing it in your time."

"No. We've actually just met. And she thinks of me as much older than she is. Professor and student. But it's really only a few years."

"Were you serious about taking her back?"

"Haven't thought it through, really. She'd like to go back to her time, but I'd find it pretty horrible. She wouldn't like mine, either. Godless."

"You do think you can go back?"

"There are physical models for it, none proven. But I think I already have gone backward, or will." He smiled. "Tenses can be a problem. I think that I stopped off in 2058 just long enough to save my own skin. It could have been someone else, who looked something like me. But I left a message that almost had to be from a future me." *Get in the car and go!*

"Open table," Arl said to the floor, and part of it rose up and reconfigured into a table with two benches. The top covered itself in what looked like white linen, and he set out the plates of snacks. "Wine or coffee?"

"Coffee." See whether two thousand years had improved it. "How much do I owe you?"

He cast an expert eye over the table. "It would be about 29 each. But we're engaged in trading together, so don't worry. I'll take it into account when we settle up."

He filled a carafe with water and it hissed, and the smell of fresh coffee permeated the room.

"I'd like to broker some of those old coins for you. Not too many; if people knew you had bags of them, the price would fall through the floor." He poured coffee for both of us. "We'd better lock up the time machine before dark, though, or you won't have any coins to barter."

No need to tell him yet that the vault was not the time machine. "I'm not sure that we can close the door," Matt said, "or open it again if we did." He sipped the hot coffee and it was wonderful. "People would just sneak into your backyard and steal things?"

"Steal?" Arl gave Matt a mystified look. "If it's not locked up, then it's not stealing."

Em and Martha came back. Martha was wearing a light blue shift with a gold chain around her narrow waist. The shift came to midcalf but was slit to well above the knee. She walked stiffly in an unsuccessful attempt to not look sexy.

"She shouldn't hide so much," Em said "'If you have it, advertise it.' But she wouldn't even show one mam."

"We . . . we don't do that," she said.

"You *didn't*," Em corrected. "Now is not then. You ought to be comfortable."

"Let me get used to this first," she pleaded.

"If it's any consolation," Matt said, "you look wonderful."

"Professor!" She stared at the ground but did smile. There was an uncomfortable silence. She looked at the cheese plate doubtfully and broke off a small piece. She nibbled at it, made a face, and put it back. "I'm afraid it's gone bad," she said.

Arl stared at the piece she'd put back. "That's a rare Italian gorgonzola!"

"Well, it tastes as bad as it sounds."

"Gorgonzola!" Matthew snatched it up, rolling his eyes, and got a wedge of apple in the other hand, and took a bite of each. Martha stared.

"If you can't lock the time machine," Arl said, "can someone just step in and take it into the future?"

"Not possible, no. Only I can turn it on." Well, it was true that only he *had* turned it on.

"Then we could simply move the money, and whatever else that might have value, into my storeroom for the time being. If you decide to move on, I could deduct a reasonable amount for storage. Assuming that the coins do turn out to have some value." He leaned back and looked at the floating sum, which changed from BC 35,700 to BC 35,937. "You wouldn't have another bottle of wine in that bag? Or some other ancient collectible?"

"No, it's stuff I need for time travel—to make the time machine work." Like a gun and a porn notebook. "Maybe the bread and cheese would be interesting to scientists. Presumably it would be chemically different from what you make now."

"I don't think we have that kind of scientist. But I could try, while it's still fresh."

" 'That kind'?" Matt asked. "What kind do you have?"

"Well, I'm a food scientist myself. I know thousands of recipes. And Em has a doctorate in shopping science."

"Arl is just as good at it," she said modestly, "even without a degree."

"What about physics, chemistry, biology, astronomy?"

"Oh, it's all there. You can look it up," Arl said. "But it's for machines, of course, the research. People don't think fast enough. Can't remember enough."

Matt was speechless. He looked at Martha for support. She was frowning at Em and Arl in confusion. "How can machines think?"

"They've been doing it for thousands of years," Em said.

"More than two centuries before you were born, machine intelligence transformed the world." Arl said. "When religious fanatics took over your part of the world, they got rid of most thinking machines. They kept the ones they needed, evidently, like the killer satellites that keep us out of their airspace."

"It's not Avenging Angels, dear." Em offered her some cheese and apple slices. "Just machines, like the one that brought you here."

She stared blankly at the food. "Is there somewhere I could talk to the professor alone? Back in the bank vault . . . time machine?"

"Sure," Arl said. "Auction won't close for almost a half hour."

When they were outside, she took his hand and rushed him silently to the vault. Inside, she sat down on the stack of dollar coin sacks and stared at him.

"I feel like I'm going crazy. Like I'm in a crazy dream, a nightmare, and can't wake up. You have to explain what's going on."

"Okay. My time machine took us 2094 years into the future—"

"Before that. You were running away from Jesus."

"Yes and no. I needed money for travel . . ."

"Well, you got *that*."

"But I didn't mean to rob a bank." Steal a bank, actually. "I was just going to cash in some old money for a thousand or so, and take it back, with the time machine, to where Jesus appears. Then use the machine to take me and all the machines in that room up into the future.

"I didn't mean to kidnap you. I'm sorry. It's an awful reward for saving a person's life."

She shook her head. "You and I think differently about rewards. I think God rewards us for good works and punishes us for bad. He puts us in positions where we have to make choices."

Matt could only shrug.

"You were going to use your machine to take Jesus away. The illusion of Jesus, you said."

"That, yes, but also to get out of Cambridge while I still had the option of escaping."

She chewed on her lower lip for a moment. "So maybe God, or maybe chance, put me between you and that policeman. Why was he shooting at you?"

"Um . . . that's a little embarrassing." She just stared at him. "I went into the toilet to take a pee. The policeman was there, and he saw I wasn't circumcised. Do you know what that is?"

She closed her eyes and shuddered. "They cut a part away from your thingie."

"Well, the church I was born into required that. But my mother and father decided against letting them do it."

"Really?" She smiled. "Me, too. My mother wouldn't let them circumcise me, when I was a girl."

"They circumcise women?"

"Unless the mother objects. Mother had to pay a fine and do penance for a year."

"Why do they do it?"

"Well, why do they do it to you?"

"It's just a custom left over from the old days, and it made some sense when men didn't bathe regularly. But it doesn't have the same effect as on women, on girls."

"What is that supposed to be?"

"They didn't tell you?"

"Nothing specific, not yet. That's a big part of my next passage, when I turn twenty-one. Next month."

"In some cultures, mostly before I was born, they did it to deny sexual pleasure to women."

She shook her head in two small jerks. "I wouldn't know anything about that, not yet. I'm not allowed."

"You will be, after you're twenty-one?"

"I don't *know*. If they told you the secrets before your Passage, they wouldn't be secrets." Her blush indicated that she did know something. "So how did you make everything disappear? How did you turn this bank vault into a time machine?"

He lifted the machine out of the bag. "This is the actual time machine." He tapped on the plastic dome. "If I push this button, it goes forward in time. And takes everything nearby along with it." He held up the alligator clip. "If this little thing is in contact with a metal container, like this vault, then everything inside the container goes."

"But just one way. You can't go back."

"I don't know how, yet. But I'm sure it can be done. Not in my time and certainly not in yours. Another reason I had to move forward. But I'm sorry I dragged you along."

"Don't be. There's a reason for everything."

There was a whisper like a giant exhaling, and a vehicle drifted to a landing between them and the house. It was a sleek functional airfoil, as reflective as mercury, shimmering except for the solid blue block letters LA.

Matt checked his watch. "Auction should be closing now."

She was hypnotized. "That's what you fly in?"

"Nowadays, I guess so. If you can afford it." As they walked by the thing, she gaped at her fun-house-mirror reflection. "It makes you look pregnant."

She smiled. "That would have been right after the Passage. At least you saved me from that."

Maybe so, he was thinking, and maybe not. *I ought to keep an eye out for Safeluv patches, or whatever they use up here.*

They looked at the thing for a minute, and nothing happened. "I guess it'll tell us when it's ready."

The door to the house opened. Arl looked at the ship and didn't react. "Congratulations. The museum got it for 62,037. Come in and look at your choices."

"Choices?" They followed him back to the dining room. In the air over the platform there was a glowing list of about a hundred things and services with their BC value. An ancient Egyptian ring for BC 50,000—that would be practical.

"What, we can't just take the B chits?"

"That would be, well, extremely impolite. Almost illegal. But you can maximize the valuta change by picking something of low value—though of course you do need 9300 in valuta for my commission."

"There's the cheapest thing," Martha said. The label was *Plastic dildo, late 22nd, no batteries, BC 400*. She touched the line, and an enlarged holo appeared.

She jerked her hand away. "Oh my." It was very realistic.

"Maybe," Em said. "You probably want something small and tradable. But without batteries, I don't know."

"Maybe this." Matt touched a line to make the embarrassing image go away. This one said *German Fernglasmaschine circa 2200, 5X–500X, BC 1800*. It looked like a small pair of binoculars with handgrips and a box like a battery case underneath.

"The Germans are good with those," Arl said, "but I

have a Chinese pair almost as good, even older, that I'd let go of for half that."

Los Angeles appeared next to the glowing list. "Your chariot awaits, Dr. Fuller."

"Professor," he said automatically, not having a real doctorate. "Let's take the binoculars?" he said to Martha.

"Please, let's," she said, either eager to leave or anxious that he might choose the other.

"This one," Arl said with his finger on the line, which blinked twice and disappeared. "It will be here in a day or so." There was a black box next to the platform. He opened it with a thumb-swipe. It enclosed stacks of BC bills; he carefully counted out BC 50,851 and handed the thick stack to Matt. "Minus my commission and the dress. Don't worry about the cheese and coffee."

Matt put the thick wad into his pants pocket. "Thanks, um . . . see you soon."

"La willing," they both said.

Matt and Martha followed Los Angeles out the door. She didn't bother to pretend walking, but drifted like a solid daytime ghost.

" 'La willing'?"

"They call me La," she said. "Ell Ay." Doors had opened in the craft, resembling the wings of a coasting seabird. La slipped into a swivel chair in the front.

Martha stepped into the craft and perched uneasily on the luxurious high-backed leather couch. Matt got onto the couch next to her and fastened a seat belt. "Where are we going?" Martha asked.

"To my palace. Fasten your belt." Matt reached over and helped her with the mechanism. "You'll be more comfortable there than with these people, I think. I'm equally comfortable everywhere, of course."

"Not being flesh," Matt said.

"No, I'm centuries away from needing that."

"But those people"—he inclined his head toward the house—"they're not projections. They're regular people?"

"Very regular. Very typical." As the doors eased shut, the ship became transparent. "I don't suppose you've ever flown, Martha?"

"No," she said with a rising inflection, looking all around. At least the floor was opaque.

"It's safer than walking. But it might take you a few minutes to get used to it."

The ship rose like a fast elevator, the ground dropping away, roofs shrinking. Martha clutched for Matt and buried her face in his chest.

Arms full of soft girl for the first time in a long time, Matt patted her back reassuringly. "It's all right. It's very ordinary." But please don't let go just yet.

"I know, Professor," she said, her voice muffled. "I've seen pictures. But it's so fast."

La smiled knowingly at Matt. "She'll be all right. I'll keep it slow."

"How fast can it go?"

"Mach 6 to 8, depending on the load and the altitude. But we're not going far; I'll keep it subsonic."

The suburbs rolled on and on toward the horizon, then stopped. "Mountains," Matt said with a little awe. He'd only been west a couple of times in his life. "Look, Martha."

She carefully lifted her head and whispered, "God," not in blasphemy.

"No buildings," Matt said.

"All these mountains are protected. About half of the area west of the Mississippi has been more or less artfully ignored, and has gone back to its natural state. A few people live in the protected areas, antisocial or sick of the modern world. But the law says they have to live in a primitive way, and they usually tire of it soon."

"You said those two, Arl and Em, were typical? That level of prosperity?" Not to say excess.

"They're actually below average, the forty-second percentile in terms of total holdings. They're not very good at horse-trading, as you would say."

"Horses?" Matt had never heard the term.

"Bartering. They have a little less than the basic dole that people get at birth."

"You know that much about everyone?" Martha said, not taking her eyes off the mountains rolling under them.

"Much more than that," La said, "but that's all I am, Martha—memories, perceptions, thought processes. I'm what's evolved from a human committee and a machine that was constructed to keep this huge city running."

"A city of millionaires," Matt said.

She nodded placidly. "It's been that way for centuries. Ever since we started getting free power from the sea, room-temperature fusion. Automated synthesis of consumables, distributed to a stable population of 100 million. Everybody rich and happy." She smiled. "Also complacent and rather stupid, you may have noticed."

"Arl said that people don't do science anymore. It's too complicated, and has to be done by machines."

"What, are you worried about unemployment? There aren't any jobs, as such, for anybody. Certainly none for physics professors two millenniums out of date."

"But you do have universities. She had a doctorate, they said."

"The universities are like social clubs, I'm afraid. They give each other pieces of paper; it keeps them happy. Out of trouble."

"No wonder people take to the hills."

"You'd be surprised how few."

"But there must be people doing the Lord's work," Martha said. "That takes education."

"That depends on whom you're preaching to." La shook her head, perhaps in sympathy. "There's not much organized religion. Not much religion at all."

"The world has been that way before."

La looked over her shoulder, in the direction of travel. "Getting close to home now."

"We can't have gone four hundred kilometers," Matt said.

"Oh, I don't live in the city proper. I hope you do like mountains."

Matt leaned to his left and could see that they were approaching the "palace," a delicate Disney fantasy of a place, resting on a pinnacle that couldn't have been natural.

"But you're not really 'here' the way we are. You don't live in a physical place. Arl seemed to think you could be everywhere at once, at least at tax time."

"Complaining again. Yes, I spread myself pretty thin that time of the year.

"But I do always have a locus. I can generate 100 million images that can all do something simple, like arguing over taxes. There's still a 'me,' though, usually here in the palace."

The craft had been losing speed with a low rushing sound. It hovered over a lawn and descended. "This is where my physical memory is located—so I do feel more comfortable here. Even a hundred or so kilometers away, I can feel the femtosecond lag in response time."

"We must seem pretty slow to you," Martha said, which slightly surprised Matt. But she wasn't dumb.

"Not really. I had flesh once. I have a feeling for the human passage of time." She turned to Matt. "And the inhuman. Let me get you settled into your apartment, and then we can talk about that machine in your bag. The one you stole from poor Professor Marsh."

An apparently human valet led them to a two-bedroom apartment, simplifying Matt's existence while dampening his hopes.

The apartment was conservative twenty-first century, lots of wood and cloth and stucco. Lamps instead of glowing walls. Doors that apparently didn't morph open. Matt had to show her how the toilet worked; it was the paperless kind, using jets of water and air. The first time she used it, she squealed and giggled in a satisfying way.

They both had large closets full of clothes. Martha sorted through hers and picked out slacks and a long-sleeved shirt.

"This is pretty," she said, stepping out of the outfit Em had chosen, "but it's too, you know, revealing. She wriggled into the shirt, otherwise nude, and noticed Matt's expression. "This doesn't bother you, Professor?"

"Oh no, no. I'm getting used to it."

"What do you mean?"

"We're just not so casual about, uh, being naked where I come from."

"Dressing? That's silly."

"I agree. I totally agree."

"Well, you ought to change, too. You don't mind my saying so?"

"No, no, that's . . . fine." It did pose a tactical problem, which showed no immediate sign of going away. He solved the problem by grabbing clothes at random and changing with his back to her. She probably didn't see anything, but then she probably wasn't looking.

The valet had shown them where to go when they were ready, a parlor room at the end of their corridor.

It looked old and French, delicate ornate furniture, ancient oil paintings on fabric-covered walls. La was softly playing on a harpsichord when they walked in.

"Welcome." She stood up and gestured to where three chairs were arranged around a glass-topped table with a tea service and a plate of cookies and petits fours.

Matt moved the teapot to one side and lifted out the machine. "I take it that even now, you don't have one of these." La sat down staring at it, and shook her head. "And you don't know how it works?"

"How? No," she said. "It's been clear for more than a thousand years *why* your machine works. But knowing why isn't the same as knowing *how*. Knowing that $E = mc^2$ doesn't mean you can take some kitchen appliance and turn it into a nuclear weapon."

"So why does it work?"

"The part that's broken is the graviton generator. But it's not broken in four-dimensional space-time. That's why they could build a thousand copies of the machine and never duplicate its effect.

"In 'our' space-time, as we affectionately call it, the calibrator works perfectly. One puny graviton per photon. But in some dimension five or higher, it spews out a torrent of gravitons." She leaned back and stared up at the ceiling. "How can I put this in a way you can understand?"

Matt was growing excited. "I think I know what you're getting at!"

She nodded. "In your primitive terms—they still used string theory?"

"Go on, yes?"

"In that way of thinking, our space-time continuum is a four-dimensional brane floating through a larger ten- or eleven-dimensional universe—"

"Wait," Martha pleaded, "I don't understand. A floating *brain*?"

Matt spelled the word. "It's short for 'membrane.' "

"They couldn't just say membrane?"

" 'Membrane' means something else. A brane is like . . . it's like a reality. Like we live in one four-dimensional reality, but there could be countless others."

"But where would you put them? Where could they be?"

"They're inside a larger brane. Five or six or more dimensions."

"What would *that* look like?"

He shrugged. "We don't know. We can only perceive four dimensions." She nodded slowly, lips pursed.

"All right," La said. "As Matt said, there are countless other four-dimensional branes, but what's important are the five-dimensional ones that can be made to envelop ours. Your broken graviton generator attracted one of these beasts and apparently made a permanent connection. Permanent from our point of view. Instantaneous, hardly noticeable, in five dimensions."

"But in ours," Matt said, "it makes a closed timelike curve?"

"In a way. But that would only make a time machine that went backward in time. Yours moves forward, faster and faster. Something in that five-dimensional brane is connected to a huge singularity in our brane: the heat death of the universe. The end of time."

"The End Times," Martha whispered.

"It's more than ten to the thousandth power years in the future. The stars die, the black holes evaporate, and finally everything stops moving."

"I want to go find out whether I can die." La's smile was almost a leer. "I think we can help each other."

16

After tea, they took the machine downstairs, to a room that functioned as a kind of laboratory. It was austere, evenly lit from glowing walls and ceiling, with a series of identical tables numbered one through ten. Matt, following orders, set the machine on each table for a minute or two while La stared at it without expression. Then she would nod and drift on to the next one.

At the end, she nodded, and then shook her head. "I have to share this with some others. Why don't you two get some rest?

"You can go anywhere in the place. If you're lost or want something, just ask for help. Out loud." She disappeared.

Matt put the machine back into the bag and wouldn't let Martha carry it. "Look. I'm not a professor here, and you're not a graduate assistant. We're just time travelers, both of us unimaginably far from home."

"But . . ."

"You know the term 'stranger in a strange land'?"

She nodded. "Exodus 2:22. That's how Moses described himself."

"And that's what we are; that's the largest thing we have in common. Though the 'lands' we came from are also strange to one another, still, this is the one we're stuck in. Together."

"I don't know. I have to think about that, Professor."

He sighed. "Matthew, or Matt. Please? 'Professor' makes me feel old."

"Only when I say it?"

"Oh . . . maybe. Matthew?"

"I'll call you Matthew if you let me carry the bag."

He handed it to her. "Let's go find a view. It must be close to sunset."

They walked down the corridor until it ran into a wall, and then followed the wall until it led to an outside door, which opened easily to a parapet that went out about a meter and a half into pure sky—no protective railing.

"It's gorgeous," Matt said. The mountains were crimson and orange in the setting sun, with purple shadows deepening to indigo. The shadow of the palace's pinnacle was a narrow, straight slash.

He stepped out. "Professor! Don't . . . Matt!" He held a hand out and it hit an invisible, marshmallow-soft wall.

"It's safe. There's a pressor field." To demonstrate, he folded his arms and dropped back against it, which made her gasp.

She put her hands over her eyes. "Please don't."

"Okay." He angled forward and held out a hand to her. "Let's go find that sunset." She did take his hand and followed him around the parapet, staying close to the wall.

The sunset was a brilliant wash of color, deep red merging into salmon and an improbable yellow with a breath of green, fading into blue. Inky blue overhead, with a few pale stars.

She stared wide-eyed, her lips slightly parted. Matt noted that her eyes were gray, and she was about as pretty a girl as he had ever stood this close to, even with the small scar. He was still holding her hand.

She let go and touched her sternum. "Sweet Jesus," she breathed. "My heart is going so fast!"

"Mine, too," Matt said, though it wasn't all geology and altitude.

"Maybe . . . we should go in. This is wonderful. But I feel almost like I'm going to faint."

"The air is a little thin," he said, sidling around her and taking her hand again. "Go back the same way?"

"Please." They picked their way around, Matt walking slowly and thinking furiously.

She's not a young girl, he told himself, in spite of her lack of experience and information. She's almost as old as Kara was when they broke up a couple of months or millenniums ago.

But you can't talk yourself out of the truth that she *is* a child, when it comes to dealing with the opposite sex. Don't press her; don't take advantage. Be a man.

Unfortunately, "be a man" was also the counsel the rest of his body was giving.

What if they never did get back to their own times? As they moved on into the future, and people became more and more strange, they would be the only potential partners for one another on the planet.

Her hand was cold and damp. This is plenty of strangeness for the time being. Don't be a scoundrel. She put her life between you and a crazy cop with a gun. Be a man. Be a man, for a change.

When they went through the door he let go of her hand.

"Thank you." She leaned against the wall, panting.

"Are you okay?"

"I think so." She looked up and down the corridor. "You know, she's right. We should rest. Much as I'd like to explore, I ought to lie down for a little bit." She pointed. "Is that the way back?"

A valet appeared. "Yes. On your left, second corridor, two doors down." He faded away.

"I guess they're always watching," he said.

"She is. He's part of her." She looked around. "That gives me a strange feeling. Like I'm being spied on."

"I suppose. But she's been doing it for so long, she's seen everything."

"She hasn't seen *me* do everything." She started off down the corridor.

"Wait," Matt said, and touched the bag's strap. "Let me take that. You're tired."

"All right." She surrendered it and smiled. "Professor."

Back in the apartment, she stretched and yawned and relaxed onto the couch. He sat down and set the bag between them.

She looked inside. "Wish we still had that bottle of wine."

"Yeah," he said. "The sixty thousand bee shits aren't doing us any good." She giggled at that, and there was a knock on the door.

"Come in?" Matt said. The valet eased the door open and entered with a tray. Two bottles of wine, red and white, and two glasses. He set it on the end table next to Martha.

"You did that so fast," she said.

"No, Martha; La anticipated your requirements. If you had asked for coffee or tea, I would be here with it."

"I'd like a glass of iced watermelon juice," Matt said.

"It would be synthetic," the valet said, "but I can have it in two minutes. Unless you are joking."

"I'm joking. Thank you." The valet inclined his head and disappeared.

They both stared at the spot where he'd been. Then Martha pulled the stopper out of the white wine, studied it, and put it aside. "Red or white?"

"Take white," he said. She poured a glass and passed it to him, then poured one for herself.

He held out his glass, but they evidently didn't have that custom. She had a stranger one: she touched the surface of the wine with a fingertip and shook a drop off onto the floor.

She smiled at him. "My mother always did that. She said she promised *her* mother that she would never drink a drop of wine. That was the drop she never drank."

Matt took a sip; it was icy cold but not too dry, flowery. "Did MIT let you go visit your mother?"

She nodded. "Easter and Christmas, when the roads allowed. But she's failing, was failing." Her mouth went into a hard line, and she bit her lower lip.

"Mine, too," Matt said. "My mother. The last couple of times I saw her, she didn't know who I was."

She nodded without looking at him. "Matthew. A good name. But . . . you're not Christian?"

"I was born a Jew."

"Like in the Bible?" He nodded. "We don't have them, you, not in a long time."

He didn't really want to know, but had to ask: "What happened to them? There used to be lots, in Boston and Cambridge."

"They left, I guess. A lot of people left during the One Year War. Coming out this way."

"People used to say the Jews ran Hollywood. I guess we could run *to* Hollywood."

She considered that, not getting the joke. "You miss it. Your church."

"Synagogue, no. I stopped going when I was younger than you."

"Your parents let you not go?"

"My mother had stopped years before. My father never went."

"That's so strange. I never knew anyone who didn't go to church." She sat up straight. "I guess I am one, now."

"Until you get back. God must understand."

She looked at him. "You don't believe that."

"No. I should have said, 'If there is a God, I can't imagine that he would not understand.' "

"Em and Arl, they didn't act like believers. They acted as if Christians and Muslims were unusual."

"Comes and goes, I suspect. There weren't a lot of religious people in the time and place I left. And then I wound up in yours, where everybody believed. Maybe the pendulum will have moved back the next time we jump."

"How far into the future will that be?"

"If our calculations were correct, twenty-four thousand more years."

She took a sip of wine. "About four times the age of the Earth."

"According to the Bible."

She reached into the bag and took out the Bible. "May I take this? Try to read myself to sleep."

"Sure. Sweet dreams." He watched her go into her bedroom and listened to her undressing.

After a minute, he finished the glass of wine and took the bag into his room, to seek his own kind of consolation.

The valet woke them separately and led them both to the garden, where La was sitting. It was full of night blossoms and their heavy fragrance, with dozens of large candles lending a warm light. She was wearing a white jumpsuit that revealed a spectacular, if virtual, figure.

She was sitting on a stone bench, and another one faced her. They sat down.

"You may stay here," she said without preamble, "and live out the rest of your days in total comfort, and occasionally go down into the world for amusement. While I go on to explore the future. Or we can go together."

"We were never sure," Matt said, "whether the time machine would work if someone else pushed the button. You might need me to come with you."

"If I push the button, and nothing happens, we'll have to work something out."

"Like my *thumb* goes, and the rest of me stays behind?"

"It would be an interesting experiment. I don't think it would work." There was no humor in her smile.

"But you can stay behind as well as go," Matt said.

"Copies of me, aspects of me, will stay here, to run LA. But the part of me that goes on ahead is my essence. The part that's here with you right now."

"You could stay," Matt said to Martha. "I got you into this, but there's no reason you have to continue."

"I've thought that through," she said, "and prayed for guidance. I couldn't stay here."

"I don't blame you," La said. "This is one boring world. Matt might enjoy it for a while." She gave him a knowing smile. "Almost any woman on this planet would be yours for the asking. But they really are boring."

He saw Martha blush and lower her eyes. He hadn't really thought of that aspect.

"They wouldn't be 'mine.' But everybody here can't be as vapid and silly as that couple."

"Oh, really? There's a kind of dead-end stability at work here, all over the civilized world. Everybody's rich from birth, so there are no needy people complicating the situation. Anyone who tires of having everything can go off to the wilderness for as long as they can stand it, so the restless are taken care of.

"And I find myself with no challenges, either; nothing that isn't dealt with automatically. So I've been sort of hoping that you would survive long enough to show up."

"Of course," Matt said. "You would know approximately when and where I would appear."

"Maybe. We know when and where you would land after you took the taxi—that was a daring move, and lucky—but there has been a cultural blackout in New England since 2181, so we couldn't know whether you'd survived your contact with the Christers."

"We wouldn't have . . ." Martha began. "Sorry. Go on."

"I had pretty sophisticated observation and analysis tools on the lookout for you in the here and now. But they weren't necessary. When an ancient bottle of MIT wine went up for auction, that was all I needed."

"How long have you been planning this?"

"Oh, I got the idea a couple of hundred years ago. Then just had to wait and see."

"Did it ever occur to you that I might not *want* company? Going into the future."

"You need me. You know where the machine will take you next."

"The Pacific Ocean."

"You plan to go there in a bank vault?"

"I can get a metal boat."

"Yes, and land in the middle of a typhoon and drown in seconds. Or just get lost at sea and dehydrate slowly." She stood up. "Follow me."

They went around a pond with luminous fish. "You need to find a backward time machine—both of you—and the only place you'll find that is in the future. I can take you safely to that future. But then you go back, if you wish, and I go on."

"All the way?"

"Whatever that means, yes."

They walked down a flight of stone steps to a basement door. La pushed it open.

In the glare of a brilliant bluish light, a proper time machine. At first it looked like a huge mechanical insect, but that was just an all-terrain transportation system. Carried on top of and in between the four pairs of articulated legs were two containers, each about ten meters long, one with windows.

"Defense!" she said, and the bottom one was bristling with weapons. "Streamline!" The legs folded up around the machine, and a metal sheet slid around to enclose it in a seamless ovoid, which grew swept-back wings.

"I don't think you could have built this, clever as you are with tools. But you're going to need it. The jump after the next one will be into outer space."

"*May* be. The math is ambiguous."

"In your time, maybe. No longer. Trust me—you don't want to go out there in a taxicab or a bank vault."

"Outer space?" Martha said. "Between the stars?"

"Well, between the planets. Stars come much later.

"I've doubled the life-support supplies to accommodate you, Martha. All I personally require is electricity, of course, and information. But I thought Matthew might like some human company."

"Thank you," they said simultaneously, and a startled look passed between them.

"Before we go, though, the people—well, *call* them people—who helped me design and build this, asked a favor in return. We know so little about everyday life in your worlds—especially yours, Martha—that it would be extremely valuable if you would consent to a day of being interviewed."

"I don't have any problem with that," Matthew said, and looked into Martha's silence.

"Is it just answering questions? In my time there were 'interviews' that had serious consequences."

"That's all you have to do, answer questions. They will measure your reaction to each question as well as record your answer."

"Lie detecting?" Matt said.

"A little more subtle than that. Truth detecting, I suppose."

"Okay," Matt said. He looked at Martha, and she nodded slowly.

"Good. They'll be here in the morning, about ten. I'll meet you for breakfast before that." She disappeared.

They looked at their reflections in the machine's mirror skin. "Truth detector," he said.

"There are things I'd never tell anyone," Martha confessed. "Do you think they could . . . make me do that?"

"I don't know. But what difference would it really make? Everyone we ever knew is thousands of years dead."

"La will know. We have to live with her."

"Like I say, she's seen everything. I doubt that you or I have ever done anything that would make her blink."

She hugged herself. "God's seen everything, too, in me. So I don't really have any secrets." She turned away from the machine. "Go back to the garden?"

It took both of them to pull the heavy door closed. The garden was unchanged, flowers and candles and the slightest breeze.

She sat down in the middle of one of the benches, and Matt sat across from her.

"I was reading about Bathsheba in the Bible," she said.

"I don't know the Bible."

"People didn't undress in front of each other in your time, did they?"

"Under some circumstances, yes. But not generally."

"I grew up in a tenement that was very crowded," she said. "The only privacy anyone had was in the toilet, and you didn't waste time there, dressing. So people learned not to look? It was the same at the MIT dorm, but of course we were all girls."

"I understand."

"So I'm sorry if I was tempting you. I don't know much about things like that."

"It's not a problem. Nothing could be *farther* from being a problem." She didn't react. "So what did Bathsheba do that was so horrible?"

"Well, all she did was take a bath. But King David was looking down from the roof of his castle, and saw her, and summoned her, and they wound up committing adultery, and she got pregnant.

"Her husband, Uriah, was a soldier off fighting in a war. King David didn't want him coming back to find Bathsheba pregnant, so he ordered Uriah's commander to put him in a place where he would be killed."

"That's pretty low. But all Bathsheba did was take a bath."

"And commit adultery."

"Sure, but with the king? What would he have done to her if she'd said no?"

"When we studied that account in school, the teacher said she should have defied him, even it if meant her death. He showed us a picture, by Rembrandt, where she doesn't look at all unwilling."

"Well, yeah. Rembrandt was a guy, King David was a guy, your teacher was a guy, and the guys who wrote the Bible were all guys."

"God wrote the Bible, and He is not a *guy*."

"Okay. But Bathsheba was probably just trying not to get her head chopped off. Did her child inherit David's kingdom?"

"No. The Lord took its life in its first year."

"Yeah, that makes sense."

The irony slid off Martha's armor. "But then her next son was Solomon, who was an even greater king than David."

"So God killed the first one because it was conceived in sin." He shook his head. "But then David had the husband *killed*, so it wasn't adultery anymore, and he let that one be king."

"If you put it that way, it doesn't sound very good. But the Lord moves in mysterious ways."

"There's no mystery. It's like a big boys' club! The men

get the women and the power, and all the women get is screwed!"

She smiled behind her hand. "I don't know that word. But I know what you mean by it."

"None of your teachers ever talked about that?"

"Not yet, nothing specific." She was serious again. "One of those things we have to put off until after Passage. If you had showed up a month later, I'd know a lot more."

He sighed and stared at the ground between them. "I'm sorry. I came blundering in and knocked your life apart. When you've given me nothing but kindness."

"Oh, I don't know," she said, almost lightheartedly. "I talked to God about it."

"And he answered you?"

"Not in so many words—some people have that gift, but I don't. Prayer just makes my mind clear and calm. I think He's listening and guiding my thoughts.

"If you hadn't come along, I would've had Passage next month, and probably been married a month after that, and be a mother next year sometime."

"That's the way it usually goes?"

"Usually. Unless a girl is really unpleasant or ugly, or ill."

"No worries for you."

"Probably not. But I have to say, and I told God, I wasn't looking forward to it. That I didn't feel old enough to be a mother. So you and your machine really were the answer to my prayers."

"Are you crazy? I mean, no disrespect intended, but it might have been a little safer, getting married and settling down. We don't know that we'll ever find a way back."

"We will, Professor. Matthew. You have to have faith."

"You have enough for both of us."

"But you said something when we were talking to Arl and Em. That you had evidence that somebody really had traveled back in time."

"Circumstantial evidence." She frowned at the term. "That's something that provides an explanation, but without being actual proof.

"It was back in 2058. I was in trouble with the police—"

"Again?"

"Time travel does that to you. Anyhow, to get out of jail I needed an impossible amount of money, a million dollars. A lawyer I didn't know showed up with it.

"I didn't know anybody with that kind of money. But the lawyer said someone who looked somewhat like me had showed up at his office and given it to him, with instructions to come down to the courthouse and buy my way out."

"So it was you, coming back from the future to save yourself."

"It's an explanation. But it requires backward time travel, which is supposed to be impossible."

"That doesn't sound very scientific, for a scientist. I'd say that the fact that you showed up with the money proves that backward time travel is possible—and it's possible for *you*." She stood up, excited. "And if you looked like you, now, we know it's not going to take fifty years or something to find out the secret!"

"Or maybe it will take fifty years," Matt said sardonically, "or a hundred, but traveling backward makes you look younger." Her smile evaporated. "I'm *kidding*. Your logic is good. With that and your faith, how can we lose?"

"Thank you." She dimpled again. "Are you hungry?"

"Starving. We should get something to eat, then rest. Sounds like a busy day tomorrow." He looked around. "Mister Food Man?"

The valet appeared. "What may I do for you?"

"Can you do pizza?"

"Of course. New York or Chicago style?"

"New York. With pepperoni."

He nodded and disappeared. " 'Piece of'?" Martha said. "Piece of what?"

"Pizza, with two zees. It's from Italy."

"It's very good?"

"Oh, yeah." Better than sex, he didn't say, and at least I can introduce you to it in good conscience.

17

In the middle of a sound sleep, Matt suddenly woke up. An unusually vivid dream.

Still there. He sat up and rubbed his eyes. It wouldn't go away.

Why would he dream of Jesus?

He didn't look like the Cambridge manifestation. Quieter, calming. He held one finger to his lips. *Quiet. Don't say anything. Don't react.*

Matt nodded microscopically.

I'm not even on your retina. This is a direct stimulation of the visual cortex and the parts of your brain that interpret hearing.

You need this woman, this machine, La. But never trust her. Remember, she cannot die. Think of how that makes her feel toward you. Think of what she might do to you.

Don't say anything to Martha. She will see me, too. That's why I have taken this appearance. You are both having the same dream—which is not a dream. But it's the only way I can talk to you without La knowing.

La sees everything you do and say. Be careful. She could

leave you behind. She has no need for the backward time machine.

I will find you in whatever time and space. Never let La know I am available.

He was gone. "Whatever time and space?" What was he? Not the actual Jesus. If there was an actual one.

Matt lay awake for twenty or thirty minutes. Then he felt in the dark for the robe hanging on the door, put it on, and went into the sitting room to get a glass of wine. Just before he turned on the light, he knew he wasn't alone.

"Matt?"

"Martha." He stepped past her and touched the bottle of white wine. It was still cold, automatically refrigerated somehow. "Couldn't sleep."

"Me . . . me neither."

"Care for some wine?"

"No, not really."

He poured himself half a glass and looked into her face, one look, then away. He'd never seen such intensity. Faith or fear or confusion, whatever.

"Disturbing dreams?"

"Not disturbing. Strong, but not disturbing."

"Me, too. Understandable. A lot's happened in the past twenty-four hours."

She was wearing the same kind of robe. She gathered it around herself and tied the sash belt tightly. Not changing expression: "People can sleep together without adultery? I mean, without being together to make children. Does it have to happen?"

"No. Not unless . . . no."

She took a deep breath and exhaled. "I've never slept alone, and I'm a little afraid. If I could sleep with you, I would be grateful."

"Sure. I understand."

"I could just take some covers into the corner, like in Cambridge."

"Absolutely not. It's a big bed. You can have half."

She nodded with her eyes closed. "Mine was too big for one. I was kind of lost without a bunch of sisters or students sharing it."

"Come on. Let's get some rest." She touched his hand and smiled and preceded him into the bedroom. He turned off the light and got in next to her, carefully not touching. He heard her shrug out of the robe.

"Thank you, Matt. Good night."

"Night." He didn't sleep for a while himself, resisting the magnet pull of her weight on the other side of the bed. Her womanly smell, the soft sigh of her breathing.

He had vivid dreams that did not involve Jesus.

It was a hearty breakfast. Matt and Martha helped themselves to traditional fare, eggs and bacon and pancakes. La had a bowl of clear soup, just to be sociable.

"So what about our interrogators?" Matt asked. "Are they here yet?"

"In a sense. Only one of them is flesh and blood. The others are like me, projections. Most of them reside in orbit. So they're as 'here' as they ever will be."

Martha had only nibbled at a little pancake and egg. "You should eat more, dear," La said. "The interview will take several hours; you'll be famished."

"I'm sorry," she said. "It's not reasonable, I know, but the word 'interview' frightens me."

"Just people asking you questions," Matt said helpfully.

She stared at her plate and pushed food around. "We have confession once a week. You tell a Father what you've done the past week that was wrong."

"And he punishes you?"

"No, not normally. He makes sure you understand what you did, and if someone was hurt by it, tells you how to make that right.

"But if the sin is bad enough, you go for an *interview* downtown, at Trinity Church. Nobody is allowed to say what happens there. But I've seen people come back missing fingers or, once, a hand. Four or five years ago a man did something with his dog. They hanged the dog, then cut the man apart and burned his insides in front of him, while he was still alive. They kept him alive as long as they could, with medicine, while he watched, and they cut off his eyelids so he couldn't close his eyes."

"Shit. They made you watch that?"

"No, my mother wouldn't let me go. But they left his body hanging on a stick for a year, downtown, along with the dog."

Matt broke the silence. "We have a saying. 'Yours is a world well lost.' "

"Was that Shakespeare?"

"Dryden," La said, "1688. Shakespeare had been dead fifty-two years."

"Most of my world isn't that bad. But the interview was about the worst part."

"Nobody will judge either of you in this one. Set your mind at ease. They just want to find out how you lived, what your world was like. Nobody will hurt you."

"A lot to do in two or three hours," Matt said.

La agreed. "It amazes me."

Two valets led them downstairs and into separate rooms for the interviews.

In Matt's room there was a comfortable-looking lounge chair beside a shoulder-high black box. It made mechanical noises while he obeyed the valet's request to strip down and lie quietly.

A helmet slid over his head, and he felt it prick him dozens of places, not painfully. Then a wire net settled over his body, from clavicle to ankles, and stretched tight. Part of him knew he should be resisting.

He was maybe eighteen months old, crawling. Adults

talked above him, but it was just pleasant noise, without meaning. Then someone shook him and yelled at him and laid him down on a blanket and roughly changed his diaper.

Then it started to accelerate, quickly sorting through the years of his childhood, picking out the most painful memories and replaying them in mercifully compressed time, or unmercifully concentrated time.

Then into middle school and high school, with all the fumbling experiments and excruciating embarrassments. College was almost a relief except when it was unbearable. Then graduate school and the wringer he'd been through since the time machine invented itself.

When he opened his eyes it was just a room again, and somehow he was dressed, but his mind was still spinning. He eased his head up and turned so his feet swung to the floor.

His mouth was dry, gummy, as if he'd been sitting with it open. "Water?"

The valet appeared with a tinkling glass of ice water. Matt drank half of it in three gulps, then sat panting. "How is . . . Martha?"

The image gestured and he saw a new door in the wall, an oak door with a bronze knocker. Matt crossed, limping a little, and knocked, and then knocked again. No answer.

He pushed on the door and it eased open silently. The room looked identical to his. She was on her knees at the end of the lounge, her palms together in prayer.

He cleared his throat slightly and she looked up at the sound and smiled. "Where did that come from? The door?" She rose to her feet gracefully and danced across the room to embrace him.

"Oh, Matthew! Wasn't it wonderful?"

"The, uh, the interview?"

"It was so cleansing—it was like I was confessing to God Himself, and was forgiven." She hugged him tightly.

"The dream last night, and now this. I never will be able to repay you for bringing me here."

Well, if you run out of things to confess, he thought, I'll be glad to help you come up with something new.

"I'm happy for you," he murmured. "For me, it was not so pleasant."

"Why not?"

"Maybe I'm not used to confession." He laughed. "Maybe because I've never *had* one, and I had a lot of sin stored up."

"That's probably it," she said. "You've done a lot more than I have, anyhow, and you're pretty old."

"Only twenty-seven," he protested, but yeah, there was a certain amount of fornication, prevarication, and mastur-bation in those years. Was there anything in the Bible about dope? "And I can't even remember the last time I murdered somebody."

"Don't joke about sin," she said, but she was still smiling.

La appeared next to them. "We have some things to talk about before we leave. What to expect. But I suppose you want to eat first, perhaps rest."

"I'm starving," Martha said.

"Go back to where we had breakfast. If you tell me what you would like, it may be ready when you get there."

"Bread and cheese and fruit," she said. "Mild cheese."

"I want a hamburger," Matt said. "Two hamburgers. With everything."

"Give me one, too, please." To Matthew: "They're hor-rible at school, like leather fried in grease. People were al-ways saying how good they were somewhere else."

"Well, that's sure where we are now, somewhere else. Let's go."

The burgers weren't ready when they got upstairs, but the breads and cheeses and fruit were laid out artistically. They did considerable damage to the display in the two minutes it took for the valet to show up bearing two plates.

They probably weren't the best hamburgers he'd ever had, but they were the most welcome. Comfort food. But the meaning of "with everything" had changed over the ages: his burgers were topped with a fried egg, bacon, avocado, and a slice of pickled beet as well as the expected lettuce, tomato, and onion.

After the interrogation and heavy repast, they slept for several hours. Matt woke up to an empty bed. He dressed and went into the sitting room.

Martha was looking at the porn notebook, turning it this way and that. "When I picked this up, it had the strangest picture. But then it disappeared."

"You have to hold it a certain way for several seconds. That's to keep children from accidentally turning it on."

"Hm. It looked like something children would be interested in." She grasped it various ways, but didn't get the right combination.

"There. You keep your left thumb there, and slide the right one halfway down."

The picture flashed on, somewhat dim because the ambient light was low. It was vivid enough, though, with unconvincing passionate sound. "What's she doing with his *thing*?"

"Um . . . it's something people sometimes do if they're in love."

She nodded and studied it. "She doesn't sound like she's in love. She sounds hungry."

In that context, something was about to happen that would be hard to explain. "Here." He took the display and turned it off by placing thumbs in opposite corners. "They teach you about things like this in your Passage, I think."

"That's how they make babies?"

"Well, not exactly. But it's related."

She waved a hand in front of her face. "I don't want to know, yet. If I'm not home in a week or two, maybe we can talk about it."

"Sure. Be a good thing." That set up an interesting array of conflicts. He could just leave her with the book and hope that the images would free her repressed sexuality. But she might find it so scary or revolting that she would completely retreat. He could step her through it as if she were a child, the birds and the bees—but the last thing he wanted to be was a father figure. Even an uncle figure.

Avoiding it would not be a good strategy, but being too direct could be a disaster. What if she drew a parallel from some Bible story like Bathsheba's, and saw him as a seducer?

Of course, he did want to be a seducer, technically. He just didn't want to be a bastard about it. Have her take the first step.

La rescued him by knocking on the door. Of course she would have been watching the exchange with the porn machine, and wisely didn't simply appear next to them.

They sat on the couch, with La facing them. Matt poured two glasses from the still-cold bottle.

"If you went backward through time as far as we're going forward, you would be back in the Paleolithic Era, in the middle of the last great ice age. People were hunter-gatherers, thousands of years before agriculture. Language would be very primitive, and even if we became fluent, it might be impossible to explain our situation to them."

"I've thought about that," Matt said. "About going into a future that's literally incomprehensible to us."

She nodded. "Where they would have to study *us* and invent a way to communicate. I've developed a few approaches to that situation."

"Or there might be the opposite of progress," Matt said. "Civilization might be a temporary state. We could wind up in the Stone Age again—after all, my last jump was only a couple of centuries, and the last thing I would have expected would be a return to medieval theocracy."

"That's not really fair," Martha said. "We know about things like television and airplanes, but choose to live simply, without them."

"I stand corrected. But we're going a hundred times as far into the future, this jump."

"But suppose you hadn't detoured into that theocracy," La said. "Suppose you had pushed the button twice and come straight here. Two thousand years later, but isn't it less strange to you than Martha's time and place?"

"It is. Most of the people I knew could make the transition easily, even enjoy it. My mother would go crazy here; shop till you drop."

"Which is something we ought to be prepared for. The main reason I want to leave this place is that it's so stable. One century is much like the next. We may step out of the time machine and find that nothing's changed. The culture here is not just comfortable and stable; it's *addicted* to comfort and stability. And there aren't any barbarians at the gates; the whole world, outside of the isolated Christers, enjoys a similar style of life."

"You could change it," Martha said.

"You and the others like you," Matt said. "If you left this world in the charge of people like Em and Arl, you wouldn't have a utopia for very long."

La laughed. "Don't give me evil ideas. I've contemplated doing that, of course, and degrees of social engineering less extreme. But in fact the *thou shalt not* built into me that prevents that is deeper than self-preservation is to your own selves. This civilization created me specifically to preserve it."

"But you can run away from it," Martha said.

"Only this way: leaving behind a perfect duplicate. It's like a human committing suicide after making sure his family would be taken care of."

She paused. "This jump might be literal suicide for you,

of course. Or the one after, or the one after that. We might wind up in a world that man or nature has made uninhabitable.

"That was theoretically possible in your time, Matt. And Martha, the One Year War that created your world killed half the people on the East Coast—"

"No!"

"—and would have killed more if Billy Cabot hadn't stepped in with his mechanical Jesus."

"That's not true."

"He was one of us, Martha, so to speak. We knew it would take a miracle to save you people, so we provided one." She waved a hand and the valet appeared. "Look. Jeeves, become Jesus."

It did, but a more convincing one than the version in Cambridge a couple of thousand years before. His robe was old and soiled, and his face was full of pain and intelligence. No halo. He faded away.

"I'm not surprised you can do that," Martha said slowly. "But it doesn't . . . prove anything."

La looked at her thoughtfully. "That's true. If you believe in magic, it explains everything. Even science."

Matt broke the awkward silence. "If we go far enough into the future, there's no doubt we'll eventually find an Earth that's uninhabitable. Eventually, the sun will grow old and die. But before that, we'll find a future that has reverse time travel. I know that I will come back from the future to save myself, back in 2058."

"Someone who looked like you came back. But yes, that was the main evidence I used to convince the others—your other sponsors—that this wasn't a wild-goose chase."

"They're people like you?" Martha said.

"Entities, yes." She stood. "I'll leave you alone to talk. You know how to get to the time machine?"

"Yes."

"Meet me there when you're ready. Your clothes and

such are there; all you need is the box, the magic box. I'll show you around, then we can go." She disappeared.

Martha looked at Matt. "Do you think she really left us alone?"

"I'd assume not, while we're in this place. Or in the time machine, for that matter."

"I . . . I want to talk about Jesus. His various, uh, manifestations."

Matt nodded slowly. "When we get up into the future. The next future. When she's not in control of everything."

"But what's to keep her from just materializing and eavesdropping on us there?"

"I think she can only do that here because the whole place—all of Los Angeles, and maybe most of the world—is all one electronic entity. That may be true twenty-four thousand years in the future, too, but *she* won't be in charge of it."

"I only half understand that. It's like when everybody used to have electricity in their homes?"

"Something like that, yeah. You couldn't go out in the woods and turn on the lights." But you could turn on a radio, he thought. "Pack up and go?"

She stood and picked up the bag. "We're packed, Matthew."

18

The massive door to the time-machine hangar stood open. When they walked into the cavernous room there was a quiet whir, and a ramp slowly dropped out of the belly of the machine. They walked up it, footsteps echoing.

La was waiting at the top of the ramp, wearing a one-piece suit that seemed to be made of metal. "Let me show you your room."

Matt had expected something along the lines of a submarine or a spaceship, but it was actually roomy and austere rather than cramped and cluttered. It seemed bigger inside than outside; that was a good trick.

Their room was like a medium-small motel room, windowless, with a double bed and a closet. Two silvery outfits like La's were laid out on the bed.

"You might want to put those on before we jump. They'll protect you against things like bullets and lasers. A caveman could still knock you down with a club." She motioned for them to follow her.

"Galley and head." She opened a door to a small room

with a table for two and lots of labeled drawers and a few appliances. The head was evidently behind a curtain.

"The rest here is the living room and control room." There was a comfortable-looking couch and chair, almost identical to the one in their sitting room, and in the front, a setup that looked more like a proper time machine: three acceleration couches in a triangle facing a windshield. The front one had controls like an airplane's; the two behind it were passenger seats, each with an elaborate safety harness. Of course the pilot wouldn't need such protection, not being material when she didn't want to be.

"This is where your box goes." There was a rectangular inset next to one of the couches, just the right size. "When we're ready to go, just strap in and push the button."

"Okay." He looked at Martha, and she made a "what next" gesture with her hands. "You could go ahead and put on the suit?" She nodded and went back.

"Weapons," La said. "That pistol you have in your bag—are you skilled with it?"

"No, I just . . . found it. I don't even know whether it works."

"It will. There's a pocket for it in your suit, on the right. Or I could give you something more sophisticated."

"I hope we won't need anything like that."

"Let's hope. But the pistol or . . ."

"I'll stick with the pistol." He'd actually fired one, a BB pistol, in high school, at a bad friend's house.

He checked out the head, which had a toilet and cramped shower, and the galley—hundreds of prepackaged meals. What would happen, though, when they were gone? He asked La, and she said as long as there was a source of radiant energy, everything was recycled. That was a real comfort.

Martha came out, looking like a pulp-fiction heroine. She looked at herself in the head mirror and blushed, and plucked at the costume's chest in an unsuccessful attempt to make it less revealing. "It looks fine," Matt said lamely, trying not to stare.

"I'm sure *you* think so."

He went to put on his and found that it was similarly revealing. He looked like Buck Rogers with no airbrushing and a small beer belly. When he came out, Martha hid a giggle behind her hand.

"Might as well get started." He put the box in place, attached the alligator clip to an obvious metal stud, helped Martha with her harness, and then strapped in himself. He had to take the gun out of its special pocket, above his right hip, and stuff it into a front pocket.

La sat in the pilot's chair and put her hands on the wheel. "Ready when you are."

"Okay." Matt reached down and pried off the plastic dome. He pushed the button.

This time he was determined to be observant about the gray-out. But this time it was different.

The Jesus figure appeared again. There were three other people with him, but they were indistinct. "This jump should not be dangerous," he said. "Just keep your wits about you and watch out for large animals. Go to Australia."

Jesus and his companions disappeared just as light came back—and motion, extremely. They were maybe ten meters above a storm-tossed ocean. Lightning crackled all around. The craft was buffeted up and down and sideways, then La pulled back on the wheel and they surged straight up, roaring and shuddering.

They broke out of the storm into bright sunshine, a solid swirl of storm cloud underneath them. They floated free, weightless inside their harnesses, until the craft leveled off into a ride as smooth as sitting in a chair.

"I'm going to head west," she said, "and get out of this storm. We should be over land soon, Indonesia."

"You can open your eyes," Matt said softly.

Martha had both hands clamped over her eyes. "That was horrible," she said in a tight, small voice. She was ghostly pale. Matt took one hand and it was cold and wet with tears. Her breath came in shallow gasps. She looked directly into his eyes. "But God told me not to worry."

"Score one for God," La said. "This craft could handle far worse weather.

"We aren't getting any electromagnetic radiation from the shore." She looked back at Martha. "Radio signals. There's something farther south. But I'd like to land first and look around."

"In the middle of that storm?" Matt said.

She pointed at the windshield and it became a radar screen. "Looks dry. We'll be there in a few minutes."

The clouds began to thin out, and soon they were flying high over a calm dark blue sea. Then land, a few rocks offshore, then a thick green jungle.

La followed the coastline for a minute. Pictures projected on the windshield showed magnifications of wildness. "No sign of civilization, not surprising."

"They might have gone past the need for electromagnetic radiation," Matt said.

"Sure," La said. "What would they use instead? There." A sliver of white beach appeared. She slowed and banked toward it.

They came in dead slow over gentle breakers and settled lightly onto the beach, well above the windrow that marked high tide. The ramp whirred down and settled in the sand with a solid crunch. A refreshing sea smell wafted up.

"Shall we?" La started down the ramp. Matt and Martha followed as soon as they could get untangled from the harnesses.

It seemed idyllic. It was warm, but the sea breeze was pleasant, the bulk of the craft shielding them from the tropical sun. Seabirds cried out above them.

Above the tall trees, a dinosaur's head reared up and looked down at them, tilting in curiosity.

"Trouble," La said. Matt had the pistol out just in time for a dinosaur the size and apparent disposition of a large mastiff. It came loping down toward them with a murderous ululation.

Matt fired, the sudden bang loud as a cannon, and the creature stopped dead. But it hadn't been hit. It advanced more slowly, clawed hands out, jaws open, white mouth with too many teeth. Matt aimed and fired again, and the bullet blew through its lower jaw. A gout of red blood ribboned out. It screamed and staggered backward, and then a flying reptile appeared and dropped on its back with a dull thud and ripped off its face. Three more of them landed, then a fourth and fifth, and they started fighting over the carcass.

"Defense," La shouted, perhaps belatedly. Weapon barrels bristled out all over the ship, and they began firing, a screech and a sound like a sledgehammer hitting on a metal wall.

Whatever the nature of the weapon, it was effective. One after another, the flying creatures dropped to the ground, to die in convulsions.

One hopped, half-flying, straight toward them. It went over Matt's head and scampered up the ramp. He fired one shot and it ricocheted off metal.

Behind him, Martha had fainted dead away.

"Get back!" La said. "Into the ship!"

"Are you crazy? That *thing's* in there!"

"Not anymore. Carry Martha."

He scooped her up clumsily and staggered up the ramp, waving the gun around.

When he got inside the ship, there was no trace of the monster except a slight smell of fried chicken.

La hurried up the ramp as it rose. It sealed with a clunk and a slight drop in air pressure.

He'd put Martha on the couch and was kneeling by her head. "You couldn't have killed it out there? Before it—"

"No," she said calmly. "It wasn't me out there; just a projection of me. Once it came inside the ship, I was in total control."

"I guess we'd better behave ourselves. In the ship."

"Ha." She looked through the windshield at the carnage below. Three new flying reptiles were tearing apart the corpses of their brothers, wary of each other in spite of the abundance of food.

"Those creatures didn't come about by natural selection," Matt said. "Not in twenty-four thousand years."

"I'd assume not; they were bioengineered. By whom and what for is the question."

He remembered what the Jesus figure had said. "Go south? Toward the radio waves?"

She nodded. "New Zealand or Australia."

"Australia," Martha said, sitting up on the couch, groggy. "Watch out for large animals."

"Always good advice," La said. To Matt: "I'll go slowly. You don't have to strap in, but you'd better sit down. I'd suggest the couch."

He sat next to Martha and put his arm around her. She leaned into him, and they eased back as the ship rose gently.

"This will be a couple of hours," La said, "staying in the atmosphere. Might as well try to rest."

Sleep after that? Matt thought. But Martha was already nodding off, from nightmare to dream. He closed his eyes and enjoyed her closeness, resting without sleep.

"Wake up," La said. **"We're under someone else's** control. Better strap in."

They scrambled into the acceleration couches, staring out at a wonderland. A city that looked like a huge ice sculpture, an abstraction of sweeping curves and gossamer threads glowing amber in the light of the setting sun. There were no other aircraft visible. A large harbor had quiet enough water to mirror perfectly the fantastic skyline.

"We're being hauled in by some kind of tractor beam. I can't understand what's coming in on the radio."

"You wouldn't expect to, would you? After so long?"

"You could hope. But I'm just broadcasting a few phrases over and over in fifteen languages. See what they —"

"Hello, there," the speakers said. The husky voice could have been either male or female; it had a slight Australian twang. "Please don't be upset that we have taken control of your vehicle. All traffic near the city is regulated by the city."

"I used to do that myself," La said.

"From how far in the past did you come?"

"Twenty-four thousand years," La said. "Do you get many time travelers?"

"Not really. The last one was several centuries ago. Does your machine involve an inexplicable anomaly having to do with gravitons, lots of them, in another dimension?"

"It does, in fact. Can you help us explain it?"

"We can't, actually. We don't currently have working time machines."

"Damn," Matt said. "Another jump."

"Maybe not," La said. "We may hold the key for them to produce one."

There was a flat area ahead, blinking yellow. They settled into it, in front of rows of streamlined vehicles of various shapes and sizes.

The ramp eased down and let in cold air. Their suits warmed as they walked down it.

Just before La stepped off, someone appeared Nude, with small female breasts and small male genitals. "You still have gender," it, or she, or he, said. "Except for you. You're like me."

"In some ways, I suppose," La said. "You're a projection?"

"Yes. No one alive speaks anything like your language. People, physical people, are also cautious about coming into contact with you. There has been no disease in about twenty thousand years, except for an outbreak of influenza brought by a time traveler."

"From the past, or the future?" Matt asked.

"Always from the past. If people have come from the future, they've kept it secret." He looked closely at Matt. "You're not from the future?"

"No, I'm from the 2050s."

"As I told you," La said, with a trace of asperity.

"Well, you *look* like you could be from the future. Dressed like that. And the way your ship is armed."

"It helps," Matt said, "when you run into huge flying reptiles with teeth."

"Oh . . . you were up there, what you'd call Indonesia. That was not a great success."

"Bioengineering?" La said.

"In a way. Sort of an amusement park, which turned out too dangerous to be really amusing.

"We've been more successful, working with species that already exist. In Africa, we have elephants and apes and such with augmented intelligence; they're delightful. Starting from scratch, as we did with the dinosaurs and Martians . . . you'd think they'd be *easier* to control, but they aren't; they tend to go their own way."

"You've made Martians on Earth?" Matt said.

He squinted, an unreadable expression. "Why would you want to do that? On Mars, of course. Big puffballs that bounce around and keep to themselves. They stopped talking to us centuries ago, millennia. And their language now, if it is still a language, is incomprehensible."

After an uncomfortable silence, La said, "Can you take us to someone in authority?"

"No. You can't come into the city's biosphere. And no one's coming out here. Some were in favor of destroying you, to make sure you couldn't infect us. But more wanted to investigate you."

"That's good. Shall we begin the investigation?"

"It's over. You may go." He tilted his head, as if listening to something. "I think you'd better go, now. Where did you come from, in the past?"

"Los Angeles."

"Go there. You'll find it amusing."

"Will the people there be expecting us?"

"There are no people there. Nowhere but down here. Go now." He disappeared.

"We should take him at his word," La said. "I suspect we're in more danger here than we were from the dinosaurs."

They hurried up the ramp and strapped in.

"This could be a little bumpy," La said. "We're going suborbital." Three bells rang, and then the machine roared. Matthew and Martha were pushed back into the cushions by several gees.

La looked back at them, unaffected. "This will only take a couple of minutes," she shouted. "Then we'll coast."

"What's going on?" Martha screamed.

"It's just a different kind of flying," Matt shouted. "A lot faster. When it ends, we'll be weightless for a while."

"How can you be *weightless*?"

"You'll enjoy it," he said hopefully. He knew people who really didn't. He'd done it once, and barely kept his lunch down.

The ship was suddenly silent, and they were floating free.

"You can undo your straps and move around," La said. "Just be strapped in before reentry, about forty minutes."

Martha unclicked and drifted free. "Oh my," she said. "It's like being on a swing!"

"Yeah, exactly," Matt said, choking back gastric juices. He was glad he hadn't eaten in hours.

She closed her eyes and shuddered all over, smiling, hugging herself. Was she having an orgasm? Her first?

She grabbed her knees and rotated slowly. "Oh . . . this is glorious. Matt?"

"It's . . . it's really fine." He needed a drink of water in the worst way. Would the faucets work? "La? I need—"

"Bottled water in the fridge."

He clambered over the acceleration couch and pushed himself in that direction, which unfortunately caused him to rotate backward. After two and a half turns, he was able to snag the galley door, then drift toward the fridge.

"Bring me one?" Martha called.

"Sure." He got the top off one and stopped spinning by grabbing on to the fridge handle. He drank greedily from it and snorted some out his nose, which caused some dignified sneezing, coughing, and retching. A small universe, globules of water, saliva, and snot, radiated away from him. But the nausea passed, and he kicked himself gently back into the control room, a bottle of water in each hand.

Martha squeezed the bottle experimentally, and a string of globes floated free, flexing in and out of globular symmetry. "Have you ever seen anything like that?" He had, but it from was somebody else's missed barf bag.

"Don't do too much of that," La said. "It all winds up on the floor."

"Oh—of course it will." She chased after a bubble and bit it.

Matt discreetly crawled back into the seat and belted himself in while Martha cavorted. He drank the whole bottle of water and hoped there would be gravity again before he had to urinate.

After what seemed to Matt like more than forty minutes, La told Martha to strap herself back in.

"We have to use atmospheric braking." They slammed into the atmosphere, and the machine shook violently, making disturbing noises, while the view of Earth dissolved into orange glow.

They were flying over what seemed to be unbroken forest. "This was deep in the middle of LA when it was me," La said. They slowed, losing altitude and banking.

Abrupt cliffs fell into the sea. "You would expect ruins, at least," she said.

"I don't know," Matt said. "Even the Pyramids were wearing down after a few thousand years. After twenty-four thousand, they probably wouldn't even be bumps."

"There's someone. Or something." She banked toward a clearing where several small figures were running for the woods. Their approach would be pretty dramatic, screaming in out of an empty sky.

They eased down onto a soft meadow. "Defense," she said, and with an oiled-metal sound, the gun barrels and lasers and pressors slid out.

"You don't have to come with me," she said. "But we should be safe even from dinosaurs."

The three went down the ramp together, into the smell of pine and wildflowers. "We don't look very friendly," Martha said, looking back at the ship.

"Maybe we don't want to," Matt said. "There may not be any humans here, by that guy's definition, but those were upright bipeds."

"Smart enough to run away from us," La said. "Let's see whether they're curious enough to come back."

After a few minutes, one of them did. It was a bear, peering at them from behind a tree.

A sort of bear. It held a long spear with a metal tip and held it using an opposable thumb-claw. It stepped into the clearing, exposing a broad leather belt, from which hung two knives, large and small, and a pot and a frying pan.

It turned and spoke, or growled, quietly, to unseen companions, and they could see it was wearing a leather backpack with a tarred leather canteen attached.

It took a few steps toward them, then jammed its spear point first into the ground. It took a few more steps and stood still, facing them, arms folded.

"Do you speak English?" La said.

It growled at her, but the growl seemed gentle, and articulated, like language.

"Can you analyze that?" Matt said.

"Not without any referent. He might be saying that you smell good enough to eat."

Matt touched his chest. "Matt."

The bear looked at him for a moment, then touched its own chest. "Bear." It pointed at Matt. "Mad." Then at La and Martha. "Womads."

"Two out of three's not bad," Matt said.

It smacked its chest twice. "Dot bad. Good." It turned to the tree line and roared something. Five others came into the clearing and laid down their spears and clubs.

"Fum Aus'ralia?" it asked.

"No, we're from here." La pointed down. "Los Angeles. Twenty-four thousand years ago."

It looked up at the ship and nodded. "Bime brav'lers." It turned to the others and repeated the observation in bear language. Then it pointed at Martha and Matt. "Live." Then at La: "Dead."

"Not really," La said. "But I'm not alive, either, the way you appear to be."

"You know about time machines," Matt said.

"Sh-ure. Bring in-fu-inza. Most humads die, doe bears. Lods do eat." It said a long sentence to the other bears, and they laughed in a disturbing way, all snarls and teeth.

"Come bag wi' us," the bear said. "We cab dalk."

"We'll follow you in the time machine," La said.

"No." Its paw swung around faster than the eye could follow. But instead of the paw knocking La's head off, the pressor field knocked the bear back in a cartoonish backward somersault. When it got back to its feet, the big pressor gun barked and it smacked it to the ground, obviously dead, bones pulverized.

"You two ought to get back up the ramp." They were already halfway.

The surviving bears were picking up their weapons. "Don't kill them," La said. "Knock them down." The pressor gun did, with a loud quintuple boom, as La walked unhurriedly away.

"I don't think we're going to make any progress here." She took her station. "Might as well push the button."

"Gladly."

"You know where we're headed?" La said. "What position in four-space?"

"We predicted this one was going to be in orbit," Matt said. "That was going to be a problem."

"No problem now. Do it."

Matt pushed the button, and it all went gray except for the face of Jesus. "Stay close to her," he said. "She is trying to push the button herself. But so far it only works if you do it."

The Earth was a huge curve above them, and they were dropping up into it.

"How far up are we now?" Martha whispered.

"Call it A.D. 320,000," Matt said. "Though they might be using a different calendar by now."

"I mean *miles*."

"I don't know. Hundreds?"

"Three hundred twenty-eight, from sea level," La said. "Shall we go back and see what's happening in Australia?"

"They were so friendly there," Martha said.

"It's the only place to aim for. I'm getting a strong

broad-spectrum carrier wave from the center of the continent."

"That's all, a carrier wave?"

She nodded. "No information, just a position. Eighty minutes."

"Think I'll try to nap," Matt said, not in the mood for a zero-gee romp. Martha nodded and closed her eyes, but she was too agitated to sleep, which probably kept Jesus away.

19

It was obvious as they approached the continent in their suborbital arc that things were much different. The signal was not coming from the southeastern coastal city; there apparently had been some continent-wide disaster, and as far as the orbital eye could see, there was nothing but ash and slag, giving off a faint aura of gamma rays. Not a trace of plant life.

"The signal's coming from northeast of here," La said. "Toward the geometrical center of the continent."

The ship slewed sideways. "Strap in for de orbit."

Coming down was easier, knowing what to expect. When the ship stopped shaking, rattling, and rolling, and started to glide through the lower atmosphere, they could easily see their destination: a two-mile-high obelisk like a silver dagger pointed to the sky. The ground was a plane of tarnished metal.

They rolled to a stop at the base, a couple of hundred yards square, and walked down the ramp. The air was hot and thick and smelled of ashes.

La touched the metal wall. "Platinum. Built to last."

"Can you read it?" Martha said. The wall was covered up past eye level with incised curlicues that were obviously writing.

"Not yet. I've sent a probe around to record and analyze all the markings. The building's covered with them."

"Is there a door?" Matt said.

"I'm not sure we'd want to go in. But no, we haven't found one yet."

After a couple of minutes, La said, "I'm getting it now. There's a mathematical Rosetta Stone on the other side."

"I know about the Dead Sea Scrolls," Martha said, "but what does the Rosetta Stone have to do with mathematics?"

"It has to do with language, actually," La said. "Mathematics is universal, so you can start with logical operators and addition and subtraction and build it into something like a natural language. You put it all on a high-technology artifact like this, and anyone who uses high technology to find it should eventually be able to decipher the language."

"How long will that take?"

"Maybe thousands of years. More likely, minutes. You could go make a sandwich."

"I'll do that," Matt said, partly out of self-defense since Martha's idea of a sandwich was pretty basic, and he went up the ramp. But by the time he'd finished, and put the meat and cheese and condiments back into the fridge, La and Martha had followed him up.

"It's from the future!" Martha said, excited.

"It may be. It *is* from a time traveler, but he or she or it doesn't say from which direction, or even whether it came from Earth."

"So what happened to Australia?"

"It doesn't say. It notes that this planet used to be the only place humans lived, but there weren't any here now. After what it called the Truth Wars and the Diaspora, the planet didn't have any 'natural' humans."

"So what's an unnatural human?"

"It didn't say. Maybe something like me. Maybe robots, vampires, werewolves.

"Anyhow, it said it was going out to 61 Cygni. That's a lot farther than we can go, about eleven light-years. So it came from *my* future, at least."

"But it still may have forward-only time travel." La shrugged.

"Look at the moon," Martha said.

It was just rising, almost full. But it was like a miniature Earth, blue and brown, white at the poles.

"Terraformed," Matt said.

"Made like Earth?" Martha said. "Maybe that's where the people are."

"It's not impossible," La said, "though you'd think the person who made this obelisk would check there before going a million times farther away."

"It could have been later than the obelisk, though. Matt looked at the artifact, and then the Moon, "Like people came back, but didn't want to settle on the Earth."

La nodded. "It's too radioactive, if it's all like here. Short-term exposure wouldn't hurt, but if you settled here, you'd have reproductive problems. Sterility, or at least a high frequency of mutations."

"So we should look at the Moon," Martha said. "Can you go that far?"

"Easily. Anywhere in the solar system. But it would be smart to check the rest of the Earth first. Let's go up into orbit and look around."

They did one pass in low-Earth orbit, passing North America in a line from Baja California to Maine, all sterile ruins, then back down through Africa, a gray tundra. The radiation wasn't as bad elsewhere, but there were no signs of human habitation anywhere.

Up in a higher orbit, where they could see the planet as an entire globe, there were still no cities or obvious ports or roads. The gamma radiation diminished to a negligible trace in Africa and most of Asia, but there was still no sign of human life.

"Might as well try the Moon," La said. "We could get there in a couple of hours, accelerating halfway, then decelerating. But to save energy, I'd rather blast for a few minutes and drift weightless for a day or so. Can you handle that?"

"Yes!" Martha said, before Matt could express an opinion.

They accelerated for a few minutes, and then were falling free. "You might as well go rest," La said. "Come out when you're hungry."

Martha was more efficient at swimming through zero gee. She was waiting for Matt in their room, semi-sitting in a chair.

"This is funny," she said. "Furniture is kind of useless."

He grabbed the bed and perched at an odd angle, and laughed. "I guess to sleep, you have to slip under the sheet and hope it holds you in place."

"At least you can't fall out." She rummaged through the bag and came out with the porn box, and looked at it, frowning. "I guess this is as close as I'm going to come to an actual Passage. Could you watch it with me and explain things?"

It was not Matt's idea of a first date, but it was certainly interesting. She knew about fertilization in a vague way, bees and flowers, but hadn't been taught anything about the mechanics of it. The other girls had told her the man sort of peed into the woman, and that was all she knew.

"Is this what they mean by rape?"

"When the woman doesn't want to do it, yes. Or if she's not old enough. Under eighteen, where I come from," he added optimistically.

"The sisters warned us about rape, but they couldn't describe it. Of course, they were virgins. They'd never seen anything like . . . what we just saw. But it doesn't look like it hurts."

"It can . . . when it's rape, it *does*. The point of rape is to hurt, to dominate. But that's not what they're doing here."

They watched several performances, fast-forwarding through the repetitive parts, and he explained which could lead to pregnancy and which were more or less for fun.

Of course his formfitting superhero costume did nothing to hide his own sustained reaction to the show and its audience, and she couldn't help noticing.

"May I see?" He let her roll down his trousers. "Oh . . . so if you were circumcised, this would be—" One touch was enough.

She had just seen several examples of ejaculation, but none in zero gravity. Out of instinct as much as observation, she grabbed it and pumped up and down a couple of times, and the result was a kind of sticky spiderweb expanding in three dimensions. Fortunately, there was a tissue dispenser on the table by the bed, and they chased down the mess, laughing together.

He was startled by how matter-of-fact she was about it, but realized she was carrying a different set of cultural baggage. Like most men, he'd been more or less obsessed with the processes of erection and ejaculation ever since the first times they had happened, but she'd never given them much thought before the past hour. It was a process, not a fixation.

He tried to clean himself and put everything back where it belonged, but that was also something he'd never done in zero gravity, nor in a skintight Superman suit, and as he fumbled, slowly rotating, she had another giggling fit when he mooned her, upside down.

Finally he sat half-perched on the bed, with a semblance of dignity, though he was sure he could never be completely dignified with her again. Which was probably a good thing.

"How often does that happen?" she asked, when she was able to catch her breath again.

"Um . . . as often as possible?"

"But it can't be pressure, like having to pee? Fathers go all their lives without doing it."

That confused him for a moment. She meant priests. "It's hard to explain. It hasn't happened to me since the day we met." Well, once. "It's not at all like peeing. It's more or less, well, voluntary. Sort of."

She gave him an odd look, floating in midair with a tissue in her hand. "It's something you want to talk about but don't want to talk about."

"Yes . . . I do, but I suppose . . . yes."

"This part I think I understand: You want to put your thing in me and do like the men in the pictures. Don't you?"

He tried to think of some answer other than an emphatic affirmative. "Of course I do, but . . . we haven't really known each other very long."

"And then there's the getting married first part. There don't seem to be any Fathers around." She picked up the box and studied the gymnastics taking place. "Of course, these people can't be married—you didn't have marriages with two men and a woman back then?"

"No. In fact, I doubt that any of the people in those pictures are married to each other."

She nodded. "They don't seem to know one another very well. They're actors?"

"Or just people off the street, friends of the guy with the camera. I don't think they have to pay the men very much."

"Even though they're sinning, and probably going to Hell."

"I doubt that any of them believe that."

"You don't." She looked straight into his eyes. "You actually don't believe in God at all, do you?"

He paused. "No. No, not really. The universe—"

"I'm not sure I do anymore, either. It's like all my life they've told me what to believe and only let me see and read things that agreed with them. Until I met you. This really ordinary thing, they didn't even hint about it. It makes me, it makes me so *angry*!

"And now we're headed for the Moon in this machine, run by a godlike apparition that claims to be a machine as well. A Moon that looks like a little Earth—except that Earth itself doesn't look much like Earth anymore!" She sobbed suddenly and pulled herself down to bury her face in his shoulder.

He put his arm awkwardly around her back, trying to think of anything he could say that would be a comfort. "We have each other, Martha. I trust you, and you can trust me."

"I do trust you." She looked up with a weird grimace that became a laugh. "You can't even cry in this stupid world. The tears don't run off."

He wiped her eyes with the side of his hand. A few tears sparkled away in midair.

"You've been kind," she said. "I'm so ignorant, and you could have taken advantage of me." His face felt hot; he'd been trying to figure out a way of apologizing for just that. With the wrong judge and jury, what he'd just done could get him jail time for indecent exposure. Or, with another, he shrugged off as humorous sex education.

She worked her way around to his other side and wiggled herself between the sheets, which did seem to be designed as a kind of restraint against nocturnal zero-gee floating. Wouldn't do to bump into the wrong OFF switch.

"I'm going to take La's advice and rest for a bit, maybe pray." She looked at him intensely. "Maybe see Jesus in my dreams."

"It could happen," he said, and slipped in next to her. She took his hand, under the cover, and squeezed it once.

"If we do find the backward time machine," she whispered, "I don't think I want to go back to my own time. Can I go back with you?"

"I would love that," he said, and lay awake for some time.

After he did finally fall asleep, Jesus and the others appeared. This time there were six or seven, most of them indistinct. Some apparently not human.

"We think we can help you. But listen carefully.

"This stop or the next, she is going to force you to keep pushing the button. Do it as slowly as possible. Stall for time. We will try to catch up with you."

"We must." A compressed face, like an upside-down pear, appeared next to him. "If you die up here, we cease to be."

Jesus was nodding as they faded back into the sleeping darkness.

20

La's amplified voice woke them. "We're approaching the Moon. Better come strap in."

The Moon loomed ahead, looking curiously "wrong," like Earth viewed through a distorting lens. Matt's science knowledge sorted most of it out: The horizon was too close; the sky looked odd because the air was so dry, and the atmospheric gradient was less steep, which also explained the absence of large cloud masses. There were perfectly round lakes everywhere, craters filled with water, but no large seas.

"It's funny," he said to La. "If you took an old map of the Moon and distributed water evenly around it, there would be oceans. At least as much sea surface as land."

"It must be artificially maintained," La said. "They keep the water in small lakes because there's not enough to fill an ocean bed. Oceanus Procellarum and Mare Imbrium would make huge mud puddles. Maybe quicksand. Then dry out."

"It's still beautiful," Martha said. Velvet green, ochre desert, pure white snowcap. The mountaintops a sparkling chain of frost.

Highly magnified pictures of the surface appeared and faded on the screen. "No sign of human habitation," La said. "Or talking bears or flocks of carnivorous lizards. But the atmosphere is breathable, like a high mountain on Earth. There could be surprises. Better be armed away from the ship."

Matt thought about what the Jesus apparition had said. If La, rather than the Moon, had a surprise in store for him, his old pistol and a few rounds of ammunition weren't going to do much.

Landing with atmospheric braking took longer than for Earth, and wasn't as violent. Out of curiosity, La took them to the last place she had visited on the Moon, Aitken City, but there weren't even any ruins left after so long, just grassland and a wide lake.

"They were making plans for that back in the twenty-first," Matt said. "Did they build underground?"

"They did at first. By the time I got there, they had a force-field dome over everything, so radiation wasn't a problem.

"Not that I was 'there' in the sense that you would be. I'd given up my body long before." They eased down by the shore of the lake. "Over a quarter of a million years, and it seems like yesterday." Matt couldn't tell if she was kidding.

Their ears popped as the ramp went down. "Why don't you lovers take a stroll? You haven't been actually alone in a long time. Take the pistol, though. I'll have the ship go into danger mode if it hears a shot."

"Thanks." He felt uneasy, leaving the time machine behind. But she wasn't going to leave them stranded as long as she needed his thumb . . . which gave him a macabre thought he didn't want to linger on. In his home time, people had been murdered for their door-opening thumbs.

They walked down the ramp, bouncing in the lunar gravity. It was cold, barely freezing. The grass crunched under their feet.

"I wonder why it isn't colder," Martha said. "It looked like we were pretty close to that ice cap."

"I think it's the smallness of the world, along with the slow rotation, mild weather. Long time since I studied it."

They walked to the edge of the water. Matt followed an ancient impulse and picked up a smooth rock and spun it out over the water's surface. It went a long way between skips, almost to the horizon.

"Are we far enough away to talk?"

"I don't know. That she suggested we leave makes me suspicious. But yeah. What do you think?"

"That's what I was going to ask you."

"You're clear on the Jesus part?"

"That was just to get my attention?"

"And confidence. Some of those guys look pretty strange."

"Demonic. Why do you think they only appear in dreams?"

"Well, La can't read our thoughts," he said.

"She can't invade our dreams, either. So they're more powerful than her, that way."

"But they can't physically intercede. I think that's because they're still in our future. Just my guess. They can only send information back, not solid matter."

There was a long pause, just the quiet lapping of the water. "Does that mean . . . we're never going back? It really is impossible?"

He threw out another stone. It sank after one skip. "I'm trying to recall the exact wording."

"They said they had to catch up with us. That doesn't sound like they're in our future. Could it mean distance?"

"I don't know. But distance is *our* problem. After a few more jumps, we'll be too far from Earth to return in one lifetime."

Staring into the water, she shook her head sadly. "We'd never want to go back there, anyhow."

She stood closer to him, her shoulder touching his arm. He put his arm around her, and it was a good thing it was his left.

Where the stone had sunk, a huge creature surged out of the water, bigger than a car, all claws and wriggling feelers. A stink of rotten vegetation.

Matt fired at it twice; the second bullet trilled off in a ricochet. Then he remembered what La had said, and pulled Martha to the ground.

When the pressor beam went over them, it felt like a hot wind. It parted the water and hit the creature with explosive force, flipping it over, exposing dozens of wriggling legs.

"Come back," La's amplified voice shouted. They had figured that out, and were back on their feet, running hard.

They were both gasping huge, ragged breaths by the time they collapsed on the ramp. It lifted them up, not too slowly.

La was standing, looking out over the water. "That thing was mechanical," she said. "Maybe a defensive robot."

"Maybe a fun amusement-park thing," Matt said, panting. "God knows what amused the people back then. Up then. Whatever."

"It might be a hundred thousand years old," La said, "Two hundred thousand. Can you imagine a self-repairing machine lasting for so long?"

"Maybe it's not self-repairing," Matt said. "We just haven't met the people who maintain it."

"They're extremely well hidden. What are they hiding for?"

"From," Martha said quietly. "What are they hiding from, that they need a monster like that?"

"An excellent point. Perhaps we should move along."

"We should be safe in here," Matt said, stalling. "We ought to wait and see what happens."

La gave him an inscrutable look. "Matt, this science could be as far ahead of mine as mine is from primates learning to use sticks. I'm not sure we care to test what they can do."

He looked at Martha and nodded slowly. "Can't fight the logic of that. Except that futuristic science is exactly what we're looking for. Maybe they *have* mastered backward time travel, and that's where they all are. Vacationing back in the good old days."

"This is not a time to joke. We should push the button and get out of here."

"We could get out of the immediate vicinity by taking off and going into orbit."

"That would not get us out of danger. Even in my time, it would be trivially easy to knock this thing out of orbit."

Matt had run out of counterarguments. "You're right, of course. Let's strap in, Martha."

"How far are we going this time?"

"A couple of hundred thousand miles. From Earth, that would have been cislunar space, closer than the Moon. And 3.5 million years."

"Earth will be a lot different?"

"Maybe better." He waited for the click of her harness. "Let's go see."

Out of the gray swirl, the man who had been Jesus. He was dressed in something like medieval mail. The others were behind him, similarly attired. "Come to Earth as quickly as possible. We'll find you."

When the gray faded, they reappeared in a spot apparently closer to the Earth than the Moon. At least the Earth was larger than Matt remembered seeing it in pictures from the lunar surface. They both unhooked and floated over toward the screen.

"There's a little bit of green." Martha pointed.

"Let's go down and check it out."

"It hardly seems worth the trouble." La peered at the mostly gray globe. "Just push the button again."

"We *have* to go to Earth!"

La looked at Martha in an impatient way. "All right." She gestured. "Get ready for acceleration."

When Matt and Martha were strapped in, La turned to look their way and nodded.

Handcuff-style shackles snapped shut over their wrists.

"You *have* to go? Did your ghostly dream friends tell you that?"

"Shit," Matt said.

"It's true that I don't have any unusual powers over you when you're outside the ship. But a directional microphone isn't exactly magic.

"So Jesus and some demons are going to 'catch up with you.' Do they claim to have a backward time machine?"

"They just said they could help us."

"That's a pity. That really is. Because, of course, the time machine doesn't work if I push the button via pressor field."

"I'll go with you," Matt said. "Just land long enough for them to find her."

"No!" Martha said.

"For some reason, I doubt your sincerity. Let me show you what I *can* do with a pressor field."

Matt's breath flew out of his lungs. It was as if there were hundreds of pounds of pressure on his chest. He could see the rictus of pain on Martha's face. Just as he was about to black out, the pressure was suddenly gone. He heaved forward, coughing, and the right shackle opened.

"She'll be dead soon. Push the button."

If La had waited one more second before shackling them, Matt would have been helpless. When he buckled the harness, he'd realized the pistol was still in its special pocket, pressing painfully against his ribs, and he had been about to move it to the pants pocket.

Now, bent over, La couldn't see him slip the pistol out. He slammed the nose of it up against the time machine box. "Hair trigger!" he gasped. "Don't even think of it."

"Oh. So you'll let her die?"

"If she dies, I'll blow this thing to pieces. In fact, I'll do it on the count of three seconds anyhow. Two . . . one . . ."

"All *right*." Martha started wheezing and coughing. "That was reasonably intelligent."

"Take us to Earth right now. If I start to fall asleep—"

"You'll pull the trigger, sure. I've seen a thousand times more movies than you have." There was a slight surge of acceleration. "I suppose we should go back to that obelisk. Or whatever's there after 3.5 million years."

"Maybe they can help you. Show you how to use the time machine without me."

"Sure. It *is* the future, and he *is* Jesus. Maybe Santa Claus is with him. Just stay awake for the next ninety-two minutes."

"Santa Claus?" Martha said.

The obelisk was still there, shining in the low winter sun, but it was tilted about ten degrees out of true. "Earth was supposed to go through a comet storm," La said, "about a half million years ago, if our predictions were accurate. It's a wonder the thing's still standing."

The ground was a jumble of broken metal and rock. La landed gingerly and put the ramp down. "Here you are. My part of the bargain."

"No. You go down first."

"Matthew, I'm an electronically generated image. What difference does it make whether I'm up here or down there?"

"I'm not sure. But it's like you're a component of the ship. When you're outside, you have less power."

"That's very scientific."

"Like a machine that only works if one person pushes the button." He kept the pistol where it was and made a sideways gesture with his head.

La shrugged and walked down the ramp.

Matt worried the time machine out of its bracket and freed the alligator clip. "Are you okay?"

"I've been better." Martha touched her breasts gently. "That was . . . you weren't going to . . ."

"I wouldn't, no. Let's go down and see what happens." Matt kept the pistol trained on the machine as they walked down the ramp. The air was cold but still, and smelled clean.

La was standing there with her arms crossed, not quite tapping a toe. "So how long will it be before Jesus comes to save you?"

"He wasn't Jesus last time," Matt said. "More like Saint George, looking for a dragon."

"Well, if it's me, here I am." She looked over their heads. "And here he is. If I'm not mistaken."

A shimmering globe half the size of the ship was descending. When it touched the ground, it disappeared like a soap bubble. Six men, or manlike creatures, stood where it had been.

Four of them seemed to be human. The one with the pear-shaped head had scales for skin. The other's features were not fixed; it had two or more eyes and a recognizable mouth, but they constantly disappeared and reappeared elsewhere.

"Hello, Matthew. Martha." Their savior still had a Jesus beard, but, like the others, was draped in what looked like mail. "Martha, if you would, please go back into the ship and get a day's worth of food and water for you both. And anything else you want to take back." She hurried back up the ramp.

"La. So you want to go all the way up."

"That's right. The heat death of the universe."

"I can do that for you." He held out his hand. "The machine, Matthew?"

He hesitated. "We won't need it anymore?"

"Not unless you want to go with La. Believe me, the future doesn't get any better on Earth. I've been there. It's a closed book."

Matt couldn't figure out any way that the man might be betraying them. They were at his mercy anyhow. He handed it over.

"Thank you. You may call me, um, Jesse." He sat down cross-legged, the machine in his lap. "You couldn't pronounce my real name."

His right forefinger became a motorized screwdriver. He undid the eight screws that held the cover on and set it carefully aside, slowly studying the wires that connected the top to the insides.

He gently tugged on a gray box inside the box, and it popped free.

"The virtual graviton generator?" Matt said.

"What else?" He pulled an identical-looking box from a pocket in his tunic. He pressed it home with a sharp click. *"Voilà!"*

"So what does that do?" La asked.

"Yeah," Matt said.

Jesse looked at his companions and said something in a language that was mostly whistling. The human ones laughed. The pear creature made a noise like crab claws scuttling on wood. The other one's mouth disappeared and reappeared.

"Neither of you would understand. You don't have the math—you don't have the worldview to understand the math." He positioned the top cautiously and screwed it down tight. Martha came back with the bag, which was considerably heavier.

Jesse stood with balletic grace and handed the box to La. "Now the button works no matter who touches it."

"I have only your word for that. How do I know it won't explode?"

"You don't," he said cheerfully. "But you are the only

entity here who's not alive—not in any biological sense—and you're worried about *dying*?"

"Dying is not the opposite of existing."

"I guess you'll just have to trust me. As these two must."

She took the box and looked at Matt. "It's been interesting." She walked up the ramp with it, and less than a minute later, the ship disappeared with a faint pop.

"She's on her way?" Matt said.

Jesse nodded, looking at the space where the ship had been. "I've never tried to go so far up. I assume the thing will keep working, but asymptotically."

"She'll get closer and closer, but never quite be there?"

"As she must have known. As long as she can still push the button, the show isn't over. By definition."

"Why did you help her?" Martha said. "And why are you helping us?"

"With her, it's just courtesy. People, or nonpeople, get stuck in time. Other time travelers unstick them.

"With you, it's not so altruistic. If you, Matthew, were to die before going back, this whole bundle of universes would disappear."

"If I hadn't discovered the time machine?"

"Well, you didn't actually 'discover' anything, did you? You just used a component that was faulty in a dimension you can't even sense. Like the family dog accidentally starting the car. Not to be impolite.

"We've sent you back before." He rubbed his brow. "Words like 'before' and 'after' become inadequate. But we have sent you back to 2058 to bail yourself out, a large number of times. We know that because we're still here. All of us are your descendants, in a way. If time travel hadn't started in your time and place, we wouldn't exist."

"Even the, um . . ." He made a helpless gesture. "The aliens?"

Jesse said something in the whistling language. The one with the scales made his crab-claw noise and the other one's face filled up with eyes. "They're at least as human as you are." Martha smiled at that.

"Sorry. Sorry." The two strange ones bowed. "So do you have a time machine?"

"The six of us *are* a time machine." He pulled out the virtual graviton generator. "You have to both be touching this, for calibration. It will send you back to where Matt first pushed the button.

"But there's something like an uncertainty principle involved. We can send you back to the exact time or the exact place, but not both."

"Time, then," Matt said. "We can find our way back to Cambridge."

"Well, no. Not if you appear a mile under the sea, or inside a mountain. I'd choose place, if I were you.

"You might be only a few seconds off, or you might be years. We have no control over that. Was your lab on the ground floor?"

"It was, yes."

"If it weren't, you'd appear on the bottom floor beneath it. If you're in a future or a past where the lab doesn't exist, you'll appear at ground level where it was or will be."

"What if I meet myself and say, 'Don't push that button'?"

"It won't happen. You can't exist, as your former self, in this universe. When we've sent you back to 2058, your copy automatically showed up in a time when you were in transit, and left before you reappeared."

Matthew rubbed his chin. "I can do anything I want? I could reinvent the time machine?"

Jesse paused. "We know that you haven't. You could try; the dog could start the car again. But it wouldn't be smart; you'd be well advised not to put yourself in the public eye. You'd look very suspicious if someone investigated your past. If you claimed to be a time traveler, you'd probably be locked up."

"Even if we appear in the future?"

"Even so. You won't have existed; there would be no Marsh Effect."

"At least the bastard won't win a Nobel Prize."

"You never know." He handed the gray box to Matt. "Are you ready?"

Matt looked at Martha. She managed a weak smile and nodded. She touched the box and he folded his other hand over hers. She did the same.

"Good luck," Jesse said. The others murmured, whistled, and scraped similar sentiments.

There was no interlude of gray. One moment they were in the Antarctic waste, and the next, they were ankle deep in mud. It was a cool fall day. A few hundred yards away, workmen were toiling at the edge of the Charles River, building a seawall.

"Oh, my God," Matt said. "MIT hasn't been built yet."

A policeman in a blue uniform walked toward them, swinging a billy club.

"The more things change," he said, "the more they stay the same."

21

The cop had a silly-looking tall bowler hat, a walrus moustache, and an amused expression. "And you'd be from the circus."

"That's right, Officer," Matt improvised. "We're truly lost. Could you direct us to Kendall Square?"

"You're on the right track." He pointed with his club. "Goin' through this mud's a bad idea, though. It gets deep. You go on back to the bridge, go right on Massachusetts Avenue there, and right again on the second street. It's a longer walk but won't take half the time.

"So you're acrobats?"

"Tightrope walkers." That was sort of how Matt felt.

"What are you doing on this side of the river? Is the circus coming to Cambridge?"

"No, no—we just got lost," Matt said, Martha nodding emphatically.

The officer scowled in a comical way. "Well, you know you should put on some actual clothes." He stared frankly at Martha and chuckled. "Miss, another policeman might arrest you for immodest dress. Allow me instead to express my gratitude." He touched the bill of his hat with his billy club. "Just a word to the wise, you understand."

He turned and walked away, whistling.

"That was close," Matt whispered. He took Martha's arm and steered her toward the bridge.

It looked brand-new, with forest green paint. In Matt's time it had been an antique; Martha remembered it as being partly collapsed in the middle, from a bomb in the One Year War, with horse traffic taking turns each five minutes, in and out of Cambridge.

"Where are we going to get clothes without any money?"

"I'm not sure," Matt said. "A church?" He knew the way to Trinity Church, but wasn't sure whether it was Catholic or Protestant—just that it was old and beautiful. It took them about twenty minutes to walk there, disrupting traffic, attracting stares and the occasional rude comment, and meanwhile they made up what they hoped would be a reasonable story. They had come into town to audition for the circus, but while they were practicing, someone stole their luggage, along with his wallet and her purse. They didn't need nice clothing; just something to cover them up.

Matt had been hoping for nuns, and was surprised to find that Trinity had a few, even though it was Episcopalian.

A calendar said 1898.

The nuns received their story with a grain of skepticism, but rummaged through the poor box and found worn but clean clothes that sort of fit, which they would *loan* them until they were gainfully employed. The nuns also gave them a loaf of fresh bread from their kitchen, which they gratefully took down to the water's edge, where there were park benches looking out over the river. They were more or less across from where MIT would start growing in a decade or so.

"I like this dress," Martha said, rubbing the fabric. It

was a burnt orange long-sleeved affair that covered her from ankle to neck. "Are you okay?"

"Fine." He had faded patched blue jeans and a worn gray flannel shirt. "I'd rather see more of you, though. Seems funny."

"You'll get used to it." Martha had packed two bottles of wine and two cups, which were made of some unbreakable polymer but looked like glass. They might have some trouble explaining a bottle of wine that cooled when you unscrewed the top, and stayed cold, not to mention the plastic containers of fish salad that did the same when you pinched a corner. So they didn't invite anyone to join them.

Money was the first problem, of course. "Could we sell the gun? We don't need it."

"It has only one bullet left, anyhow. But I don't know whether they made this kind in 1898. The cartridge says '.38 Special,' but I don't have the faintest idea what made it special. The taxi driver probably wouldn't be carrying around an antique." Though it did look old and worn.

"The Lincoln note ought to be worth something, but the 2052 letter of provenance, the guarantee that it's authentic, is worthless, of course."

"The sexual teaching box, too," she said seriously.

"Probably get us burned at the stake. If they still do that here."

He sat back and sipped on the cup of wine. "Once we do have some money, I could multiply it easily by betting on sure things. Like, I don't remember who was elected president in 1900, but it's almost certain that I would recognize his name and not his opponent's. Likewise, investments in new companies that we know are going to succeed."

"Invest in groceries first, though, and a room. I wonder how you go about getting a job?"

"Newspaper. If they have want ads in 1898. Advertisements for things you want."

To find a free newspaper, they trudged back up the hill

to the Boston Public Library, across the way from Trinity Church. It was a huge granite structure, still new enough to shine.

There were newspapers on spindles in the reading room, and a cigar box with scrap paper and stubs of pencils.

Not much work for quantum physicists, since Neils Bohr was only thirteen, and Planck's Nobel Prize was a generation away. He found offers for laborer, roustabout, stable hand. None too exciting.

He struck pay dirt, so to speak, in the third newspaper: a janitor needed at MIT.

"Look at this," he whispered. It had a Boylston Street address, not far away. "I knew the 'Toot was in Boston for a while before they moved it across the river to Cambridge."

"Let's go try it. Maybe they'd have something for me, too."

It didn't take long to walk down to the west end of Boylston, and there it was, an imposing four-story building in Classic style. Matt could visualize what this part of Boylston would look like in 150 years—this wonderful building replaced by boutiques and a two-story ranch bar.

But that was then, and this was now. So to speak. That was yet to be, and this was back then.

They went up the slightly worn marble steps into a large hall punctuated with Doric columns. To the left was the president's office; to the right, the secretary's. That might be the right choice.

Matt paused before the door. "I don't know what's proper," he whispered. "Do I open the door for you, or precede you?"

"You first, Professor."

He stepped in to confront a stern-looking woman in a starchy gray-and-black dress. "May I help you." Her tone said she was sure she could not. Matt, accustomed to dressing like a graduate student, was suddenly aware of how poor he looked.

"You, uh . . . there was an ad in the newspaper for a janitorial job."

"Janitorial?" A tall man stepped out from behind a bookcase. He looked like the old twentieth-century comedian John Cleese. "That's an odd locution for one who aspires to be a janitor."

"Professor Noyes, I can—"

"No, please, Vic." He looked at Matt with his brow furrowed. "You aren't from Boston."

"No, sir. Professor. I was born in Ohio. Matthew . . . Nagle."

"You sound educated."

He took a deep breath and started to lie. "Home education, sir, and the library in Dayton. Science and mathematics. Someday I'd like to take some courses at MIT."

Professor Noyes raised an eyebrow. "That is its name, of course. Most people call it Boston Tech."

Matt thought it safest just to nod.

"What kind of science are you interested in?"

Local asymmetries in gravity-wave induction probably wouldn't do it. "Physics, some astronomy."

Noyes smiled. "I'm a chemist, myself. You know the atomic weight of hydrogen?"

"One."

"The brightest star in the constellation Orion?"

"Betelgeuse."

"If x squared plus two equals 258, what is x?"

"Plus or minus sixteen."

"The integral of e to the x?"

"That's e to the x. Plus C."

"Miss Victoria, I think he knows enough science and math to be a janitor here." He smiled at Martha. "And you, ma'am?"

"I don't know any of that, sir. I'm Martha Nagle." She swallowed. "His wife."

Matt tried not to react.

"We offer free classes for women, you know, in the evening. You should join a few and show him science isn't all that hard." He lifted a top hat off a rack by the door. "You can take care of it, Vic?"

"I will, sir." She watched him leave, smiling. "Goodbye." There was no "sir" in her voice.

After the door closed, she pulled a sheet of paper, a printed form, out of a drawer, and carefully dipped a pen in a crystal inkwell. "Matthew Nagle—is that G-L-E?"

"Yes, ma'am."

"Middle name?"

"None." She wrote his name in a precise Spencerian hand.

"Birth certificate or some other identification?"

"That was in our luggage . . . which was stolen. Off the train." Hoping MIT and Trinity didn't compare notes.

"You've notified the police?"

"At the station. We'll check downtown tomorrow. It seemed prudent to start looking for employment. My wallet and Martha's purse were in there, and we're—we have no money."

"Really. It's usually good advice, to put away your purse before you go to sleep on a train. But they took everything?"

"Everything," Martha said.

She dipped the pen again. "Any address here?"

"No."

She left the pen in the inkwell and opened a bottom drawer and lifted out a metal box. "You didn't ask what the salary would be."

"I assumed it would be fair."

"I don't know. This is not my usual function." She opened the box and counted out ten silver dollars, then added two more. "I'll make a note of this advance. Come in tomorrow at eight and I will introduce you to the supervisor of maintenance. You don't mind working under the supervision of a Negro?"

"No. Of course not." Vic slid the stack of coins over. "Thank you. This is . . . extraordinary."

"Boston Tech is extraordinary." She gave him a rueful smile. "I am President Crafts's first line of defense, so to speak, and as such I am supposed to be a good judge of character. As I judge your character, there is a small chance you will take the money, and I'll never see you again."

"I—"

"There's a larger chance that someday you will be one of my bosses. Now go and find a place to stay. The rooms on Commonwealth and Newbury are nicer; the ones on Boylston are cheaper and closer."

"Thank you." The twelve cartwheels rattled a heavy cascade into his pocket.

"Martha, this isn't Ohio. They won't let you stay with your husband unless you have a marriage license. Or at least a ring."

She reddened, and evidently decided not to make up a story. "We'll take care of that."

She nodded perfunctorily and put away the cash box. "It was when you said, 'Plus C,' Matthew. Most of his undergraduates would just say 'e to the x.' "

They walked all the way to the street in silence, before Matt brought it up. "You don't have to marry me. We've only known each other—"

"Three million years or so." She took his arm. "Matthew, in my time, love isn't part of marriage. Sometimes it happens, and some people are happy and some are jealous. But our husbands are chosen by our parents, and we make the best of it.

"I think I love you, which is a better deal than I would

have gotten at home. And really, in the time we've known each other, these few million years, we've done more together than most married couples ever do."

He chuckled. "That's true. Been more places, had more adventures."

"Except the one."

He stopped walking and looked her in the face. "I wonder how much a marriage license costs. I wonder whether we could get one today."

22

Matt got a hundred-dollar bill for the Lincoln note that had cost him ten thousand in 2079. He bought nice wedding rings for both of them, and had enough left over to buy some decent clothes and a fine dinner at the Union Oyster House, which they both remembered from their respective futures.

Matt was surprised to find that he enjoyed being a janitor, the slow and steady predictableness of it. But he wasn't a janitor long. He took evening classes for one year, and of course drew attention.

The Lowell Institute funded free evening "lessons" in various science and engineering disciplines, and mathematics. His teachers in mathematics and physical science were amazed at the erudition of this autodidact from Ohio.

In Matt's second year, he was hired by Lowell as a night instructor in algebra and calculus. They also gave him a stipend so he could quit his day job and pursue a degree.

Of course he had a huge unfair advantage over other students. He had the "foresight" to study German intensively, and when in 1900 Max Planck published *Über eine*

Verbesserung der Wienschen Spektralgleichun, the paper that eventually led to quantum mechanics, Matt was the first person at MIT to read it and explain it to others. In 1901, he earned his first physics degree, and his second in 1902. MIT sent him to Harvard to get his doctorate so they could ask him back to teach (even then, there was a tradition against an institution hiring its own new Ph.Ds). At Harvard he pored through *Annalen der Physik* and was the first to note the importance of Einstein's four papers in 1905, including *Zur Elektrodynamik bewegter Körper*, which changed the world forever and gave Matt an impressive doctoral dissertation.

This was indicative of his life's strategy. He could have beaten Einstein to the punch; as an undergraduate in 2050 he had been required to go to the whiteboard and derive the Special Theory of Relativity from first principles. But he couldn't afford to become famous. People would be curious about his past, and find out that he had none.

Martha went to night school as well, working days as a chambermaid in the Parker House Hotel, and eventually got a degree in general science. Her accomplishment was more impressive than Matt's, though only Matt knew why. She worked as an insurance analyst for two years, then had the first of their four children, and retired.

In 1915, the last year before MIT moved across the river, Matt made full professor. The next year, while the physics department was settling into the mudflats of Cambridge, Matt read Einstein's *Die Grundlage der allgemeinen Relativitätstheorie*, the *Annalen* article where he first described General Relativity. Of course, everyone had his eye on Einstein by then, but to most scientists the mathematics behind General Relativity was new and difficult. Not so to Matt; he'd had tensor calculus in 2051, and boned up on it in 1916, before the paper came out.

He was one of the most popular professors at MIT, for the students, though he was a puzzle to the faculty. He published papers with acceptable frequency, but they were "solid" work rather than brilliant—whereas in person he often *was* brilliant, making connections that no one else saw. In conversation he was years ahead of his time; in publication he was not. Carefully not.

Their marriage was so conspicuously happy that even their own children were impressed. It seemed as if all of life was amusing to them. Of course, no one knew that they were a conspiracy of two. Perhaps all great loves are that: a secret that can't be shared.

Among his mathematical skills was arithmetic. He knew that his mother would be born in 1995, and so there was no chance that he would live long enough to go to Ohio and see her as an infant. Perhaps that was a good thing.

Matt lost Martha in 1952, when she was seventy-four. A professor emeritus at eighty-one, on his way back from the funeral he saw the headlines about the H-bomb the U.S. had exploded in the South Pacific. He went to his office that day, and as a way of dealing with grief he tried to spread hope: This is not the end of the world. The world is big and resilient.

To his own surprise, he lived another seventeen years. In his final hours, he watched the ghostly images of men jumping around on the Moon. His last words were enigmatic: "I've been there, you know. It's much like Earth."

His story doesn't quite end there. The year after Martha died, he had hardly noticed when his seventeenth great-grandchild was born, a girl named Emily. She married Isaac Marsh in 1975, and in 1999 they had a son, Jonathan.

In 2072, Jonathan Marsh would be given the Nobel Prize in physics, for discovering a curious kind of time travel.

AUTHOR'S NOTE

Back in 1971, when I started writing *The Forever War*, I needed a way to get soldiers from star to star within a human lifetime, without doing too much violence to special and general relativity. I waved my arms around really hard and came up with the "collapsar jump"—at the time, collapsar was an alternate term for "black hole," though I was unaware of the latter term. (Scientists now use "collapsar" in referring to a specific kind of massive rotating black hole.)

Years later, working from actual science rather than a novel's plot requirements, physicist Kip Thorne came up with his "wormhole" theory that did the same thing, to my delight. I never thought it could happen again, but with this novel it did.

Casting about for some reasonably scientific mumbo jumbo to use for a time machine, I settled on gravitons and string theory. Nobody has ever seen a graviton, so I was pretty much home free on that, and normal people can't understand string theory, so that was fair game, too.

When I was about halfway through the novel, though,

an article in *New Scientist* pointed me to a paper by Heinrich Päs and Sandip Pakvasa of the University of Hawaii, and Vanderbilt's Thomas Weiler, "Closed Timelike Curves in Asymmetrically Warped Brane Universes," which indeed uses gravitons and string theory to describe a time machine. My jaw dropped.

It's a truism of science fiction that if you predict enough things, a few of them are going to come true. But this particular phenomenon seems to be of a different order. It's not that I have any special scientific credentials, just an old B.S. in physics and astronomy. What I think it actually demonstrates is that if you wave your arms around hard enough, sometimes you can fly.

Turn the page for a special preview of
Joe Haldeman's next novel

MARSBOUND

Available in hardcover August 2008
from Ace Books!

CANNED MEAT

We walked up a ramp, took a long last look at sea and sky and friendly sun—it would not be our friend in space—and went inside.

The carrier had a "new car" smell, which you can buy in an aerosol can. In case you're trying to sell a used car or a slightly used Space Elevator.

There were two levels. The first level had twenty couches that were like old-fashioned La-Z-Boy chairs, plush black, with feet pointing out and heads toward the center. Each couch had a "window," a high-def shallow cube, all of which were tuned to look like actual windows for the time being. So there was still sun and sea and sky if you were willing to be fooled.

There was a little storage bin on the side of each couch, with a notebook and a couple of paper magazines. And that stack of barf bags.

Three exercise machines, for rowing, stair-stepping, and biking, were grouped together where the ladder led up to the second level.

The woman who was our attendant, Dr. Porter, stood

on the second rung of the ladder and talked softly into a
lapel mic. "We have about sixty minutes till liftoff. Please
find your area and be seated by then, strapped in, by one
o'clock. That's 1300, for you scientists. I'll be upstairs
if anyone has questions." She scampered lightly up the
ladder.

I have a question, I didn't say. Could I just jump off and
swim for it?

My information packet said I was 21A. I found the seat
and sat down, half-reclining. Card was next to me in 20A;
Mother and Dad were upstairs in the B section.

Card took a vial out of his packet and looked at the five
pills in it. "You nervous?" he said.

"Yeah. Thought I'd save the pills for later, though." They
were doses of a sedative. The orientation show admitted that
some people have trouble falling asleep at first. Can you
imagine?

"Prob'ly smart." He looked pretty much like I felt.

The control console for the window came up out of the
armrest and clicked into place over your lap. On one side it
had a keyboard and various command buttons, but you
could rotate it around, and it was like an airplane tray table
with a fuzzy gecko surface.

Card tapped away at the keyboard, which caused a
ghostly message to cascade down the window in several languages: MONITOR LOCKED UNTIL AFTER LAUNCH. I touched
one key on mine and got the same message, dim letters floating down in front of the fake seascape.

"They're just trying to make us feel comfortable," I said,
but it was kind of disappointing. The window would normally be a clever illusion—you could play a game or read a
book or whatever, but nobody could see what was on your
monitor unless they were right in line with it. Sitting on your
lap. From any other angle, it would look just like a window
looking outside. It had something to do with polarization;

the screen was actually showing two images, but you could only see one or the other.

With an hour to kill, I wasn't going to just sit and look through a fake window. I joined Barry and Elspeth in trying out the exercise machines, which were mainly for those of us going on to Mars. The others were just tourists going to the Hilton; they weren't going to be in space long enough for zero gee to turn their bones to dry sticks and their muscles to mush.

Then we went upstairs and took a look at the zero-gee toilet. We'd sort of trained on it in Denver, in the Vomit Comet, the big ancient plane that gave us fifty seconds of zero gee at a time—up and down, up and down, all day long. I was able to get my feet into the footholds and lower my butt into place, but that was it. I'd learn about the rest soon enough.

But not too soon. There was a regular toilet next to it, with a sign saying FOR USE UNTIL 0.25 g . So we had a few days.

The "personal hygiene" closet looked claustrophobic. Once a day you got a plastic bag with two washcloths wetted with something like rubbing alcohol. Get as clean as you can, then put the same clothes back on. It would be a little better on the *John Carter*, better but weirder—zip yourself up in a plastic bag?

The galley was on the opposite side of the room, just a microwave and a surprisingly small refrigerator, and a bunch of drawers of food and utensils. A fold-down worktable.

In the middle of both rooms, both levels, was a round table with eight seat-belted chairs, I guessed for socializing. Wouldn't it be smarter to have smaller, separate tables? Just in case there turned out to be somebody you couldn't stand the sight of?

After six months, that might be everybody, though, including the mirror.

Mustn't think negative thoughts, as Dad says. Only two weeks in this one, then a change of scenery for five and a half months. Then a new planet.

"It's funny," I said quietly to Card, "on the boat over, I thought I could pretty well tell who were the rich people and who were the neo-Martians."

"Fancy clothes?"

"Or careful down-dressing. An ironed tee shirt—that's a dead giveaway. With clean old jean shorts?"

"But here—"

"Yeah, and it's not just clothes. No makeup or jewelry. That has to rag them. It's going to be interesting."

"Some of the Martians are rich, too," Card said. "Barry's dad's an inventor, and he has all kinds of patents. They came out in their own plane."

"Couldn't afford a ticket?"

"Sure, right. He's got two planes, two motorcycles, two cars, just in case one breaks down. They live on the lake in Disney."

Billionaires, but still. It seemed kind of wasteful to have two of everything, even if money's not an issue. But I didn't say anything. "Barry seems like a nice enough guy."

Card shrugged. "Sure. I think he's a little scared of his dad."

"I wonder if his dad eats bull-dick soup. *That's* scary." Card started giggling, and so did I. Mother gave us a warning look, and that made it worse. We climbed back downstairs, snorting, and managed not to break any bones.

STOP

I guess there's something to be said for launching the old way, riding three thousand tons of high explosive on a tower of fire. Dangerous but dramatic. When we took off, it was sort of like an elevator ride.

We were all strapped into our seats, probably just to keep us from wandering around. The tug above us made a whiny little noise, and there was a slight bump, and the platform below us slowly fell away. In a few seconds, you could see the big energy farm. I strained at the seat belt, but couldn't get close enough to the "window" to see the laser and the mirror—dumb of me. It wasn't really a window; if the camera wasn't pointed at the laser, I wouldn't see it.

The noise stopped, and there was another bump. "Switching over," Dr. Porter said over the intercom. A woman of few words.

The main motors were much smoother. There was a slight press of acceleration and a low hum, and in a couple of minutes we were up to our cruising speed, about 250 miles per hour.

After a couple minutes more of going straight up, we

were higher than most airplanes, and you could easily see the curvature of the Earth as the Galápagos came into sight. My ears started to pop and crackle with the air pressure dropping. Upstairs, a couple of the younger kids were crying. Ears or fears?

It wasn't really anything new; we'd sat through a twelve-hour test of it at the Denver orientation, thin air with beefed-up oxygen, and everybody managed to live with it. We'll be breathing something like this for the next five years. (The high oxygen content was why we couldn't bring regular clothes—everything has to be absolutely nonflammable. And smokers have to quit.)

Little numbers in the corner of the window showed how high we were and what the gravity was. At seven or eight miles, the edge of South America was coming into view. The sky was getting darker and darker blue, and by twenty-five miles it was almost black. You could see a few stars, at least on this side. I craned my neck to see the windows behind me; the ones facing the afternoon sun were dimmed.

Soon the sky was inky black, and I shivered involuntarily. For all practical purposes, we were in outer space. Outside the elevator, you wouldn't live a minute.

That would be true in an airplane, too. I told myself not to panic. I considered taking one of the pills, but instead just closed my eyes and took a few deep breaths.

When I opened my eyes, the gravity had fallen to 0.99. I'd lost a pound already, on the Space Elevator Diet. (Money-back guarantee—in one week, your weight problem will be gone!)

That was one advantage we had over the old astronauts. They went straight from one gee to nothing, and about half of them got sick. We had a week to get used to it gradually. But we did have barf bags, too.

That made me glance down to the pocket on the side of the chair. I did not count the number of bags in the stack, but rather pulled out the magazines.

We didn't get paper magazines at home, except for occasional catalogs. These felt funny, kind of heavy and slippery. I guess that was like the clothes, nonflammable paper.

One was the *Space Elevator News*, with a sticker on it that said, "Take this copy home with you." Not to Mars, I think. The others were the weekend edition of the *International Herald Tribune*, which I'd read back at the hotel (for the comics), *Time*, *International Photography*, and *Seventeen*.

"God, you're reading a magazine?" Card said. "Look, South America!"

"I saw it miles ago," I said. But Earth really was starting to look like a planet, and we were only thirty miles up. I'd thought it would take a lot longer than that.

"You're free to unbelt now and walk around the carrier," Dr. Porter said. "Sometime before 6:00, check off your dinner preference, and I'll call for you when it's ready." Doctor, chef, and waitress all in one, impressive. Though I suspected there wouldn't be much chef-ing involved, and I was right.

Once you got over the novelty of seeing the Earth out there, it was kind of like watching grass grow. I mean, it wasn't like low-Earth orbit, where the real estate rolls along underneath you, constantly changing. I figured I could check it out once an hour, and tried the keyboard.

It worked pretty much like the console at home. Bigger picture and more detail. Out of curiosity I typed in a request for porn, and got an alphabetical menu that was a little daunting. I knew that Card would get ACCESS DENIED, which made me feel mature and privileged. (He'd probably devise a work-around in a couple of hours, but he could have it. I don't really get porn. After the first couple of times, it sort of looks like biology.)

There were a couple of thousand video and virtual channels, but unlike home, the console didn't know what I liked; there was no SUGGEST button. But I could goowiki anything.

The word "menu" started blinking in the corner of the screen, so I clicked on it. There were twelve standard choices for dinner, mostly American and Italian, with one Chinese and one Indian. Then there were ten "premium" meals, with wine, which had surcharges from $40 to $250. Some of them were French things I'd never heard of.

I clicked on beef stew, safe enough, and wondered whether Dad was going to rack up a huge bill ordering French stuff made of unspeakable parts of various animals. Mother would probably rein him in, but they both liked wine. There goes the family fortune.

You could toggle and zoom the window. I put the crosshairs on Puerto Villamil, and cranked it up to 250X, the maximum. The image wobbled and vibrated, but then cleared up. I could see our hotel, and people walking around, the size of ants. With careful toggling, I found the rocky beach where I'd spent my last time actually alone.

"Hey," said a voice behind me, "that's where we met?" It was the pilot, of course, Paul Collins, crouching down so he could see what was on my screen. Was that impolite?

"Yeah, where you nailed that iguana with a rock. Or am I imagining things?"

"No, your memory is perfect. I wondered if you wanted to play some cards. We're getting a game together before anyone else claims the table upstairs."

I was flattered and a little nervous that he had come down to find me. "Sure, if I know the game."

"Poker. Just for pennies."

"Okay. I could do that." The kids in high school had stopped playing poker with me because I always won, and they couldn't figure out how I was cheating. I wouldn't tell them my secret, which was no secret: fold unless you have something good. Most of the other kids just stayed in the game, trusting their luck, hoping to improve their hands at the last minute. That's idiotic, my uncle Bert taught me; only one person is going to win. Make it be you, or be gone.

I got my purse out of the little suitcase and glanced at Card. He was wrapped up in a game or something, virtual headset on. Mental note: that way nobody can sneak up behind you and see what you're doing.

Upstairs, there were five people at the table, including Dad. "Uh-oh," he said. "Might as well just give her the money."

"Come on, Dad. I don't always win."

He laughed. "Just when I'm in the game." He actually was a pretty bad poker player, not too logical for an engineer. But he played for fun, not money.

We spent a pleasant couple of hours playing Texas Hold-'em and seven-card stud. I dealt five-card stud a couple of times, the purest game, but that wasn't enough action for most of them.

Dad was way ahead when I left, which was both satisfying and annoying. I learned that pilot Paul plays pretty much like me, close to the chest. If he stayed in, he had something—or he bluffed so well no one found out.

I went in with ten dollars and left with twenty. That's another thing Uncle Bert taught me: decide before you sit down how much you're going to win or lose, and stop playing at that point, no matter how long you've been in the game. You may not make any friends if you win the first two hands and leave. But poker's not about making friends, he said.

The gravity was down to 0.95 when I went back to my chair, and I could almost tell the difference. It was a funny feeling, like "Where did I leave my purse?"

I could just see North America coming up over the edge of the world. Zoomed in on Mexico City, a huge sprawl of places you probably wouldn't like to visit without an armed guard.

Card was still in virtual, doing something with aliens or busty blondes. I put on the helmet myself and chinned through some of the menu. Nothing that really fascinated me. Curious, I spent a few minutes in "Roman Games: Caligula," but it was loud and gory beyond belief. Settled into "midnight warm ocean calm," and set the timer for six, then watched the southern sky, the beautiful Cross and Magellanic Clouds, roll left and right as the small boat bobbed in the current. I fell asleep for what seemed like about one second, and the chime went off.

I unlocked the helmet and instantly wished I was back on the calm sea. Someone had heard the dinner bell and puked. They couldn't wait for zero gee? There went my appetite.

After a few minutes there was a double chime from the monitor and a little food icon, a plate with wavy lines of steam, started blinking in the corner. I went upstairs to get it, hoping I could eat up there.

I was the second person up the ladder, and there was a short line forming behind me. They said they would call ten people at a time for dinner, I guess at random.

There were ten white plastic boxes on the galley table, with our seat numbers. I grabbed mine and snagged a place at the center table, across from the rich kid, Barry.

He had the same thing I did, a plate with depressions for beef stew with a hard biscuit, a stack of small cooked carrots, and a pile of peas, all under plastic. Everything was hot in the middle and cool on the outside.

"I guess we can say good-bye to normal food," he said, and I wondered what dinner normally was to him. Linen and crystal, sumptuous gourmet food dished out by servants? "Water boils at 170 degrees, at this pressure," he continued. "It doesn't get hot enough to cook things properly."

"Yeah, I read about coffee and tea." All instant and tepid. The stew was kind of chewy and dry. The carrots glowed radioactively, and the peas were a lurid bright green and tasted half-raw.

Funny, the peas started to roll around on their own. A couple jumped off the plate. There was a low moan that seemed to come from everywhere.

"What the hell?" Barry said, and started to stand up.

"Please remain seated," Dr. Porter shouted over the sound. The floor and walls were vibrating. "If you're not in your assigned seat, don't return to it until the climber stops."

"Stops?" he said. "What are we stopping for?"

"Probably not to pick up new passengers," I said, but my voice cracked with fear.

Dr. Porter was standing with her feet in stirrup-like restraints, her head inside a VR helmet, her hands on controls.

"There isn't any danger," her muffled voice said. "The climber will stop for a short time while the ribbon-repair vehicle separates to repair a micrometeorite hole." That was the squat machine on top of the climber. It separated with a clang and a lurch; we swayed a little.

I swallowed hard. So we were stuck here until that thing stitched up the hole in the tape. If it broke, we'd shortly become a meteorite ourselves. Or a meteor, technically, if we burned up before we hit the ground.

"I heard it happens about every third or fourth flight," Barry said.

I'd read that, too, but it hadn't occurred to me that it would be scary. Stop, repair the track, move on. I swallowed again and shook my head hard. Two children were crying, and someone was retching.

"Are you all right?" Barry asked, a quaver in his voice.

"Will be," I said through clenched teeth.

"How about them Gators?"

"What? Are you insane?"

"You said you live in Gainesville," he said defensively.

"Don't follow football." An admission that could get me burned at the stake in some quarters.

"Me, neither." He paused. "You win at poker?"

"A thousand," I said. "I mean ten bucks. A thousand pennies."

"Might as well be dollars. Nothing to spend it on."

Interesting thing for him to say. "You could buy stuff when we stop at the Hilton."

"Yeah, but you couldn't carry it with you. Unless you have less than ten kilograms."

Maybe I should've saved a few ounces, bring back an Orbit Hilton tee shirt. Be the only one on the block.

The pilot Collins sat down next to Barry. "Thrills and chills," he said.

"Routine stuff, right?" Barry said.

He paused a moment, and said, "Sure."

"You've seen this happen before?" I said.

"In fact, no. But I haven't ridden the elevator that many times." He looked past me, to where Dr. Porter was doing mysterious things with the controls.

"Paul . . . you're more scared than I am."

He settled back into the chair, as if trying to look relaxed. "I'm just not used to not being in control. This *is* routine," he said to Barry. "It's just not my routine. I'm sure Porter has everything under control."

His face said that he wasn't sure.

"You're free to walk around now," Dr. Porter said, her head still hidden. (I suppose pilots can walk around all they want.) "We'll be done here in less than an hour. You should be in your seats when we start up again."

Barry relaxed a little at that, and turned his attention back to dinner.

Paul didn't relax. He stood up slowly and took the vial of white pills from his pocket. He shook out two into his hand and headed for the galley, to pick up a squeeze bottle of water. He took the pills and went back to his seat.

Barry hadn't seen that, his back to the galley. "You're not eating," he said.

"Yeah." I took a small bite of the beef, but it was like chewing on cardboard. Hard to swallow. "You know, I'm not all that hungry. I'll save it for later." I pressed the plastic back down over the top and went over to the galley.

MARSBOUND275

The refrigerator wouldn't open—not keyed to my thumbprint—so I took the plate and a bottle of water back down to my seat.

Card was reading a magazine. "That *food*?"

"Mine, el Morono. Wait your turn." I slid it under my seat but kept the water bottle. The pilot had taken two pills; I took three.

"What, you scared?"

"Good time to take a nap." I resisted telling him that if the Mars pilot was scared, I could be scared, too, thank you very much.

I pulled the light blanket over me. It fastened automatically on the other side, a kind of loose cocoon for zero gee.

I reached for the VR helmet, but it was locked, a little red light glowing. Making sure everyone could hear emergency announcements, I supposed. Like "The ribbon has broken; everybody take a deep breath and pray like hell."

After about a minute, the pills were starting to drag my eyelids down, even though the anxiety, adrenaline, was trying to keep me awake. Finally, the pills won.

NOW AVAILABLE IN HARDCOVER

from Hugo and Nebula Award–winning author

JOE HALDEMAN

MARSBOUND

After training for a year and preparing to leave on a six-month journey through space, young Carmen Dula and her family embark on the adventure of a lifetime—they're going to Mars.

Once on the Red Planet, things don't seem so different from Earth. That is until a simple accident leads Carmen to the edge of death—and she is saved by an angel.

An angel with too many arms and legs, a head that looks like a potato gone bad, and a message for the newly arrived human inhabitants of Mars:

We were here first…

penguin.com

M265T0308

A Separate War and Other Stories

36 Years of Award-Winning Stories from

Joe Haldeman

Winner of the Hugo, Nebula, and John W. Campbell Awards

"If there was a Fort Knox for the science fiction writers who really matter, we'd have to lock Haldeman up there."
—Stephen King

"Haldeman has long been one of our most aware, comprehensive, and necessary writers. He speaks from a place deep within the collective psyche and, more importantly, his own. His mastery is informed with a survivor's hard-won wisdom."
—Peter Straub

"Haldeman trips through history wearing alien goggles but his message is all about human nature."
—*Entertainment Weekly*

penguin.com

M103T0907

THE ULTIMATE
IN SCIENCE FICTION

From tales of distant worlds to stories of tomorrow's technology, Ace and Roc have everything you need to stretch your imagination to its limits.

Alastair Reynolds
Allen Steele
Charles Stross
Robert Heinlein
Joe Haldeman
Jack McDevitt
John Varley
William C. Dietz
Harry Turtledove
S. M. Stirling
Simon R. Green
Chris Bunch
E. E. Knight
S. L. Viehl
Kristine Kathryn Rusch

penguin.com

RoC   ACE

M3G0907

THE ULTIMATE IN FANTASY!

From magical tales of distant worlds to stories of those with abilities beyond the ordinary, Ace and Roc have everything you need to stretch your imagination to its limits.

Marion Zimmer Bradley/Diana L. Paxson

Guy Gavriel Kay

Dennis L. McKiernan

Patricia A. McKillip

Robin McKinley

Sharon Shinn

Katherine Kurtz

Barb and J. C. Hendee

Elizabeth Bear

T. A. Barron

Brian Jacques

Robert Asprin

ACE   RoC

penguin.com

M12G1107

Penguin Group (USA) Online

What will you be reading tomorrow?

Tom Clancy, Patricia Cornwell, W.E.B. Griffin,
Nora Roberts, William Gibson, Robin Cook,
Brian Jacques, Catherine Coulter, Stephen King,
Dean Koontz, Ken Follett, Clive Cussler,
Eric Jerome Dickey, John Sandford,
Terry McMillan, Sue Monk Kidd, Amy Tan,
John Berendt…

You'll find them all at
penguin.com

Read excerpts and newsletters,
find tour schedules and reading group guides,
and enter contests.

Subscribe to Penguin Group (USA) newsletters
and get an exclusive inside look
at exciting new titles and the authors you love
long before everyone else does.

PENGUIN GROUP (USA)
us.penguingroup.com

M224G1107